T0276962

New York Stories

EDITED BY BOB BLAISDELL

DOVER PUBLICATIONS, INC.
Mineola, New York

ACKNOWLEDGMENTS: See page v.

Copyright

Copyright © 2016 by Dover Publications, Inc.
All rights reserved.

Bibliographical Note

New York Stories, first published by Dover Publications, Inc., in 2016, is a new compilation of short stories, reprinted from standard editions. Bob Blaisdell has selected the stories and provided the introductory Note and brief biographies.

Library of Congress Cataloging-in-Publication Data
Names: Blaisdell, Robert, editor.
Title: New York stories / edited by Bob Blaisdell.
Description: Mineola, New York : Dover Publications, 2016. |
    Includes bibliographical references.
Identifiers: LCCN 2015049491| ISBN 9780486802534 (paperback) |
    ISBN 0486802531 (paperback)
Subjects: LCSH: New York (N.Y.)—Fiction. | Short stories, American. |
    American fiction—19th century. | American fiction—20th century. |
    BISAC: FICTION / Classics.
Classification: LCC PS648.N39 N47 2016 | DDC 813/.01083587471—dc23
LC record available at http://lccn.loc.gov/2015049491

Printed in Canada
80253102   2024
www.doverpublications.com

Introduction

BESIDES TAKING PLACE in one of the five boroughs of New York City, what makes a New York short story a "New York" story? After compiling this anthology, I can answer only the obvious: a New York story couldn't have happened as it happened if it hadn't occurred in New York City. "I remembered the bright silks and sparkling faces I had seen that day, in gala trim, swanlike sailing down the Mississippi of Broadway . . ." writes Herman Melville's New York-smitten narrator in "Bartleby, the Scrivener." But it's not the landmarks or the names of famous streets that evoke the city; it's the characters themselves who have expectations of New York: they know or imagine that something special has to happen here. From Rocky's aunt (in P. G. Wodehouse's "The Aunt and the Sluggard") to Yunior's Papi (in Junot Díaz's "Negocios"), New York is the place where dreams *could* come true: living the high life or simply getting a job that will lead to another job up the long ladder of success.

The three husbands in Edith Wharton's "The Other Two" must all adapt in a New York minute to modern life and morals. There is no avoiding the strong currents of New York that sweep them all into its swirling pool; New York life is the most distinctive of American lives, and we hear, see and smell its distinctiveness in these stories. In Edwidge Danticat's "New York Day Women," a daughter comments on the daily life and habits of her Haitian mother, a member of the ranks of the city's immigrant women. While New York's expanse isn't representable, and its worst sides are mostly out of the picture, the characters sense, hope or fear that everything that's ever been possible in New York is potentially going to happen.

Does anybody want to say that New York City is a character in these stories? Well, it's not; it's simply the big bold intrusive *nonfictional* setting. The New York of these stories *is* New York. It has no stand-in, as it sometimes does in the movies. The geographical references—among them, Harlem, Brighton Beach, Midtown Manhattan, Washington Heights, Wall Street—are electrically *charged*, and when we readers feel that New York City current, we're prepared for anything.

Bob Blaisdell
New York City
July 15, 2015

Acknowledgments

Danticat, Edwidge. "New York Day Women" from *Krik? Krak!*, copyright © 1991, 1995 by Edwidge Danticat reprinted by permission of Soho Press, Inc. All rights reserved.

Díaz, Junot. "Negocios," from *Drown* by Junot Díaz, copyright © 1996 by Junot Díaz. Used by permission of Riverhead, an imprint of Penguin Publishing Group, a division of Penguin Random House LLC.

Hughes, Langston. "Midsummer Madness" from *The Best of Simple* by Langston Hughes. Copyright © 1961 by Langston Hughes. Copyright renewed 1989 by George Houston Bass. Reprinted by permission of Hill and Wang, a division of Farrar, Strauss and Giroux, LLC.

Parker, Dorothy. "Glory in the Daytime," copyright © 1933, renewed 1961 by Dorothy Parker, from *The Portable Dorothy Parker* by Dorothy Parker, edited by Marion Meade. Used by permission of Viking Books, an imprint of Penguin Random House LLC.

Parker, Dorothy. "Glory in the Daytime," from *The Complete Dorothy Parker*, reprinted by permission of Gerald Duckworth & Co. Ltd.

Rich, Simon. "Sirens of Gowanus" from *The Last Girlfriends on Earth and Other Stories* by Simon Rich. Copyright © 2013 by Simon Rich. Reprinted by permission of Little, Brown and Company.

Vapnyar, Lara. "Mistress" from *There Are Jews in My House: Stories* by Lara Vapnyar. Copyright © 2003 by Lara Vapnyar. Used by permission of Pantheon Books, an imprint of the Knopf Doubleday Publishing Group, a division of Penguin Random House LLC. All rights reserved.

Contents

New York Stories

BARTLEBY, THE SCRIVENER

A Story of Wall Street (1853)

Herman Melville

"Bartleby, the Scrivener" ("scrivener" means scribe, *someone paid to copy written materials) is a comedy of peculiar poignancy set in the bustling New York City business world of the early 1850s. Bartleby, "a scrivener of the strangest I ever saw or heard of," is the title character, but the tale is narrated by Bartleby's boss, a curious-minded, reflective, unnamed "rather elderly man." Poor Bartleby has become famous for his automatic response to any request for work or cooperation: "I would prefer not to." We have* preferred *to use the original* Putnam's Monthly Magazine *version of the story published in November and December 1853, before it was collected (and slightly revised) in* The Piazza Tales *(1856).*

Born in New York in 1819, Melville, besides serving as a sailor as a young man, also worked in banking and teaching. After some literary success, his writing career faltered, and he took a job at the New York Custom House. He died in 1891, overlooked at the time as one of the most significant American authors. Melville was buried in Woodlawn Cemetery in the Bronx.

I AM A rather elderly man. The nature of my avocations for the last thirty years has brought me into more than ordinary contact with what would seem an interesting and somewhat singular set of men, of whom, as yet, nothing that I know of has ever been written—I mean the law-copyists, or scriveners. I have known very many of them, professionally and privately, and, if I pleased, could relate divers histories at which good-natured gentlemen might smile and sentimental souls might weep. But I waive the biographies of all other scriveners for a few passages in the life of Bartleby, who was a scrivener, the strangest I ever saw or heard of. While of other law-copyists I might write the complete life of Bartleby nothing of that sort can be done. I believe that no materials exist for a full and satisfactory biography of this man. It is an irreparable loss to literature. Bartleby was one of those beings of whom nothing is ascertainable except from the original sources, and, in his case, those are very small. What my own astonished eyes saw of Bartleby, *that* is all I know of him, except, indeed, one vague report, which will appear in the sequel.

Ere introducing the scrivener as he first appeared to me, it is fit I make some mention of myself, my employees, my business, my chambers and general surroundings, because some such description is indispensable to an adequate understanding of the chief character about to be presented. *Imprimis:* I am a man who, from his youth upwards, has been filled with a profound conviction that the easiest way of life is the best. Hence, though I belong to a profession proverbially energetic and nervous even to turbulence at times, yet nothing of that sort have I ever suffered to invade my peace. I am one of those unambitious lawyers who never addresses a jury or in any way draws down public applause, but, in the cool tranquillity of a snug retreat, do a snug business among rich men's bonds, and mortgages, and title-deeds. All who know me consider me an eminently *safe* man. The late John Jacob Astor, a personage little given to poetic enthusiasm, had no hesitation in pronouncing my first grand point to be prudence, my next, method. I do not speak it in vanity, but simply record the fact that I was not unemployed in my profession by the late John Jacob Astor, a name which, I admit, I love to repeat, for it hath a rounded and orbicular sound to it, and rings like unto bullion. I will freely add that I was not insensible to the late John Jacob Astor's good opinion.

Some time prior to the period at which this little history begins my avocations had been largely increased. The good old office, now extinct in the State of New York, of a Master in Chancery, had been conferred upon me. It was not a very arduous office, but very pleasantly remunerative. I seldom lose my temper, much more seldom indulge in dangerous indignation at wrongs and outrages, but I must be permitted to be rash here and declare that I consider the sudden and violent abrogation of the office of Master in Chancery, by the new Constitution, as a —— premature act, inasmuch as I had counted upon a life lease of the profits, whereas I only received those of a few short years. But this is by the way.

My chambers were upstairs at No. —— Wall Street. At one end they looked upon the white wall of the interior of a spacious skylight shaft, penetrating the building from top to bottom.

This view might have been considered rather tame than otherwise, deficient in what landscape painters call "life." But, if so, the view from the other end of my chambers offered at least a contrast, if nothing more. In that direction, my windows commanded an unobstructed view of a lofty brick wall, black by age and everlasting shade, which wall required no spyglass to bring out its lurking beauties, but, for the benefit of all nearsighted spectators, was pushed up to within ten feet of my window-panes. Owing to the great height of the surrounding buildings, and my chambers being on the second floor, the interval between this wall and mine not a little resembled a huge square cistern.

At the period just preceding the advent of Bartleby, I had two persons as copyists in my employment, and a promising lad as an office boy. First, Turkey; second, Nippers; third, Ginger Nut. These may seem names the like of which are not usually found in the Directory. In truth, they were nicknames, mutually conferred upon each other by my three clerks, and were deemed expressive of their respective persons or characters. Turkey was a short, pursy Englishman, of about my own age—that is, somewhere not far from sixty. In the morning, one might say, his face was of a fine florid hue, but after twelve o'clock, meridian—his dinner hour—it blazed like a grate full of Christmas coals; and continued blazing—but, as it were, with a gradual wane—till 6 o'clock, P.M., or thereabouts; after which I saw no more of the proprietor of the face, which, gaining its meridian with the sun, seemed to set with it, to rise, culminate, and decline the following day, with the like regularity and undiminished glory. There are many singular coincidences I have known in the course of my life, not the least among which was the fact, that, exactly when Turkey displayed his fullest beams from his red and radiant countenance, just then, too, at that critical moment, began the daily period when I considered his business capacities as seriously disturbed for the remainder of the twenty-four hours. Not that he was absolutely idle or averse to business then; far from it. The difficulty was, he was apt to be altogether too energetic. There was a strange, inflamed, flurried, flighty recklessness of activity about him. He would be incautious in dipping his pen into his inkstand. All his blots upon my documents were dropped there after twelve o'clock, meridian. Indeed, not only would he be reckless and sadly given to making blots in the afternoon, but some days he went further and was rather noisy. At such times, too, his face flamed with augmented blazonry, as if cannel coal had been heaped on anthracite. He made an unpleasant racket with his chair; spilled his sandbox; in mending his pens, impatiently split them all to pieces and threw them on the floor in a sudden passion; stood up and leaned over his table, boxing his papers about in a most indecorous manner, very sad to behold in an elderly man like him. Nevertheless, as he was in many ways a most valuable person to me, and all the time before twelve o'clock, meridian, was the quickest, steadiest creature, too, accomplishing a great deal of work in a style not easily to be matched—for these reasons I was willing to overlook his eccentricities, though indeed, occasionally, I remonstrated with him. I did this very gently, however, because, though the civilest, nay, the blandest and most reverential of men in the morning, yet, in the afternoon he was disposed, upon provocation, to be slightly rash with his tongue—in fact, insolent. Now, valuing his morning services as I did, and resolved not to lose them—yet, at the same time, made uncomfortable by his inflamed ways after twelve o'clock—and being a man of peace, unwilling by my admonitions to call forth unseemly retorts from him, I took upon me one Saturday noon (he was always worse on Saturdays) to hint to him, very kindly, that perhaps, now that he was growing old, it might be well to abridge his labors; in short, he need not come to my chambers after twelve o'clock, but, dinner over, had best go home to his lodgings and rest himself till teatime. But no; he insisted upon his afternoon devotions. His countenance became intolerably fervid, as he oratorically assured me—gesticulating with a long ruler at the other end of the room—that if his services in the morning were useful, how indispensable, then, in the afternoon?

"With submission, sir," said Turkey, on this occasion, "I consider myself your right-hand man. In the morning I but marshal and deploy my columns, but in the afternoon I put myself at their head, and gallantly charge the foe, thus"—and he made a violent thrust with the ruler.

"But the blots, Turkey," intimated I.

"True; but, with submission, sir, behold these hairs! I am getting old. Surely, sir, a blot or two of a warm afternoon is not to be severely urged against gray hairs. Old age—even if it blot the page—is honorable. With submission, sir, we *both* are getting old."

This appeal to my fellow feeling was hardly to be resisted. At all events, I saw that go he would not. So I made up my mind to let him stay, resolving, nevertheless, to see to it that, during the afternoon, he had to do with my less important papers.

Nippers, the second on my list, was a whiskered, sallow, and, upon the whole rather piratical-looking young man of about five and twenty. I always deemed him the victim of two evil powers—ambition and indigestion. The ambition was evinced by a certain impatience of the duties of a mere copyist, an unwarrantable usurpation of strictly professional affairs, such as the original drawing up of legal documents. The indigestion seemed betokened in an occasional nervous testiness and grinning irritability, causing the teeth to audibly grind together over mistakes committed in copying; unnecessary maledictions, hissed rather than spoken, in the heat of business; and especially by a continual discontent with the height of the table where he worked. Though of a very ingenious mechanical turn, Nippers could never get this table to suit him. He put chips under it, blocks of various sorts, bits of pasteboard, and at last went so far as to attempt an exquisite adjustment by final pieces of folded blotting paper. But no invention would answer. If, for the sake of easing his back, he brought the table lid at a sharp angle well up towards his chin, and wrote there like a man using the steep roof of a Dutch house for his desk, then he declared that it stopped the circulation in his arms. If now he lowered the table to his waistbands and stooped over it in writing, then there was a sore aching in his back. In short, the truth of the matter was Nippers knew not what he wanted. Or, if he wanted any thing, it was to be rid of a scrivener's table altogether. Among the manifestations of his diseased ambition was a fondness he had for receiving visits from certain ambiguous-looking fellows in seedy coats, whom he called his clients. Indeed, I was aware that not only was he, at times, considerable of a ward politician, but he occasionally did a little business at the Justices' courts, and was not unknown on the steps of the Tombs. I have good reason to believe, however, that one individual who called upon him at my chambers, and who, with a grand air, he insisted was his client, was no other than a dun, and the alleged title deed, a bill. But, with all his failings, and the annoyances he caused me, Nippers, like his compatriot Turkey, was a very useful man to me; wrote a neat, swift hand; and, when he chose, was not deficient in a gentlemanly sort of deportment. Added to this, he always dressed in a gentlemanly sort of way, and so, incidentally, reflected credit upon my chambers. Whereas, with respect to Turkey, I had much ado to keep him from being a reproach to me. His clothes were apt to look oily, and smell of eating houses. He wore his pantaloons very loose and baggy in summer. His coats were execrable, his hat not to be handled. But while the hat was a thing of indifference to me, inasmuch as his natural civility and deference, as a dependent Englishman, always led him to doff it the moment he entered the room, yet his coat was another matter. Concerning his coats, I reasoned with him, but with no effect. The truth was, I suppose, that a man of so small an income could not afford to sport such a lustrous face and a lustrous coat at one and the same time. As Nippers once observed, Turkey's money went chiefly for red ink. One winter day, I presented Turkey with a highly respectable-looking coat of my own—a padded gray coat of a most comfortable warmth, and which buttoned straight up from the knee to the neck. I thought Turkey would appreciate the favor and abate his rashness and obstreperousness of afternoons. But no; I verily believe that buttoning himself up in so downy and blanketlike a coat had a pernicious effect upon him—upon the same principle that too much oats are bad for horses. In fact, precisely as a rash, restive horse is said to feel his oats, so Turkey felt his coat. It made him insolent. He was a man whom prosperity harmed.

Though, concerning the self-indulgent habits of Turkey I had my own private surmises, yet, touching Nippers, I was well persuaded that, whatever might be his faults in other respects, he was, at least, a temperate young man. But indeed, nature herself seemed to have been his vintner, and, at his birth, charged him so thoroughly with an irritable, brandylike disposition that all subsequent potations were needless. When I consider how, amid the stillness of my chambers, Nippers would sometimes impatiently rise from his seat, and, stooping over his table, spread his arms wide apart, seize the whole desk, and move it, and jerk it, with a grim, grinding motion on the floor, as if the table were a perverse voluntary agent, intent on thwarting and vexing him, I plainly perceive that, for Nippers, brandy-and-water were altogether superfluous.

It was fortunate for me that, owing to its peculiar cause—indigestion—the irritability and consequent nervousness of Nippers were mainly observable in the morning, while in the afternoon he was comparatively mild. So that, Turkey's paroxysms only coming on about twelve o'clock, I never had to do with their eccentricities at one time. Their fits relieved each other, like guards. When Nippers's was on, Turkey's was off; and vice versa. This was a good natural arrangement, under the circumstances.

Ginger Nut, the third on my list, was a lad some twelve years old. His father was a carman, ambitious of seeing his son on the bench instead of a cart before he died. So he sent him to my office, as student at law, errand boy, cleaner and sweeper, at the rate of one dollar a week. He had a little desk to himself, but he did not use it much. Upon inspection, the drawer exhibited a great array of the shells of various sorts of nuts. Indeed, to this quick-witted youth, the whole noble science of the law was contained in a nutshell. Not the least among the employments of Ginger Nut, as well as one which he discharged with the most alacrity, was his duty as cake and apple purveyor for Turkey and Nippers. Copying law papers being proverbially a dry, husky sort of business, my two scriveners were fain to moisten their mouths very often with Spitzenbergs, to be had at the numerous stalls nigh the Custom House and Post Office. Also, they sent Ginger Nut very frequently for that peculiar cake—small, flat, round, and very spicy—after which he had been named by them. Of a cold morning, when business was but dull, Turkey would gobble up scores of these cakes, as if they were mere wafers—indeed, they sell them at the rate of six or eight for a penny—the scrape of his pen blending with the crunching of the crisp particles in his mouth. Of all the fiery afternoon blunders and flurried rashnesses of Turkey was his once moistening a ginger cake between his lips and clapping it on to a mortgage for a seal. I came within an ace of dismissing him then. But he mollified me by making an Oriental bow, and saying:

"With submission, sir, it was generous of me to find you in stationery on my own account."

Now my original business—that of a conveyancer and tide hunter, and drawer-up of recondite documents of all sorts—was considerably increased by receiving the Master's office. There was now great work for scriveners. Not only must I push the clerks already with me, but I must have additional help.

In answer to my advertisement, a motionless young man one morning stood upon my office threshold, the door being open, for it was summer. I can see that figure now—pallidly neat, pitiably respectable, incurably forlorn! It was Bartleby.

After a few words touching his qualifications, I engaged him, glad to have among my corps of copyists a man of so singularly sedate an aspect, which I thought might operate beneficially upon the flighty temper of Turkey and the fiery one of Nippers.

I should have stated before that ground-glass folding doors divided my premises into two parts, one of which was occupied by my scriveners, the other by myself. According to my humor, I threw open these doors or closed them. I resolved to assign Bartleby a corner by the folding doors, but on my side of them, so as to have this quiet man within easy call, in case any trifling thing was to be done. I placed his desk close up to a small side window in that part of the room, a window which originally had afforded a lateral view of certain grimy back yards and bricks, but which, owing to subsequent erections, commanded at present no view at all, though it gave some light. Within three feet of the panes was a wall, and the light came down from far above, between two lofty buildings, as from a very small opening in a dome. Still further to a satisfactory arrangement, I procured a high green folding screen, which might entirely isolate Bartleby from my sight, though not remove him from my voice. And thus, in a manner, privacy and society were conjoined.

At first, Bartleby did an extraordinary quantity of writing. As if long famishing for something to copy, he seemed to gorge himself on my documents. There was no pause for digestion. He ran a day and night line, copying by sunlight and by candlelight. I should have been quite delighted with his application, had he been cheerfully industrious. But he wrote on silently, palely, mechanically.

It is, of course, an indispensable part of a scrivener's business to verify the accuracy of his copy, word by word. Where there are two or more scriveners in an office, they assist each other in this examination, one reading from the copy, the other holding the original. It is a very dull, wearisome, and lethargic affair. I can readily imagine that, to some sanguine temperaments, it would be altogether intolerable. For example, I cannot credit that the mettlesome poet, Byron, would have contentedly sat down with Bartleby to examine a law document of, say five hundred pages, closely written in a crimpy hand.

Now and then, in the haste of business, it had been my habit to assist in comparing some brief document myself, calling Turkey or

Nippers for this purpose. One object I had in placing Bartleby so handy to me behind the screen was to avail myself of his services on such trivial occasions. It was on the third day, I think, of his being with me, and before any necessity had arisen for having his own writing examined, that, being much hurried to complete a small affair I had in hand, I abruptly called to Bartleby. In my haste and natural expectancy of instant compliance, I sat with my head bent over the original on my desk, and my right hand sideways, and somewhat nervously extended with the copy, so that, immediately upon emerging from his retreat, Bartleby might snatch it and proceed to business without the least delay.

In this very attitude did I sit when I called to him, rapidly stating what it was I wanted him to do—namely, to examine a small paper with me. Imagine my surprise, nay, my consternation, when, without moving from his privacy, Bartleby, in a singularly mild, firm voice, replied, "I would prefer not to."

I sat awhile in perfect silence, rallying my stunned faculties. Immediately it occurred to me that my ears had deceived me, or Bartleby had entirely misunderstood my meaning. I repeated my request in the clearest tone I could assume; but in quite as clear a one came the previous reply, "I would prefer not to."

"Prefer not to," echoed I, rising in high excitement, and crossing the room with a stride. "What do you mean? Are you moon-struck? I want you to help me compare this sheet here—take it," and I thrust it towards him.

"I would prefer not to," said he.

I looked at him steadfastly. His face was leanly composed; his gray eyes dimly calm. Not a wrinkle of agitation rippled him. Had there been the least uneasiness, anger, impatience or impertinence in his manner; in other words, had there been anything ordinarily human about him, doubtless I should have violently dismissed him from the premises. But as it was I should have as soon thought of turning my pale plaster-of-Paris bust of Cicero out of doors. I stood gazing at him awhile, as he went on with his own writing, and then reseated myself at my desk. This is very strange, thought I. What had one best do? But my business hurried me. I concluded to forget the matter for the present, reserving it for my future leisure. So calling Nippers from the other room, the paper was speedily examined.

A few days after this, Bartleby concluded four lengthy documents, being quadruplicates of a week's testimony taken before me in my High Court of Chancery. It became necessary to examine them. It was an important suit, and great accuracy was imperative. Having all things arranged, I called Turkey, Nippers, and Ginger Nut from the next room, meaning to place the four copies in the hands of my four clerks, while I should read from the original. Accordingly, Turkey, Nippers, and Ginger Nut had taken their seats in a row, each with his document in his hand, when I called to Bartleby to join this interesting group.

"Bartleby! quick, I am waiting."

I heard a slow scrape of his chair legs on the uncarpeted floor, and soon he appeared standing at the entrance of his hermitage.

"What is wanted?" said he mildly.

"The copies, the copies," said I, hurriedly. "We are going to examine them. There"—and I held towards him the fourth quadruplicate.

"I would prefer not to," he said, and gently disappeared behind the screen.

For a few moments I was turned into a pillar of salt, standing at the head of my seated column of clerks. Recovering myself, I advanced towards the screen and demanded the reason for such extraordinary conduct.

"*Why* do you refuse?"

"I would prefer not to."

With any other man I should have flown outright into a dreadful passion, scorned all further words, and thrust him ignominiously from my presence. But there was something about Bartleby that not only strangely disarmed me, but, in a wonderful manner, touched and disconcerted me. I began to reason with him.

"These are your own copies we are about to examine. It is labor saving to you, because one examination will answer for your four papers. It is common usage. Every copyist is bound to help examine his copy. Is it not so? Will you not speak? Answer!"

"I prefer not to," he replied in a flutelike tone. It seemed to me that, while I had been addressing him, he carefully revolved every statement that I made; fully comprehended the meaning; could not gainsay the irresistible conclusion but, at the same time, some paramount consideration prevailed with him to reply as he did.

"You are decided, then, not to comply with my request—a request made according to common usage and common sense?"

He briefly gave me to understand that on that point my judgment was sound. Yes: his decision was irreversible.

It is not seldom the case that, when a man is browbeaten in some unprecedented and violently unreasonable way, he begins to stagger in his own plainest faith. He begins, as it were, vaguely to surmise that, wonderful as it may be, all the justice and all the reason is on the other side. Accordingly, if any disinterested persons are present, he turns to them for some reinforcement for his own faltering mind.

"Turkey," said I, "what do you think of this? Am I not right?"

"With submission, sir," said Turkey, with his blandest tone, "I think that you are."

"Nippers," said I, "what do *you* think of it?"

"I think I should kick him out of the office."

(The reader of nice perceptions will here perceive that, it being morning, Turkey's answer is couched in polite and tranquil terms, but Nippers replies in ill-tempered ones. Or, to repeat a previous sentence, Nippers's ugly mood was on duty, and Turkey's off.)

"Ginger Nut," said I, willing to enlist the smallest suffrage in my behalf, "what do *you* think of it?"

"I think, sir, he's a little *luny*," replied Ginger Nut, with a grin.

"You hear what they say," said I, turning towards the screen, "come forth and do your duty."

But he vouchsafed no reply. I pondered a moment in sore perplexity. But once more business hurried me. I determined again to postpone the consideration of this dilemma to my future leisure. With a little trouble we made out to examine the papers without Bartleby, though at every page or two Turkey deferentially dropped his opinion that this proceeding was quite out of the common; while Nippers, twitching in his chair with a dyspeptic nervousness, ground out between his set teeth occasional hissing maledictions against the stubborn oaf behind the screen. And for his (Nippers's) part, this was the first and the last time he would do another man's business without pay.

Meanwhile Bartleby sat in his hermitage, oblivious to everything but his own peculiar business there.

Some days passed, the scrivener being employed upon another lengthy work. His late remarkable conduct led me to regard his ways narrowly. I observed that he never went to dinner; indeed, that he never went any where. As yet I had never, of my personal knowledge, known him to be outside of my office. He was a perpetual sentry in the corner. At about eleven o'clock, though, in the morning, I noticed that Ginger Nut would advance towards the opening in Bartleby's screen, as if silently beckoned thither by a gesture invisible to me where I sat. The boy would then leave the office jingling a few pence, and reappear with a handful of ginger-nuts, which he delivered in the hermitage, receiving two of the cakes for his trouble.

He lives, then, on gingernuts, thought I; never eats a dinner, properly speaking; he must be a vegetarian, then; but no, he never eats even vegetables, he eats nothing but gingernuts. My mind then ran on in reveries concerning the probable effects upon the human constitution of living entirely on gingernuts. Gingernuts are so called because they contain ginger as one of their peculiar constituents, and the final flavoring one. Now, what was ginger? A hot, spicy thing. Was Bartleby hot and spicy? Not at all. Ginger, then, had no effect upon Bartleby. Probably he preferred it should have none.

Nothing so aggravates an earnest person as a passive resistance. If the individual so resisted be of a not inhumane temper, and the resisting one perfectly harmless in his passivity, then, in the better moods of the former, he will endeavor charitably to construe to his imagination what proves impossible to be solved by his judgment. Even so, for the most part, I regarded Bartleby and his ways. Poor fellow! thought I, he means no mischief; it is plain he intends no insolence; his aspect sufficiently evinces that his eccentricities are involuntary. He is useful to me. I can get along with him. If I turn him away, the chances are he will fall in with some less indulgent employer, and then he will be rudely treated, and perhaps driven forth miserably to starve. Yes. Here I can cheaply purchase a delicious self-approval. To befriend Bartleby, to humor him in his strange willfulness, will cost me little or nothing, while I lay up in my soul what will eventually prove a sweet morsel for my conscience. But this mood was not invariable with me. The passiveness of Bartleby sometimes irritated me. I felt strangely goaded on to encounter him in new opposition—to elicit some angry spark from him answerable to my own. But, indeed, I might as well have essayed to strike fire with my knuckles against a bit of Windsor soap. But one afternoon the evil impulse in me mastered me, and the following little scene ensued:

"Bartleby," said I, "when those papers are all copied, I will compare them with you."

"I would prefer not to."

"How? Surely you do not mean to persist in that mulish vagary?"
No answer.

I threw open the folding doors near by, and, turning upon Turkey and Nippers, exclaimed:

"Bartleby a second time says he won't examine his papers. What do you think of it, Turkey?"

It was afternoon, be it remembered. Turkey sat glowing like a brass boiler, his bald head steaming, his hands reeling among his blotted papers.

"Think of it?" roared Turkey. "I think I'll just step behind his screen and black his eyes for him!"

So saying, Turkey rose to his feet and threw his arms into a pugilistic position. He was hurrying away to make good his promise when I detained him, alarmed at the effect of incautiously rousing Turkey's combativeness after dinner.

"Sit down, Turkey," said I, "and hear what Nippers has to say. What do you think of it, Nippers? Would I not be justified in immediately dismissing Bartleby?"

"Excuse me, that is for you to decide, sir. I think his conduct quite unusual, and indeed, unjust, as regards Turkey and myself. But it may only be a passing whim."

"Ah," exclaimed I, "you have strangely changed your mind, then— you speak very gently of him now."

"All beer," cried Turkey; "gentleness is effects of beer—Nippers and I dined together today. You see how gentle *I* am, sir. Shall I go and black his eyes?"

"You refer to Bartleby, I suppose. No, not today, Turkey," I replied; "pray, put up your fists."

I closed the doors and again advanced towards Bartleby. I felt additional incentives tempting me to my fate. I burned to be rebelled against again. I remembered that Bartleby never left the office.

"Bartleby," said I, "Ginger Nut is away; just step round to the Post Office, won't you? (it was but a three minutes' walk), and see if there is any thing for me."

"I would prefer not to."

"You *will* not?"

"I *prefer* not."

I staggered to my desk and sat there in a deep study. My blind inveteracy returned. Was there any other thing in which I could procure myself to be ignominiously repulsed by this lean, penniless wight?—my hired clerk? What added thing is there, perfectly reasonable, that he will be sure to refuse to do?

"Bartleby!"

No answer.

"Bartleby," in a louder tone.

No answer.

"Bartleby," I roared.

Like a very ghost, agreeably to the laws of magical invocation, at the third summons he appeared at the entrance of his hermitage.

"Go to the next room, and tell Nippers to come to me."

"I prefer not to," he respectfully and slowly said, and mildly disappeared.

"Very good, Bartleby," said I, in a quiet sort of serenely severe self-possessed tone, intimating the unalterable purpose of some terrible retribution very close at hand. At the moment I half intended something of the kind. But upon the whole, as it was drawing towards my dinner hour, I thought it best to put on my hat and walk home for the day, suffering much from perplexity and distress of mind.

Shall I acknowledge it? The conclusion of this whole business was that it soon became a fixed fact of my chambers, that a pale young scrivener by the name of Bartleby had a desk there; that he copied for me at the usual rate of four cents a folio (one hundred words); but he was permanently exempt from examining the work done by him, that duty being transferred to Turkey and Nippers, out of compliment, doubtless, to their superior acuteness; moreover, said Bartleby was never, on any account, to be dispatched on the most trivial errand of any sort; and that even if entreated to take upon him such a matter, it was generally understood that he would "prefer not to"—in other words, that he would refuse point-blank.

As days passed on, I became considerably reconciled to Bartleby. His steadiness, his freedom from all dissipation, his incessant industry (except when he chose to throw himself into a standing reverie behind his screen), his great stillness, his unalterableness of demeanor under all circumstances, made him a valuable acquisition. One prime thing was this—*he was always there*—first in the morning, continually through the day, and the last at night. I had a singular confidence in his honesty. I felt my most precious papers perfectly safe in his hands. Sometimes, to be sure, I could not, for the very soul of me, avoid falling into sudden spasmodic passions with him. For it was exceeding difficult to bear in mind all the time those strange peculiarities, privileges, and unheard-of exemptions, forming the tacit stipulations on Bartleby's part under which he remained in my office. Now and then, in the eagerness of dispatching pressing business, I would inadvertently summon Bartleby, in a short, rapid tone, to put his finger, say, on the incipient tie of a bit of red tape with which I was about compressing some papers. Of course, from behind the screen the usual answer, "I prefer not to," was sure to come; and then, how could a human creature, with the common infirmities of our nature, refrain from bitterly exclaiming upon such perverseness—such unreasonableness? However, every added repulse of this sort which I received only tended to lessen the probability of my repeating the inadvertence.

Here it must be said that, according to the custom of most legal gentlemen occupying chambers in densely populated law buildings, there were several keys to my door. One was kept by a woman residing in the attic, which person weekly scrubbed and daily swept and dusted my apartments. Another was kept by Turkey for convenience' sake. The third I sometimes carried in my own pocket. The fourth I knew not who had.

Now, one Sunday morning I happened to go to Trinity Church, to hear a celebrated preacher, and finding myself rather early on the ground I thought I would walk round to my chambers for a while. Luckily I had my key with me, but upon applying it to the lock, I found it resisted by something inserted from the inside. Quite surprised, I called out, when to my consternation a key was turned from within, and, thrusting his lean visage at me, and holding the door ajar, the apparition of Bartleby appeared, in his shirt sleeves, and otherwise in a strangely uttered deshabille, saying quietly that he was sorry, but he was deeply engaged just then, and—preferred not admitting me at present. In a brief word or two, he moreover added, that perhaps I had better walk around the block two or three times, and by that time he would probably have concluded his affairs.

Now, the utterly unsurmised appearance of Bartleby, tenanting my law chambers of a Sunday morning, with his cadaverously gentlemanly *nonchalance,* yet withal firm and self-possessed, had such a strange effect upon me that incontinently I slunk away from my own door and did as desired. But not without sundry twinges

of impotent rebellion against the mild effrontery of this unaccountable scrivener. Indeed, it was his wonderful mildness, chiefly,
which not only disarmed me but unmanned me, as it were. For I
consider that one, for the time, is sort of unmanned when he tranquilly permits his hired clerk to dictate to him and order him away
from his own premises. Furthermore, I was full of uneasiness as to
what Bartleby could possibly be doing in my office in his shirt
sleeves, and in an otherwise dismantled condition, of a Sunday
morning. Was anything amiss going on? Nay, that was out of the
question. It was not to be thought of for a moment that Bartleby
was an immoral person. But what could he be doing there?—
copying? Nay again, whatever might be his eccentricities, Bartleby
was an eminently decorous person. He would be the last man to sit
down to his desk in any state approaching to nudity. Besides, it was
Sunday; and there was something about Bartleby that forbade the
supposition that he would by any secular occupation violate the
proprieties of the day.

Nevertheless, my mind was not pacified, and, full of a restless
curiosity, at last I returned to the door. Without hindrance I
inserted my key, opened it, and entered. Bartleby was not to be
seen. I looked round anxiously, peeped behind his screen, but it
was very plain that he was gone. Upon more closely examining the
place, I surmised that for an indefinite period Bartleby must have
ate, dressed, and slept in my office, and that, too, without plate,
mirror, or bed. The cushioned seat of a rickety old sofa in one
corner bore the faint impress of a lean, reclining form. Rolled away
under his desk I found a blanket; under the empty grate, a blacking
box and brush; on a chair, a tin basin, with soap and a ragged towel;
in a newspaper a few crumbs of gingernuts and a morsel of cheese.
Yes, thought I, it is evident enough that Bartleby has been making
his home here, keeping bachelor's hall all by himself. Immediately
then the thought came sweeping across me, what miserable friend-
lessness and loneliness are here revealed. His poverty is great, but
his solitude, how horrible! Think of it. Of a Sunday, Wall Street is
deserted as Petra, and every night of every day it is an emptiness.
This building, too, which of weekdays hums with industry and life,
at nightfall echoes with sheer vacancy, and all through Sunday is
forlorn. And here Bartleby makes his home, sole spectator of a
solitude which he has seen all populous—a sort of innocent and
transformed Marius brooding among the ruins of Carthage!

For the first time in my life a feeling of overpowering stinging melancholy seized me. Before, I had never experienced aught but a not unpleasing sadness. The bond of a common humanity now drew me irresistibly to gloom. A fraternal melancholy! For both I and Bartleby were sons of Adam. I remembered the bright silks and sparkling faces I had seen that day, in gala trim, swanlike sailing down the Mississippi of Broadway; and I contrasted them with the pallid copyist, and thought to myself, Ah, happiness courts the light, so we deem the world is gay, but misery hides aloof, so we deem that misery there is none. These sad fancyings—chimeras, doubtless, of a sick and silly brain—led on to other and more special thoughts, concerning the eccentricities of Bartleby. Presentiments of strange discoveries hovered round me. The scrivener's pale form appeared to me laid out, among uncaring strangers in its shivering winding sheet.

Suddenly I was attracted by Bartleby's closed desk, the key in open sight left in the lock.

I mean no mischief, seek the gratification of no heartless curiosity, thought I; besides, the desk is mine, and its contents, too, so I will make bold to look within. Everything was methodically arranged, the papers smoothly placed. The pigeonholes were deep, and, removing the files of documents, I groped into their recesses. Presently I felt something there, and dragged it out. It was an old bandanna handkerchief, heavy and knotted. I opened it, and saw it was a savings bank.

I now recalled all the quiet mysteries which I had noted in the man. I remembered that he never spoke but to answer; that, though at intervals he had considerable time to himself, yet I had never seen him reading—no, not even a newspaper; that for long periods he would stand looking out, at his pale window behind the screen, upon the dead brick wall; I was quite sure he never visited any refectory or eating house, while his pale face clearly indicated that he never drank beer like Turkey, or tea and coffee even, like other men; that he never went anywhere in particular that I could learn; never went out for a walk, unless, indeed, that was the case at present; that he had declined telling who he was, or whence he came, or whether he had any relatives in the world; that though so thin and pale, he never complained of ill health. And more than all I remembered a certain unconscious air of pallid—how shall I call it?—of pallid haughtiness, say, or rather an austere reserve about him, which had positively awed me into my tame compliance with his eccentricities, when I had feared to ask him to do the slightest incidental thing for me, even though I might know, from his long-continued motionlessness, that behind his screen he must be standing in one of those dead-wall reveries of his.

Revolving all these things, and coupling them with the recently discovered fact that he made my office his constant abiding place and home, and not forgetful of his morbid moodiness—revolving all these things, a prudential feeling began to steal over me. My first emotions had been those of pure melancholy and sincerest pity; but just in proportion as the forlornness of Bartleby grew and grew to my imagination, did that same melancholy merge into fear, that pity into repulsion. So true it is, and so terrible too, that up to a certain point the thought or sight of misery enlists our best affections; but, in certain special cases, beyond that point it does not. They err who would assert that invariably this is owing to the inherent selfishness of the human heart. It rather proceeds from a certain hopelessness of remedying excessive and organic ill. To a sensitive being, pity is not seldom pain. And when at last it is perceived that such pity cannot lead to effectual succor, common sense bids the soul be rid of it. What I saw that morning persuaded me that the scrivener was the victim of innate and incurable disorder. I might give alms to his body, but his body did not pain him—it was his soul that suffered, and his soul I could not reach.

I did not accomplish the purpose of going to Trinity Church that morning. Somehow, the things I had seen disqualified me for the time from churchgoing. I walked homeward, thinking what I would do with Bartleby. Finally, I resolved upon this—I would put certain calm questions to him the next morning, touching his history, etc., and if he declined to answer them openly and unreservedly (and I supposed he would prefer not), then to give him a twenty-dollar bill over and above whatever I might owe him, and tell him his services were no longer required; but that if in any other way I could assist him, I would be happy to do so, especially if he desired to return to his native place, wherever that might be, I would willingly help to defray the expenses. Moreover, if, after reaching home, he found himself at any time in want of aid, a letter from him would be sure of a reply.

The next morning came.

"Bartleby," said I, gently calling to him behind his screen.

No reply.

"Bartleby," said I, in a still gentler tone, "come here; I am not going to ask you to do anything you would prefer not to do—I simply wish to speak to you."

Upon this he noiselessly slid into view.

"Will you tell me, Bartleby, where you were born?"

"I would prefer not to."

"Will you tell me *anything* about yourself?"

"I would prefer not to."

"But what reasonable objection can you have to speak to me? I feel friendly towards you."

He did not look at me while I spoke, but kept his glance fixed upon my bust of Cicero, which, as I then sat, was directly behind me, some six inches above my head.

"What is your answer, Bartleby?" said I, after waiting a considerable time for a reply, during which his countenance remained immovable, only there was the faintest conceivable tremor of the white attenuated mouth.

"At present I prefer to give no answer," he said, and retired into his hermitage.

It was rather weak in me I confess, but his manner, on this occasion, nettled me. Not only did there seem to lurk in it a certain calm disdain, but his perverseness seemed ungrateful, considering the undeniable good usage and indulgence he had received from me.

Again I sat ruminating what I should do. Mortified as I was at his behavior, and resolved as I had been to dismiss him when I entered my office, nevertheless I strangely felt something superstitious knocking at my heart, and forbidding me to carry out my purpose, and denouncing me for a villain if I dared to breathe one bitter word against this forlornest of mankind. At last, familiarly drawing my chair behind his screen, I sat down and said: "Bartleby, never mind, then, about revealing your history; but let me entreat you, as a friend, to comply as far as may be with the usages of this office. Say now, you will help to examine papers tomorrow or next day: in short, say now, that in a day or two you will begin to be a little reasonable:—say so, Bartleby."

"At present I would prefer not to be a little reasonable," was his mildly cadaverous reply.

Just then the folding doors opened and Nippers approached. He seemed suffering from an unusually bad night's rest, induced by severer indigestion than common. He overheard those final words of Bartleby.

"*Prefer not,* eh?" gritted Nippers—"I'd *prefer* him, if I were you, sir," addressing me—"I'd *prefer* him; I'd give him preferences, the stubborn mule! What is it, sir, pray, that he *prefers* not to do now?"

Bartleby moved not a limb.

"Mr. Nippers," said I, "I'd prefer that you would withdraw for the present."

Somehow, of late, I had got into the way of involuntarily using this word "prefer" upon all sorts of not exactly suitable occasions. And I trembled to think that my contact with the scrivener had already and seriously affected me in a mental way. And what further and deeper aberration might it not yet produce? This apprehension had not been without efficacy in determining me to summary measures.

As Nippers, looking very sour and sulky, was departing, Turkey blandly and deferentially approached.

"With submission, sir," said he, "yesterday I was thinking about Bartleby here, and I think that if he would but prefer to take a quart of good ale every day, it would do much towards mending him, and enabling him to assist in examining his papers."

"So you have got the word, too," said I, slightly excited.

"With submission, what word, sir?" asked Turkey, respectfully crowding himself into the contracted space behind the screen, and by so doing making me jostle the scrivener. "What word, sir?"

"I would prefer to be left alone here," said Bartleby, as if offended at being mobbed in his privacy.

"*That's* the word, Turkey," said I—"*that's* it."

"Oh, prefer? oh yes—queer word. I never use it myself. But, sir, as I was saying, if he would but prefer——"

"Turkey," interrupted I, "you will please withdraw."

"Oh certainly, sir, if you prefer that I should."

As he opened the folding door to retire, Nippers at his desk caught a glimpse of me, and asked whether I would prefer to have a certain paper copied on blue paper or white. He did not in the least roguishly accent the word prefer. It was plain that it involuntarily rolled from his tongue. I thought to myself, surely I must get rid of a demented man, who already has in some degree turned the tongues, if not the heads, of myself and clerks. But I thought it prudent not to break the dismission at once.

The next day I noticed that Bartleby did nothing but stand at his window in his dead-wall reverie. Upon asking him why he did not write, he said that he had decided upon doing no more writing.

"Why, how now? what next?" exclaimed I, "do no more writing?"

"No more."

"And what is the reason?"

"Do you not see the reason for yourself?" he indifferently replied. I looked steadfastly at him, and perceived that his eyes looked dull and glazed. Instantly it occurred to me that his unexampled diligence in copying by his dim window for the first few weeks of his stay with me might have temporarily impaired his vision.

I was touched. I said something in condolence with him. I hinted that of course he did wisely in abstaining from writing for a while; and urged him to embrace that opportunity of taking wholesome exercise in the open air. This, however, he did not do. A few days after this, my other clerks being absent, and being in a great hurry to dispatch certain letters by the mail, I thought that, having nothing else earthly to do, Bartleby would surely be less inflexible than usual, and carry these letters to the Post Office. But he blankly declined. So, much to my inconvenience, I went myself.

Still added days went by. Whether Bartleby's eyes improved or not, I could not say. To all appearance, I thought they did. But when I asked him if they did, he vouchsafed no answer. At all events, he would do no copying. At last, in reply to my urgings, he informed me that he had permanently given up copying.

"What!" exclaimed I; "suppose your eyes should get entirely well—better than ever before—would you not copy then?"

"I have given up copying," he answered, and slid aside.

He remained as ever, a fixture in my chamber. Nay—if that were possible—he became still more of a fixture than before. What was to be done? He would do nothing in the office; why should he stay there? In plain fact, he had now become a millstone to me, not only useless as a necklace, but afflictive to bear. Yet I was sorry for him. I speak less than truth when I say that, on his own account, he occasioned me uneasiness. If he would but have named a single relative or friend, I would instantly have written and urged their taking the poor fellow away to some convenient retreat. But he seemed alone, absolutely alone in the universe. A bit of wreck in the mid-Atlantic. At length, necessities connected with my business tyrannized over all other considerations. Decently as I could, I told Bartleby that in six days' time he must unconditionally leave the office. I warned him to take measures, in the interval, for procuring some other abode. I offered to assist him in this endeavor, if he himself would but take the first step towards a removal. "And when you finally quit me, Bartleby," added I, "I shall see that you go not away entirely unprovided. Six days from this hour, remember."

At the expiration of that period, I peeped behind the screen, and lo! Bartleby was there.

I buttoned up my coat, balanced myself, advanced slowly towards him, touched his shoulder, and said, "The time has come; you must quit this place; I am sorry for you; here is money; but you must go."

"I would prefer not," he replied, with his back still towards me.

"You *must*."

He remained silent.

Now I had an unbounded confidence in this man's common honesty. He had frequently restored to me sixpences and shillings carelessly dropped upon the floor, for I am apt to be very reckless in such shirt-button affairs. The proceeding, then, which followed will not be deemed extraordinary.

"Bartleby," said I, "I owe you twelve dollars on account; here are thirty-two; the odd twenty are yours.—Will you take it?" and I handed the bills towards him.

But he made no motion.

"I will leave them here, then," putting them under a weight on the table. Then taking my hat and cane and going to the door, I tranquilly turned and added—"After you have removed your things from these offices, Bartleby, you will of course lock the door—since everyone is now gone for the day but you—and if you please, slip your key underneath the mat, so that I may have it in the morning. I shall not see you again; so good-bye to you. If, hereafter, in your new place of abode, I can be of any service to you, do not fail to advise me by letter. Good-bye, Bartleby, and fare you well."

But he answered not a word; like the last column of some ruined temple, he remained standing mute and solitary in the middle of the otherwise deserted room.

As I walked home in a pensive mood, my vanity got the better of my pity. I could not but highly plume myself on my masterly management in getting rid of Bartleby. Masterly I call it, and such it must appear to any dispassionate thinker. The beauty of my procedure seemed to consist in its perfect quietness. There was no vulgar bullying, no bravado of any sort, no choleric hectoring and striding to and fro across the apartment, jerking out vehement commands for Bartleby to bundle himself off with his beggarly traps. Nothing of the kind. Without loudly bidding Bartleby depart—as an inferior genius might have done—I *assumed* the ground that depart he must, and upon that assumption built all I had to say. The more I thought over my procedure, the more I was charmed with it. Nevertheless, next morning, upon awakening, I had my doubts—I had somehow slept off the fumes of vanity. One of the coolest and wisest hours a man has is just after he awakes in the morning. My procedure seemed as sagacious as ever—but only in theory. How it would prove in practice—there was the rub. It was truly a beautiful thought to have assumed Bartleby's departure; but, after all, that assumption was simply my own, and none of Bartleby's. The great point was, not whether I had assumed that he would quit me, but whether he would prefer so to do. He was more a man of preferences than assumptions.

After breakfast, I walked downtown, arguing the probabilities pro and con. One moment I thought it would prove a miserable failure, and Bartleby would be found all alive at my office as usual; the next moment it seemed certain that I should find his chair empty. And so I kept veering about. At the corner of Broadway and Canal Street, I saw quite an excited group of people standing in earnest conversation.

"I'll take odds he doesn't," said a voice as I passed.

"Doesn't go?—done!" said I, "put up your money."

I was instinctively putting my hand in my pocket to produce my own, when I remembered that this was an election day. The words I had overheard bore no reference to Bartleby but to the success or nonsuccess of some candidate for the mayoralty. In my intent frame of mind, I had, as it were, imagined that all Broadway shared in my excitement, and were debating the same question with me. I passed on, very thankful that the uproar of the street screened my momentary absent-mindedness.

As I had intended, I was earlier than usual at my office door. I stood listening for a moment. All was still. He must be gone. I tried the knob. The door was locked. Yes, my procedure had worked to a charm; he indeed must be vanished. Yet a certain melancholy mixed with this: I was almost sorry for my brilliant success. I was fumbling under the door mat for the key, which Bartleby was to have left there for me, when accidentally my knee knocked against a panel, producing a summoning sound, and in response a voice came to me from within—"Not yet; I am occupied."

It was Bartleby.

I was thunderstruck. For an instant I stood like the man who, pipe in mouth, was killed one cloudless afternoon long ago in Virginia by summer lightning; at his own warm open window he was killed, and remained leaning out there upon the dreamy afternoon, till someone touched him, when he fell.

"Not gone!" I murmured at last. But again obeying that wondrous ascendancy which the inscrutable scrivener had over me, and from which ascendancy, for all my chafing, I could not completely escape, I slowly went downstairs and out into the street, and while walking round the block considered what I should next do in this unheard-of perplexity. Turn the man out by an actual thrusting I could not; to drive him away by calling him hard names would not do; calling in the police was an unpleasant idea; and yet, permit him to enjoy his cadaverous triumph over me—this, too, I could not think of. What was to be done? or, if nothing could be done, was there anything further that I could *assume* in the matter? Yes, as before I had prospectively assumed that Bartleby would depart, so now I might retrospectively assume that departed he was. In the legitimate carrying out of this assumption I might enter my office in a great hurry, and, pretending not to see Bartleby at all, walk straight against him as if he were air. Such a proceeding would in a singular degree have the appearance of a home thrust. It was hardly possible that Bartleby could withstand such an application of the doctrine of assumptions. But upon second thoughts the success of the plan seemed rather dubious. I resolved to argue the matter over with him again.

"Bartleby," said I, entering the office, with a quietly severe expression, "I am seriously displeased. I am pained, Bartleby. I had thought better of you. I had imagined you of such a gentlemanly organization that in any delicate dilemma a slight hint would suffice—in short, an assumption. But it appears I am deceived. Why," I added unaffectedly starting, "you have not even touched that money yet," pointing to it, just where I had left it the evening previous.

He answered nothing.

"Will you, or will you not, quit me?" I now demanded in a sudden passion, advancing close to him.

"I would prefer *not* to quit you," he replied, gently emphasizing the *not*.

"What earthly right have you to stay here? Do you pay any rent? Do you pay my taxes? Or is this property yours?"

He answered nothing.

"Are you ready to go on and write now? Are your eyes recovered? Could you copy a small paper for me this morning? or help examine a few lines? or step round to the Post Office? In a word, will you do any thing at all to give a coloring to your refusal to depart the premises?"

He silently retired into his hermitage.

I was now in such a state of nervous resentment that I thought it but prudent to check myself at present from further demonstrations. Bartleby and I were alone. I remembered the tragedy of the unfortunate Adams and the still more unfortunate Colt in the solitary office of the latter; and how poor Colt, being dreadfully incensed by Adams, and imprudently permitting himself to get wildly excited, was at unawares hurried into his fatal act—an act which certainly no man could possibly deplore more than the actor himself. Often it had occurred to me in my ponderings upon the subject that had that altercation taken place in the public street, or at a private residence, it would not have terminated as it did. It was the circumstance of being alone in a solitary office, upstairs, of a building entirely unhallowed by humanizing domestic associations—an uncarpeted office, doubtless, of a dusty, haggard sort of appearance;—this it must have been which greatly helped to enhance the irritable desperation of the hapless Colt.

But when this old Adam of resentment rose in me and tempted me concerning Bartleby, I grappled him and threw him. How? Why, simply by recalling the divine injunction: "A new commandment give I unto you, that ye love one another." Yes, this it was that saved me. Aside from higher considerations, charity often operates as a vastly wise and prudent principle—a great safeguard to its possessor. Men have committed murder for jealousy's sake, and anger's sake, and hatred's sake, and selfishness' sake, and spiritual pride's sake: but no man that ever I heard of ever committed a diabolical murder for sweet charity's sake. Mere self-interest, then, if no better motive can be enlisted, should, especially with high-tempered men, prompt all beings to charity and philanthropy. At any rate, upon the occasion in question, I strove to drown my exasperated feelings towards the scrivener by benevolently construing his conduct. Poor fellow, poor fellow! thought I, he don't mean anything, and besides, he has seen hard times, and ought to be indulged.

I endeavored, also, immediately to occupy myself, and at the same time to comfort my despondency. I tried to fancy that in the course of the morning, at such time as might prove agreeable to him, Bartleby, of his own free accord, would emerge from his hermitage and take up some decided line of march in the direction of the door. But no. Half-past twelve o'clock came; Turkey began to glow in the face, overturn his inkstand, and become generally obstreperous; Nippers abated down into quietude and courtesy; Ginger Nut munched his noon apple; and Bartleby remained standing at his window in one of his profoundest dead-wall reveries. Will it be credited? Ought I to acknowledge it? That afternoon I left the office without saying one further word to him.

Some days now passed during which, at leisure intervals, I looked a little into "Edwards on the Will," and "Priestley on Necessity." Under the circumstances, those books induced a salutary feeling. Gradually I slid into the persuasion that these troubles of mine touching the scrivener had been all predestinated from eternity and Bartleby was billeted upon me for some mysterious purpose of an all-wise Providence, which it was not for a mere mortal like me to fathom. Yes, Bartleby, stay there behind your screen, thought I; I shall persecute you no more; you are harmless and noiseless as any of these old chairs; in short, I never feel so private as when I know you are here. At last I see it, I feel it; I penetrate to the predestinated purpose of my life. I am content. Others may have loftier parts to enact, but my mission in this world, Bartleby, is to furnish you with office room for such period as you may see fit to remain.

I believe that this wise and blessed frame of mind would have continued with me had it not been for the unsolicited and uncharitable remarks obtruded upon me by my professional friends who visited the rooms. But thus it often is that the constant friction of illiberal minds wears out at last the best resolves of the more generous. Though, to be sure, when I reflected upon it it was not strange that people entering my office should be struck by the peculiar aspect of the unaccountable Bartleby, and so be tempted to throw out some sinister observations concerning him. Sometimes an attorney having business with me, and calling at my office, and finding no one but the scrivener there, would undertake to obtain some sort of precise information from him touching my whereabouts; but without heeding his idle talk, Bartleby would remain standing immovable in the middle of the room. So, after contemplating him in that position for a time, the attorney would depart no wiser than he came.

Also, when a reference was going on, and the room full of lawyers and witnesses, and business was driving fast, some deeply-occupied legal gentleman present, seeing Bartleby wholly unemployed, would request him to run round to his (the legal gentleman's) office and fetch some papers for him. Thereupon Bartleby would tranquilly decline, and yet remain idle as before. Then the lawyer would give a great stare, and turn to me. And what could I say? At last I was made aware that all through the circle of my professional acquaintance a whisper of wonder was running round, having reference to the strange creature I kept at my office. This worried me very much. And as the idea came upon me of his possibly turning out a longlived man, and keep occupying my chambers, and denying my authority; and perplexing my visitors; and scandalizing my professional reputation; and casting a general gloom over the premises; keeping soul and body together to the last upon his savings (for doubtless he spent but half a dime a day), and in the end perhaps outlive me, and claim possession of my office by right of his perpetual occupancy—as all these dark anticipations crowded upon me more and more, and my friends continually intruded their relentless remarks upon the apparition in my room, a great change was wrought in me. I resolved to gather all my faculties together and forever rid me of this intolerable incubus.

Ere revolving any complicated project, however, adapted to this end, I first simply suggested to Bartleby the propriety of his permanent departure. In a calm and serious tone, I commended the idea to his careful and mature consideration. But, having taken three days to meditate upon it, he apprised me that his original determination remained the same; in short, that he still preferred to abide with me.

What shall I do? I now said to myself, buttoning up my coat to the last button. What shall I do? what ought I to do? what does conscience say I *should* do with this man, or, rather, ghost. Rid myself of him, I must; go, he shall. But how? You will not thrust him, the poor, pale, passive mortal—you will not thrust such a helpless creature out of your door? you will not dishonor yourself by such cruelty? No, I will not, I cannot do that. Rather would I let him live and die here, and then mason up his remains in the wall. What, then, will you do? For all your coaxing, he will not budge. Bribes he leaves under your own paperweight on your table; in short, it is quite plain that he prefers to cling to you.

Then something severe, something unusual, must be done. What! surely you will not have him collared by a constable, and commit his innocent pallor to the common jail? And upon what ground could you procure such a thing to be done?—a vagrant, is he? What! he a vagrant, a wanderer, who refuses to budge? It is because he will *not* be a vagrant, then, that you seek to count him *as* a vagrant. That is too absurd. No visible means of support: there I have him. Wrong again: for indubitably he *does* support himself, and that is the only unanswerable proof that any man can show of his possessing the means so to do. No more, then. Since he will not quit me, I must quit him. I will change my offices; I will move elsewhere, and give him fair notice that if I find him on my new premises I will then proceed against him as a common trespasser.

Acting accordingly, next day I thus addressed him: "I find these chambers too far from the City Hall; the air is unwholesome. In a word, I propose to remove my offices next week, and shall no longer require your services. I tell you this now, in order that you may seek another place."

He made no reply, and nothing more was said.

On the appointed day I engaged carts and men, proceeded to my chambers, and, having but little furniture, everything was removed in a few hours. Throughout, the scrivener remained standing behind the screen, which I directed to be removed the last thing. It was withdrawn; and being folded up like a huge folio, left him the motionless occupant of a naked room. I stood in the entry watching him a moment, while something from within me upbraided me.

I re-entered, with my hand in my pocket—and—and my heart in my mouth.

"Good-bye, Bartleby; I am going—good-bye; and God some way bless you; and take that," slipping something in his hand. But it dropped upon the floor, and then—strange to say—I tore myself from him whom I had so longed to be rid of.

Established in my new quarters, for a day or two I kept the door locked, and started at every footfall in the passages. When I returned to my rooms after any little absence, I would pause at the threshold for an instant and attentively listen ere applying my key. But these fears were needless. Bartleby never came nigh me.

I thought all was going well, when a perturbed-looking stranger visited me, inquiring whether I was the person who had recently occupied rooms at No. —— Wall Street.

Full of forebodings, I replied that I was.

"Then, sir," said the stranger, who proved a lawyer, "you are responsible for the man you left there. He refuses to do any copying; he refuses to do anything; he says he prefers not to; and he refuses to quit the premises."

"I am very sorry, sir," said I, with assumed tranquillity, but an inward tremor, "but, really, the man you allude to is nothing to me—he is no relation or apprentice of mine, that you should hold me responsible for him."

"In mercy's name, who is he?"

"I certainly cannot inform you. I know nothing about him. Formerly I employed him as a copyist; but he has done nothing for me now for some time past."

"I shall settle him, then,—good morning, sir."

Several days passed, and I heard nothing more; and though I often felt a charitable prompting to call at the place and see poor Bartleby, yet a certain squeamishness, of I know not what, withheld me.

All is over with him, by this time, thought I at last, when through another week, no further intelligence reached me. But, coming to my room the day after, I found several persons waiting at my door in a high state of nervous excitement.

"That's the man—here he comes," cried the foremost one, whom I recognized as the lawyer who had previously called upon me alone.

"You must take him away, sir, at once," cried a portly person among them, advancing upon me, and whom I knew to be the landlord of No. —— Wall Street. "These gentlemen, my tenants, cannot stand it any longer; Mr. B ——," pointing to the lawyer, "has turned him out of his room, and he now persists in haunting the building generally, sitting upon the banisters of the stairs by day, and sleeping in the entry by night. Everybody is concerned; clients are leaving the offices; some fears are entertained of a mob; something you must do, and that without delay."

Aghast at this torrent, I fell back before it, and would fain have locked myself in my new quarters. In vain I persisted that Bartleby was nothing to me—no more than to anyone else. In vain—I was the last person known to have anything to do with him, and they held me to the terrible account. Fearful, then, of being exposed in the papers (as one person present obscurely threatened), I considered the matter, and at length said that if the lawyer would give me a confidential interview with the scrivener, in his (the lawyer's) own room, I would, that afternoon strive my best to rid them of the nuisance they complained of.

Going upstairs to my old haunt, there was Bartleby silently sitting upon the banister at the landing.

"What are you doing here, Bartleby?" said I.

"Sitting upon the banister," he mildly replied.

I motioned him into the lawyer's room, who then left us.

"Bartleby," said I, "are you aware that you are the cause of great tribulation to me, by persisting in occupying the entry after being dismissed from the office?"

No answer.

"Now one of two things must take place. Either you must do something, or something must be done to you. Now what sort of business would you like to engage in? Would you like to re-engage in copying for someone?"

"No; I would prefer not to make any change."

"Would you like a clerkship in a dry-goods store?"

"There is too much confinement about that. No, I would not like a clerkship; but I am not particular."

"Too much confinement," I cried; "why you keep yourself confined all the time!"

"I would prefer not to take a clerkship," he rejoined, as if to settle that little item at once.

"How would a bartender's business suit you? There is no trying of the eyesight in that."

"I would not like it at all; though, as I said before, I am not particular."

His unwonted wordiness inspirited me. I returned to the charge.

"Well, then, would you like to travel through the country collecting bills for the merchants? That would improve your health."

"No, I would prefer to be doing something else."

"How, then, would going as a companion to Europe, to entertain some young gentleman with your conversation—how would that suit you?"

"Not at all. It does not strike me that there is anything definite about that. I like to be stationary. But I am not particular."

"Stationary you shall be, then," I cried, now losing all patience, and, for the first time in all my exasperating connection with him, fairly flying into a passion. "If you do not go away from these premises before night, I shall feel bound—indeed, I *am* bound—to—to—to quit the premises myself!" I rather absurdly concluded, knowing not with what possible threat to try to frighten his immobility into compliance. Despairing of all further efforts, I was precipitately leaving him, when a final thought occurred to me—one which had not been wholly unindulged before.

"Bartleby," said I, in the kindest tone I could assume under such exciting circumstances, "will you go home with me now—not to my office, but my dwelling—and remain there till we can conclude upon some convenient arrangement for you at our leisure? Come, let us start now, right away."

"No; at present I would prefer not to make any change at all."

I answered nothing, but, effectually dodging everyone by the suddenness and rapidity of my flight, rushed from the building, ran up Wall Street towards Broadway, and, jumping into the first omnibus, was soon removed from pursuit. As soon as tranquillity returned, I distinctly perceived that I had now done all that I possibly could, both in respect to the demands of the landlord and his tenants, and with regard to my own desire and sense of duty, to benefit Bartleby, and shield him from rude persecution. I now strove to be entirely carefree and quiescent, and my conscience justified me in the attempt, though, indeed, it was not so successful as I could have wished. So fearful was I of being again hunted out by the incensed landlord and his exasperated tenants that, surrendering my business to Nippers for a few days, I drove about the upper part of the town and through the suburbs in my rockaway; crossed over to Jersey

City and Hoboken, and paid fugitive visits to Manhattanville and Astoria. In fact, I almost lived in my rockaway for the time.

When again I entered my office, lo, a note from the landlord lay upon the desk. I opened it with trembling hands. It informed me that the writer had sent to the police, and had Bartleby removed to the Tombs as a vagrant. Moreover, since I knew more about him than anyone else, he wished me to appear at that place and make a suitable statement of the facts. These tidings had a conflicting effect upon me. At first I was indignant, but at last almost approved. The landlord's energetic, summary disposition had led him to adopt a procedure which I do not think I would have decided upon myself; and yet, as a last resort, under such peculiar circumstances, it seemed the only plan.

As I afterwards learned, the poor scrivener, when told that he must be conducted to the Tombs, offered not the slightest obstacle, but, in his pale, unmoving way, silently acquiesced.

Some of the compassionate and curious bystanders joined the party; and, headed by one of the constables arm in arm with Bartleby, the silent procession filed its way through all the noise, and heat, and joy of the roaring thoroughfares at noon.

The same day I received the note, I went to the Tombs, or, to speak more properly, the Halls of Justice. Seeking the right officer, I stated the purpose of my call, and was informed that the individual I described was indeed within. I then assured the functionary that Bartleby was a perfectly honest man, and greatly to be compassionated, however unaccountably eccentric. I narrated all I knew, and closed by suggesting the idea of letting him remain in as indulgent confinement as possible till something less harsh might be done—though, indeed, I hardly knew what. At all events, if nothing else could be decided upon, the almshouse must receive him. I then begged to have an interview.

Being under no disgraceful charge, and quite serene and harmless in all his ways, they had permitted him freely to wander about the prison, and, especially, in the inclosed grass-platted yards thereof. And so I found him there, standing all alone in the quietest of the yards, his face towards a high wall, while all around, from the narrow slits of the jail windows, I thought I saw peering out upon him the eyes of murderers and thieves.

"Bartleby!"

"I know you," he said, without looking round—"and I want nothing to say to you."

"It was not I that brought you here, Bartleby," said I, keenly pained at his implied suspicion. "And, to you, this should not be so vile a place. Nothing reproachful attaches to you by being here. And see, it is not so sad a place as one might think. Look, there is the sky, and here is the grass."

"I know where I am," he replied, but would say nothing more, and so I left him.

As I entered the corridor again, a broad meatlike man in an apron accosted me, and, jerking his thumb over his shoulder, said—"Is that your friend?"

"Yes."

"Does he want to starve? If he does, let him live on the prison fare, that's all."

"Who are you?" asked I, not knowing what to make of such an unofficially speaking person in such a place.

"I am the grubman. Such gentlemen as have friends here hire me to provide them with something good to eat."

"Is this so?" said I, turning to the turnkey.

He said it was.

"Well, then," said I, slipping some silver into the grubman's hands (for so they called him), "I want you to give particular attention to my friend there; let him have the best dinner you can get. And you must be as polite to him as possible."

"Introduce me, will you?" said the grubman, looking at me with an expression which seemed to say he was all impatience for an opportunity to give a specimen of his breeding.

Thinking it would prove of benefit to the scrivener, I acquiesced, and, asking the grubman his name, went up with him to Bartleby.

"Bartleby, this is a friend; you will find him very useful to you."

"Your sarvant, sir, your sarvant," said the grubman, making a low salutation behind his apron. "Hope you find it pleasant here, sir; nice grounds—cool apartments—hope you'll stay with us some time—try to make it agreeable. What will you have for dinner today?"

"I prefer not to dine today," said Bartleby, turning away. "It would disagree with me; I am unused to dinners." So saying, he slowly moved to the other side of the inclosure and took up a position fronting the dead-wall.

"How's this?" said the grubman, addressing me with a stare of astonishment. "He's odd, ain't he?"

"I think he is a little deranged," said I, sadly.

"Deranged? deranged is it? Well, now, upon my word, I thought that friend of yourn was a gentleman forger; they are always pale and genteel-like, them forgers. I can't help pity 'em—can't help it, sir. Did you know Monroe Edwards?" he added, touchingly, and paused. Then, laying his hand pityeously on my shoulder, sighed, "He died of consumption at Sing-Sing. So you weren't acquainted with Monroe?"

"No, I was never socially acquainted with any forgers. But I cannot stop longer. Look to my friend yonder. You will not lose by it. I will see you again."

Some few days after this, I again obtained admission to the Tombs, and went through the corridors in quest of Bartleby; but without finding him.

"I saw him coming from his cell not long ago," said a turnkey. "Maybe he's gone to loiter in the yards."

So I went in that direction.

"Are you looking for the silent man?" said another turnkey, passing me. "Yonder he lies—sleeping in the yard there. 'Tis not twenty minutes since I saw him lie down."

The yard was entirely quiet. It was not accessible to the common prisoners. The surrounding walls, of amazing thickness, kept off all sounds behind them. The Egyptian character of the masonry weighed upon me with its gloom. But a soft imprisoned turf grew underfoot. The heart of the eternal pyramids, it seemed, wherein, by some strange magic, through the clefts, grass-seed, dropped by birds, had sprung.

Strangely huddled at the base of the wall, his knees drawn up and lying on his side, his head touching the cold stones, I saw the wasted Bartleby. But nothing stirred. I paused, then went close up to him, stooped over, and saw that his dim eyes were open; otherwise he seemed profoundly sleeping. Something prompted me to touch him. I felt his hand, when a tingling shiver ran up my arm and down my spine to my feet.

The round face of the grubman peered upon me now. "His dinner is ready. Won't he dine today, either? Or does he live without dining?"

"Lives without dining," said I, and closed the eyes.

"Eh!—He's asleep, ain't he?"

"With kings and counselors," murmured I.

★ ★ ★

There would seem little need for proceeding further in this history. Imagination will readily supply the meager recital of poor Bartleby's interment. But, ere parting with the reader, let me say that if this little narrative has sufficiently interested him to awaken curiosity as to who Bartleby was, and what manner of life he led prior to the present narrator's making his acquaintance, I can only reply that in such curiosity I fully share, but am wholly unable to gratify it. Yet here I hardly know whether I should divulge one little item of rumor which came to my ear a few months after the scrivener's decease. Upon what basis it rested, I could never ascertain, and hence how true it is I cannot now tell. But, inasmuch as this vague report has not been without a certain suggestive interest to me, however sad, it may prove the same with some others, and so I will briefly mention it. The report was this: that Bartleby had been a subordinate clerk in the Dead Letter Office at Washington, from which he had been suddenly removed by a change in the administration. When I think over this rumor, hardly can I express the emotions which seize me. Dead letters! does it not sound like dead men? Conceive a man by nature and misfortune prone to a pallid hopelessness, can any business seem more fitted to heighten it than that of continually handling these dead letters, and assorting them for the flames? For by the cartload they are annually burned. Sometimes from out the folded paper the pale clerk takes a ring— the finger it was meant for, perhaps, moulders in the grave; a bank note sent in swiftest charity—he whom it would relieve nor eats nor hungers any more; pardon for those who died despairing; hope for those who died unhoping; good tidings for those who died stifled by unrelieved calamities. On errands of life, these letters speed to death.

Ah, Bartleby! Ah, humanity!

ADVENTURES OF A NOVELIST (1896)

Stephen Crane

Stephen Crane (1871–1900), born in New Jersey, began visiting New York City around 1891. He based "Adventures of a Novelist" on an actual event, converting into the third-person his experience of testifying to the police and in court in defense of a prostitute. He publicized the event himself, and explained his participation in it in this way: "I am studying the life of the Tenderloin for the purpose of getting material for some sketches."[1] (Indeed, he did gather material, and was the renowned author of The Red Badge of Courage, *as well as of the notorious (at the time) New York novella* Maggie: A Girl of the Streets.) *On September 20, 1896, in the* New York Journal, *Crane narrated his "adventure" with his character in the role of "the reluctant witness"; Crane's fictionalized dramatization was meant to depict not only police abuse of power but also the typical wavering New York witness, whose conscience is addressed with the admonition: "If you don't go to court and speak for that girl you are no man!" As it happened, Crane was indeed a man and, like his protagonist, did testify and exonerate "that girl." Crane traveled the world, reporting on wars and civil strife. He died at twenty-eight of tuberculosis.*

THIS IS A plain tale of two chorus girls, a woman of the streets and a reluctant laggard witness. The tale properly begins in a resort on Broadway, where the two chorus girls and the reluctant witness sat the entire evening. They were on the verge of departing their several ways when a young woman approached one of the chorus girls, with outstretched hand.

"Why, how do you do?" she said. "I haven't seen you for a long time."

---

[1] *The New York Sun.* September 17, 1896. Cited in Stanley Wertheim and Paul Sorrentino's *The Crane Log: A Documentary Life of Stephen Crane, 1871–1900.* New York: G. K. Hall and Company, 1995. 207.

The chorus girl recognized some acquaintance of the past, and the young woman then took a seat and joined the party. Finally they left the table in this resort, and the quartet walked down Broadway together. At the corner of Thirty-first street one of the chorus girls said that she wished to take a car immediately for home, and so the reluctant witness left one of the chorus girls, and the young woman on the corner of Thirty-first street while he placed the other chorus girl aboard an uptown cable car. The two girls who waited on the corner were deep in conversation.

The reluctant witness was returning leisurely to them. In the semi-conscious manner in which people note details which do not appear at the time important, he saw two men passing along Broadway. They passed swiftly, like men who are going home. They paid attention to none, and none at the corner of Thirty-first street and Broadway paid attention to them.

The two girls were still deep in conversation. They were standing at the curb facing the street. The two men passed unseen—in all human probability—by the two girls. The reluctant witness continued his leisurely way. He was within four feet of these two girls when suddenly and silently a man appeared from nowhere in particular and grabbed them both.

The astonishment of the reluctant witness was so great for the ensuing seconds that he was hardly aware of what transpired during that time, save that both girls screamed. Then he heard this man, who was now evidently an officer, say to them: "Come to the station house. You are under arrest for soliciting two men."

With one voice the unknown woman, the chorus girl and the reluctant witness cried out: "What two men?"

The officer said: "Those two men who have just passed."

And here began the wildest and most hysterical sobbing of the two girls, accompanied by spasmodic attempts to pull their arms away from the grip of the policeman. The chorus girl seemed nearly insane with fright and fury. Finally she screamed:

"Well, he's my husband." And with her finger she indicated the reluctant witness. The witness at once replied to the swift, questioning glance of the officer, "Yes; I am."

If it was necessary to avow a marriage to save a girl who is not a prostitute from being arrested as a prostitute, it must be done, though the man suffer eternally. And then the officer forgot immediately—without a second's hesitation, he forgot that a moment previously he had arrested this girl for soliciting, and so, dropping her arm, released her.

"But," said he, "I have got this other one." He was as picturesque as a wolf.

"Why arrest her, either?" said the reluctant witness.

"For soliciting those two men."

"But she didn't solicit those two men."

"Say," said the officer, turning, "do you know this woman?"

The chorus girl had it in mind to lie then for the purpose of saving this woman easily and simply from the palpable wrong she seemed to be about to experience. "Yes; I know her"—"I have seen her two or three times"—"Yes; I have met her before———" But the reluctant witness said at once that he knew nothing whatever of the girl.

"Well," said the officer, "she's a common prostitute."

There was a short silence then, but the reluctant witness presently said: "Are you arresting her as a common prostitute? She has been perfectly respectable since she has been with us. She hasn't done anything wrong since she has been in our company."

"I am arresting her for soliciting those two men," answered the officer, "and if you people don't want to get pinched, too, you had better not be seen with her."

Then began a parade to the station house—the officer and his prisoner ahead and two simpletons following.

At the station house the officer said to the sergeant behind the desk that he had seen the woman come from the resort on Broadway alone, and on the way to the corner of Thirty-first street solicit two men, and that immediately afterward she had met a man and a woman—meaning the chorus girl and the reluctant witness— on the said corner, and was in conversation with them when he arrested her. He did not mention to the sergeant at this time the arrest and release of the chorus girl.

At the conclusion of the officer's story the sergeant said, shortly: "Take her back." This did not mean to take the woman back to the corner of Thirty-first street and Broadway. It meant to take her back to the cells, and she was accordingly led away.

The chorus girl had undoubtedly intended to be an intrepid champion; she had avowedly come to the station house for that purpose, but her entire time had been devoted to sobbing in the wildest form of hysteria. The reluctant witness was obliged to devote his entire time to an attempt to keep her from making an uproar of some kind. This paroxysm of terror, of indignation, and the extreme mental anguish caused by her unconventional and strange situation, was so violent that the reluctant witness could not take time from her to give any testimony to the sergeant.

After the woman was sent to the cell the reluctant witness reflected a moment in silence; then he said:

"Well, we might as well go."

On the way out of Thirtieth street the chorus girl continued to sob. "If you don't go to court and speak for that girl you are no man!" she cried. The arrested woman had, by the way, screamed out a request to appear in her behalf before the Magistrate.

"By George! I cannot," said the reluctant witness. "I can't afford to do that sort of thing. I—I——"

After he had left this girl safely, he continued to reflect: "Now this arrest I firmly believe to be wrong. This girl may be a courtesan, for anything that I know at all to the contrary. The sergeant at the station house seemed to know her as well as he knew the Madison square tower. She is then, in all probability a courtesan. She is arrested, however, for soliciting those two men. If I have ever had a conviction in my life, I am convinced that she did not solicit those two men. Now, if these affairs occur from time to time, they must be witnessed occasionally by men of character. Do these reputable citizens interfere? No, they go home and thank God that they can still attend piously to their own affairs. Suppose I were a clerk and I interfered in this sort of a case. When it became known to my employers they would say to me: 'We are sorry, but we cannot have men in our employ who stay out until 2:30 in the morning in the company of chorus girls.'

"Suppose, for instance, I had a wife and seven children in Harlem. As soon as my wife read the papers she would say: 'Ha! You told me you had a business engagement! Half-past two in the morning with questionable company!'

"Suppose, for instance, I were engaged to the beautiful Countess of Kalamazoo. If she were to hear it, she would write: 'All is over between us. My future husband cannot rescue prostitutes at 2:30 in the morning.'

"These, then, must be three small general illustrations of why men of character say nothing if they happen to witness some possible affair of this sort, and perhaps these illustrations could be multiplied to infinity. I possess nothing so tangible as a clerkship, as a wife and seven children in Harlem, as an engagement to the beautiful Countess of Kalamazoo; but all that I value may be chanced in this affair. Shall I take this risk for the benefit of a girl of the streets?

"But this girl, be she prostitute or whatever, was at this time manifestly in my escort, and—Heaven save the blasphemous philosophy—a wrong done to a prostitute must be as purely a wrong as a wrong done to a queen," said the reluctant witness—this blockhead.

"Moreover, I believe that this officer has dishonored his obligation as a public servant. Have I a duty as a citizen, or do citizens have duty, as a citizen, or do citizens have no duties? Is it a mere myth that there was at one time a man who possessed a consciousness of civic responsibility, or has it become a distinction of our municipal civilization that men of this character shall be licensed to deprecate in such a manner upon those who are completely at their mercy?"

He returned to the sergeant at the police station, and, after asking if he could send anything to the girl to make her more comfortable for the night, he told the sergeant the story of the arrest, as he knew it.

"Well," said the sergeant, "that may be all true. I don't defend the officer. I do not say that he was right, or that he was wrong, but it seems to me that I have seen you somewhere before and know you vaguely as a man of good repute; so why interfere in this thing? As for this girl, I know her to be a common prostitute. That's why I sent her back."

"But she was not arrested as a common prostitute. She was arrested for soliciting two men, and I know that she didn't solicit the two men."

"Well," said the sergeant, "that, too, may all be true, but I give you the plain advice of a man who has been behind this desk for years, and knows how these things go, and I advise you simply to stay home. If you monkey with this case, you are pretty sure to come out with mud all over you."

"I suppose so," said the reluctant witness. "I haven't a doubt of it. But I don't see how I can, in honesty, stay away from court in the morning."

"Well, do it anyhow," said the sergeant.

"But I don't see how I can do it."

The sergeant was bored. "Oh, I tell you, the girl is nothing but a common prostitute," he said, wearily.

The reluctant witness on reaching his room set the alarm clock for the proper hour.

In the court at 8:30 he met a reporter acquaintance. "Go home," said the reporter, when he had heard the story. "Go home; your own participation in the affair doesn't look very respectable. Go home."

"But it is a wrong," said the reluctant witness.

"Oh, it is only a temporary wrong," said the reporter. The definition of a temporary wrong did not appear at that time to the reluctant witness, but the reporter was too much in earnest to consider terms. "Go home," said he.

Thus—if the girl was wronged—it is to be seen that all circumstances, all forces, all opinions, all men were combined to militate against her. Apparently the united wisdom of the world declared that no man should do anything but throw his sense of justice to the winds in an affair of this description. "Let a man have a conscience for the daytime," said wisdom. "Let him have a conscience for the daytime, but it is idiocy for a man to have a conscience at 2:30 in the morning, in the case of an arrested prostitute."

The officer who had made the arrest told a story of the occurrence. The girl at the bar told a story of the occurrence. And the girl's story as to this affair was, to the reluctant witness, perfectly true. Nevertheless, her word could not be accounted of any value. It was impossible that any one in the courtroom could suppose that she was telling the truth, save the reluctant witness and the reporter to whom he had told the tale.

The reluctant witness recited what he believed to be a true accounting, and the Magistrate discharged the prisoner.

The reluctant witness has told this story merely because it is a story which the public of New York should know for once.

THE OTHER TWO (1904)

Edith Wharton

Edith Wharton (1862–1937) hit her stride as an author of fiction in her early forties. "The qualities that make Wharton a great writer," observes that great biographer Hermione Lee, "her mixture of harshly detached, meticulously perceptive, disabused realism, with a language of poignant feeling and deep passion, and her setting of the most confined of private lives in a thick, complex network of social forces—were the product of years of observation, reading, practice and refinement."* In the quietly comic "The Other Two," a wealthy Wall Street man marries a twice-divorced mother, the flighty Alice. "He had known when he married that his wife's former husbands were both living," writes Wharton, sympathetically but wryly, "and that amid the multiplied contacts of modern existence there were a thousand chances to one that he would run against one or the other . . ." He didn't know, however, that he would figure in a short story called "The Other Two," where the chances would be considerably higher. Two of Wharton's classic novels, The House of Mirth *(1905) and* The Age of Innocence *(1920), are set in New York City.*

I

WAYTHORN, ON THE drawing-room hearth, waited for his wife to come down to dinner.

It was their first night under his own roof, and he was surprised at his thrill of boyish agitation. He was not so old, to be sure—his glass gave him little more than the five-and-thirty years to which his wife confessed—but he had fancied himself already in the temperate zone; yet here he was listening for her step with a tender sense of all it symbolized, with some old trail of verse about the

---

* Hermione Lee. *Edith Wharton: A Biography.* New York: Knopf. 2007. 349.

garlanded nuptial doorposts floating through his enjoyment of the pleasant room and the good dinner just beyond it.

They had been hastily recalled from their honeymoon by the illness of Lily Haskett, the child of Mrs. Waythorn's first marriage. The little girl, at Waythorn's desire, had been transferred to his house on the day of her mother's wedding, and the doctor, on their arrival, broke the news that she was ill with typhoid, but declared that all the symptoms were favorable. Lily could show twelve years of unblemished health, and the case promised to be a light one. The nurse spoke as reassuringly, and after a moment of alarm Mrs. Waythorn had adjusted herself to the situation. She was very fond of Lily—her affection for the child had perhaps been her decisive charm in Waythorn's eyes—but she had the perfectly balanced nerves which her little girl had inherited, and no woman ever wasted less tissue in unproductive worry. Waythorn was therefore quite prepared to see her come in presently a little late because of a last look at Lily, but as serene and well-appointed as if her good-night kiss had been laid on the brow of health. Her composure was restful to him; it acted as ballast to his somewhat unstable sensibilities. As he pictured her bending over the child's bed he thought how soothing her presence must be in illness: her very step would prognosticate recovery.

His own life had been a gray one, from temperament rather than circumstance, and he had been drawn to her by the unperturbed gaiety which kept her fresh and elastic at an age when most women's activities are growing either slack or febrile. He knew what was said about her; for, popular as she was, there had always been a faint undercurrent of detraction. When she had appeared in New York, nine or ten years earlier, as the pretty Mrs. Haskett whom Gus Varick had unearthed somewhere—was it in Pittsburgh or Utica?—society, while promptly accepting her, had reserved the right to cast a doubt on its own indiscrimination. Inquiry, however, established her undoubted connection with a socially reigning family, and explained her recent divorce as the natural result of a runaway match at seventeen; and as nothing was known of Mr. Haskett it was easy to believe the worst of him.

Alice Haskett's remarriage with Gus Varick was a passport to the set whose recognition she coveted, and for a few years the Varicks were the most popular couple in town. Unfortunately the alliance was brief and stormy, and this time the husband had his champions.

Still, even Varick's stanchest supporters admitted that he was not meant for matrimony, and Mrs. Varick's grievances were of a nature to bear the inspection of the New York courts. A New York divorce is in itself a diploma of virtue, and in the semiwidowhood of this second separation Mrs. Varick took on an air of sanctity, and was allowed to confide her wrongs to some of the most scrupulous ears in town. But when it was known that she was to marry Waythorn there was a momentary reaction. Her best friends would have preferred to see her remain in the role of the injured wife, which was as becoming to her as crepe to a rosy complexion. True, a decent time had elapsed, and it was not even suggested that Waythorn had supplanted his predecessor. People shook their heads over him, however, and one grudging friend, to whom he affirmed that he took the step with his eyes open, replied oracularly: "Yes— and with your ears shut."

Waythorn could afford to smile at these innuendoes. In the Wall Street phrase, he had "discounted" them. He knew that society has not yet adapted itself to the consequences of divorce, and that till the adaptation takes place every woman who uses the freedom the law accords her must be her own social justification. Waythorn had an amused confidence in his wife's ability to justify herself. His expectations were fulfilled, and before the wedding took place Alice Varick's group had rallied openly to her support. She took it all imperturbably: she had a way of surmounting obstacles without seeming to be aware of them, and Waythorn looked back with wonder at the trivialities over which he had worn his nerves thin. He had the sense of having found refuge in a richer, warmer nature than his own, and his satisfaction, at the moment, was humorously summed up in the thought that his wife, when she had done all she could for Lily, would not be ashamed to come down and enjoy a good dinner.

The anticipation of such enjoyment was not, however, the sentiment expressed by Mrs. Waythorn's charming face when she presently joined him. Though she had put on her most engaging tea gown she had neglected to assume the smile that went with it, and Waythorn thought he had never seen her look so nearly worried.

"What is it?" he asked. "Is anything wrong with Lily?"

"No; I've just been in and she's still sleeping." Mrs. Waythorn hesitated. "But something tiresome has happened."

He had taken her two hands, and now perceived that he was crushing a paper between them. "This letter?"

"Yes—Mr. Haskett has written—I mean his lawyer has written."

Waythorn felt himself flush uncomfortably. He dropped his wife's hands.

"What about?"

"About seeing Lily. You know the courts—"

"Yes, yes," he interrupted nervously.

Nothing was known about Haskett in New York. He was vaguely supposed to have remained in the outer darkness from which his wife had been rescued, and Waythorn was one of the few who were aware that he had given up his business in Utica and followed her to New York in order to be near his little girl. In the days of his wooing, Waythorn had often met Lily on the doorstep, rosy and smiling, on her way "to see papa."

"I am so sorry," Mrs. Waythorn murmured.

He roused himself. "What does he want?"

"He wants to see her. You know she goes to him once a week."

"Well—he doesn't expect her to go to him now, does he?"

"No—he has heard of her illness; but he expects to come here."

"*Here?*"

Mrs. Waythorn reddened under his gaze. They looked away from each other.

"I'm afraid he has the right . . . You'll see. . . ." She made a proffer of the letter.

Waythorn moved away with a gesture of refusal. He stood staring about the softly-lighted room, which a moment before had seemed so full of bridal intimacy.

"I'm so sorry," she repeated. "If Lily could have been moved—"

"That's out of the question," he returned impatiently.

"I suppose so."

Her lip was beginning to tremble, and he felt himself a brute.

"He must come, of course," he said. "When is—his day?"

"I'm afraid—tomorrow."

"Very well. Send a note in the morning."

The butler entered to announce dinner.

Waythorn turned to his wife. "Come—you must be tired. It's beastly, but try to forget about it," he said, drawing her hand through his arm.

"You're so good, dear. I'll try," she whispered back.

Her face cleared at once, and as she looked at him across the flowers, between the rosy candleshades, he saw her lips waver back into a smile.

"How pretty everything is!" she sighed luxuriously.

He turned to the butler. "The champagne at once, please. Mrs. Waythorn is tired."

In a moment or two their eyes met above the sparkling glasses. Her own were quite clear and untroubled: he saw that she had obeyed his injunction and forgotten.

II

Waythorn, the next morning, went downtown earlier than usual. Haskett was not likely to come till the afternoon, but the instinct of flight drove him forth. He meant to stay away all day—he had thoughts of dining at his club. As his door closed behind him he reflected that before he opened it again it would have admitted another man who had as much right to enter it as himself, and the thought filled him with a physical repugnance.

He caught the elevated at the employees' hour, and found himself crushed between two layers of pendulous humanity. At Eighth Street the man facing him wriggled out, and another took his place. Waythorn glanced up and saw that it was Gus Varick. The men were so close together that it was impossible to ignore the smile of recognition on Varick's handsome overblown face. And after all—why not? They had always been on good terms, and Varick had been divorced before Waythorn's attentions to his wife began. The two exchanged a word on the perennial grievance of the congested trains, and when a seat at their side was miraculously left empty the instinct of self-preservation made Waythorn slip into it after Varick.

The latter drew the stout man's breath of relief. "Lord—I was beginning to feel like a pressed flower." He leaned back, looking unconcernedly at Waythorn. "Sorry to hear that Sellers is knocked out again."

"Sellers?" echoed Waythorn, starting at his partner's name.

Varick looked surprised. "You didn't know he was laid up with the gout?"

"No. I've been away—I only got back last night." Waythorn felt himself reddening in anticipation of the other's smile.

"All—yes; to be sure. And Sellers' attack came on two days ago. I'm afraid he's pretty bad. Very awkward for me, as it happens, because he was just putting through a rather important thing for me."

"Ah?" Waythorn wondered vaguely since when Varick had been dealing in "important things." Hitherto he had dabbled only in the shallow pools of speculation, with which Waythorn's office did not usually concern itself.

It occurred to him that Varick might be talking at random to relieve the strain of their propinquity. That strain was becoming momentarily more apparent to Waythorn, and when, at Cortlandt Street, he caught sight of an acquaintance and had a sudden vision of the picture he and Varick must present to an initiated eye, he jumped up with a muttered excuse.

"I hope you'll find Sellers better," said Varick civilly, and he stammered back: "If I can be of any use to you—" and let the departing crowd sweep him to the platform.

At his office he heard that Sellers was in fact ill with the gout, and would probably not be able to leave the house for some weeks.

"I'm sorry it should have happened so, Mr. Waythorn," the senior clerk said with affable significance. "Mr. Sellers was very much upset at the idea of giving you such a lot of extra work just now."

"Oh, that's no matter." said Waythorn hastily. He secretly welcomed the pressure of additional business, and was glad to think that, when the day's work was over, he would have to call at his partner's on the way home.

He was late for luncheon, and turned in at the nearest restaurant instead of going to his club. The place was full, and the waiter hurried him to the back of the room to capture the only vacant table. In the cloud of cigar smoke Waythorn did not at once distinguish his neighbors: but presently, looking about him, he saw Varick seated a few feet off. This time, luckily, they were too far apart for conversation, and Varick, who faced another way, had probably not even seen him; but there was an irony in their renewed nearness.

Varick was said to be fond of good living, and as Waythorn sat dispatching his hurried luncheon he looked across half enviously at the other's leisurely degustation of his meal. When Waythorn first saw him he had been helping himself with critical deliberation to a bit of Camembert at the ideal point of liquefaction, and now, the cheese removed, he was just pouring his *café double*[1] from its little two-storied earthen pot. He poured slowly, his ruddy profile bent over the task, and one beringed white hand steadying the lid of the coffeepot; then he stretched his other hand to the decanter of cognac at his elbow, filled a liqueur glass, took a tentative sip, and poured the brandy into his coffee cup.

Waythorn watched him in a kind of fascination. What was he thinking of—only of the flavor of the coffee and the liqueur? Had the morning's meeting left no more trace in his thoughts than on his face? Had his wife so completely passed out of his life that even this odd encounter with her present husband, within a week after her remarriage, was no more than an incident in his day? And as Waythorn mused, another idea struck him: had Haskett ever met Varick as Varick and he had just met? The recollection of Haskett perturbed him, and he rose and left the restaurant, taking a circuitous way out to escape the placid irony of Varick's nod.

It was after seven when Waythorn reached home. He thought the footman who opened the door looked at him oddly.

"How is Miss Lily?" he asked in haste.

"Doing very well, sir. A gentleman—"

"Tell Barlow to put off dinner for half an hour," Waythorn cut him off, hurrying upstairs.

He went straight to his room and dressed without seeing his wife. When he reached the drawing room she was there, fresh and radiant. Lily's day had been good; the doctor was not coming back that evening.

At dinner Waythorn told her of Sellers' illness and of the resulting complications. She listened sympathetically, adjuring him not to let himself be overworked, and asking vague feminine questions about the routine of the office. Then she gave him the chronicle of Lily's day; quoted the nurse and doctor, and told him who had called to inquire. He had never seen her more serene and unruffled. It struck him with a curious pang, that she was very happy in being with him, so happy that she found a childish pleasure in rehearsing the trivial incidents of her day.

After dinner they went to the library, and the servant put the coffee and liqueurs on a low table before her and left the room. She

---

[1] *[café double]* very strong coffee.

looked singularly soft and girlish in her rosy-pale dress, against the
dark leather of one of his bachelor armchairs. A day earlier the
contrast would have charmed him.

He turned away now, choosing a cigar with affected deliberation.

"Did Haskett come?" he asked, with his back to her.

"Oh, yes—he came."

"You didn't see him, of course?"

She hesitated a moment. "I let the nurse see him."

That was all. There was nothing more to ask. He swung round
toward her, applying a match to his cigar. Well, the thing was over
for a week, at any rate. He would try not to think of it. She looked
up at him, a trifle rosier than usual, with a smile in her eyes.

"Ready for your coffee, dear?"

He leaned against the mantelpiece, watching her as she lifted the
coffeepot. The lamplight struck a gleam from her bracelets and
tipped her soft hair with brightness. How light and slender she was,
and how each gesture flowed into the next! She seemed a creature
all compact of harmonies. As the thought of Haskett receded,
Waythorn felt himself yielding again to the joy of possessorship.
They were his, those white hands with their flitting motions, his
the light haze of hair, the lips and eyes. . . .

She set down the coffeepot, and reaching for the decanter of
cognac, measured off a liqueur glass and poured it into his cup.

Waythorn uttered a sudden exclamation.

"What is the matter?" she said, startled.

"Nothing; only—I don't take cognac in my coffee."

"Oh, how stupid of me," she cried.

Their eyes met, and she blushed a sudden agonized red.

III

Ten days later, Mr. Sellers, still housebound, asked Waythorn to
call on his way downtown.

The senior partner, with his swaddled foot propped up by the
fire, greeted his associate with an air of embarrassment.

"I'm sorry, my dear fellow; I've got to ask you to do an awkward thing for me."

Waythorn waited, and the other went on, after a pause apparently given to the arrangement of his phrases: "The fact is, when

I was knocked out I had just gone into a rather complicated piece of business for—Gus Varick."

"Well?" said Waythorn, with an attempt to put him at his ease.

"Well—it's this way: Varick came to me the day before my attack. He had evidently had an inside tip from somebody, and had made about a hundred thousand. He came to me for advice, and I suggested his going in with Vanderlyn."

"Oh, the deuce!" Waythorn exclaimed. He saw in a flash what had happened. The investment was an alluring one, but required negotiation. He listened quietly while Sellers put the case before him, and, the statement ended, he said: "You think I ought to see Varick?"

"I'm afraid I can't as yet. The doctor is obdurate. And this thing can't wait. I hate to ask you, but no one else in the office knows the ins and outs of it."

Waythorn stood silent. He did not care a farthing for the success of Varick's venture, but the honor of the office was to be considered, and he could hardly refuse to oblige his partner.

"Very well," he said, "I'll do it."

That afternoon, apprised by telephone, Varick called at the office. Waythorn, waiting in his private room, wondered what the others thought of it. The newspapers, at the time of Mrs. Waythorn's marriage, had acquainted their readers with every detail of her previous matrimonial ventures, and Waythorn could fancy the clerks smiling behind Varick's back as he was ushered in.

Varick bore himself admirably. He was easy without being undignified, and Waythorn was conscious of cutting a much less impressive figure. Varick had no experience of business, and the talk prolonged itself for nearly an hour while Waythorn set forth with scrupulous precision the details of the proposed transaction.

"I'm awfully obliged to you," Varick said as he rose. "The fact is I'm not used to having much money to look after, and I don't want to make an ass of myself—" He smiled, and Waythorn could not help noticing that there was something pleasant about his smile. "It feels uncommonly queer to have enough cash to pay one's bills. I'd have sold my soul for it a few years ago!"

Waythorn winced at the allusion. He had heard it rumored that a lack of funds had been one of the determining causes of the Varick separation, but it did not occur to him that Varick's words were intentional. It seemed more likely that the desire to keep clear of embarrassing topics had fatally drawn him into one. Waythorn did not wish to be outdone in civility.

"We'll do the best we can for you," he said. "I think this is a good thing you're in."

"Oh, I'm sure it's immense. It's awfully good of you—" Varick broke off, embarrassed. "I suppose the thing's settled now—but if—"

"If anything happens before Sellers is about, I'll see you again," said Waythorn quietly. He was glad, in the end, to appear the more self-possessed of the two.

The course of Lily's illness ran smooth, and as the days passed Waythorn grew used to the idea of Haskett's weekly visit. The first time the day came round, he stayed out late, and questioned his wife as to the visit on his return. She replied at once that Haskett had merely seen the nurse downstairs, as the doctor did not wish anyone in the child's sickroom till after the crisis.

The following week Waythorn was again conscious of the recurrence of the day, but had forgotten it by the time he came home to dinner. The crisis of the disease came a few days later, with a rapid decline of fever, and the little girl was pronounced out of danger. In the rejoicing which ensued the thought of Haskett passed out of Waythorn's mind, and one afternoon, letting himself into the house with a latchkey, he went straight to his library without noticing a shabby hat and umbrella in the hall.

In the library he found a small effaced-looking man with a thinnish gray beard sitting on the edge of a chair. The stranger might have been a piano tuner, or one of those mysteriously efficient persons who are summoned in emergencies to adjust some detail of the domestic machinery. He blinked at Waythorn through a pair of gold-rimmed spectacles and said mildly: "Mr. Waythorn, I presume? I am Lily's father."

Waythorn flushed. "Oh—" he stammered uncomfortably. He broke off, disliking to appear rude. Inwardly he was trying to adjust the actual Haskett to the image of him projected by his wife's reminiscences. Waythorn had been allowed to infer that Alice's first husband was a brute.

"I am sorry to intrude," said Haskett, with his over-the-counter politeness.

"Don't mention it," returned Waythorn, collecting himself. "I suppose the nurse has been told?"

"I presume so. I can wait," said Haskett. He had a resigned way of speaking, as though life had worn down his natural powers of resistance.

Waythorn stood on the threshold, nervously pulling off his gloves.

"I'm sorry you've been detained. I will send for the nurse," he said; and as he opened the door he added with an effort: "I'm glad we can give you a good report of Lily." He winced as the *we* slipped out, but Haskett seemed not to notice it.

"Thank you, Mr. Waythorn, it's been an anxious time for me."

"Ah, well, that's past. Soon she'll be able to go to you." Waythorn nodded and passed out.

In his own room he flung himself down with a groan. He hated the womanish sensibility which made him suffer so acutely from the grotesque chances of life. He had known when he married that his wife's former husbands were both living, and that amid the multiplied contacts of modern existence there were a thousand chances to one that he would run against one or the other, yet he found himself as much disturbed by his brief encounter with Haskett as though the law had not obligingly removed all difficulties in the way of their meeting.

Waythorn sprang up and began to pace the room nervously. He had not suffered half as much from his two meetings with Varick. It was Haskett's presence in his own house that made the situation so intolerable. He stood still, hearing steps in the passage.

"This way, please," he heard the nurse say. Haskett was being taken upstairs, then: not a corner of the house but was open to him. Waythorn dropped into another chair, staring vaguely ahead of him. On his dressing table stood a photograph of Alice, taken when he had first known her. She was Alice Varick then—how fine and exquisite he had thought her! Those were Varick's pearls about her neck. At Waythorn's instance they had been returned before her marriage. Had Haskett ever given her any trinkets—and what had become of them, Waythorn wondered? He realized suddenly that he knew very little of Haskett's past or present situation; but from the man's appearance and manner of speech he could reconstruct with curious precision the surroundings of Alice's first marriage. And it startled him to think that she had, in the background of her life, a phase of existence so different from anything with which he had connected her. Varick, whatever his faults, was a gentleman, in the conventional, traditional sense of the term: the sense which at that moment seemed, oddly enough, to have most meaning to Waythorn. He and Varick had the same social habits, spoke the same language, understood the same allusions. But this other man . . . it was grotesquely uppermost in Waythorn's mind that Haskett had worn a made-up tie attached with an elastic. Why should that ridiculous detail symbolize the whole man? Waythorn was exasperated by his own paltriness, but the fact of the tie expanded, forced itself on him, became as it were the key to Alice's past. He could see her, as Mrs. Haskett, sitting in a "front parlor" furnished in plush, with a pianola, and copy of *Ben Hur* on the center table. He could see her going to the theater with Haskett—or perhaps even to a "Church Sociable"—she in a "picture hat" and Haskett in a black frock coat, a little creased, with the made-up tie on an elastic. On the way home they would stop and look at the illuminated shop windows, lingering over the photographs of New York actresses. On Sunday afternoons Haskett would take her for a walk, pushing Lily ahead of them in a white enameled perambulator, and Waythorn had a vision of the people they would stop and talk to. He could fancy how pretty Alice must have looked, in a dress adroitly constructed from the hints of a New York fashion paper, and how she must have looked down on the other women, chafing at her life, and secretly feeling that she belonged in a bigger place.

For the moment his foremost thought was one of wonder at the way in which she had shed the phase of existence which her marriage with Haskett implied. It was as if her whole aspect, every gesture, every inflection, every allusion, were a studied negation of that period of her life. If she had denied being married to Haskett she could hardly have stood more convicted of duplicity than in this obliteration of the self which had been his wife.

Waythorn started up, checking himself in the analysis of her motives. What right had he to create a fantastic effigy of her and then pass judgment on it? She had spoken vaguely of her first marriage as unhappy, had hinted, with becoming reticence, that Haskett had wrought havoc among her young illusions. . . . It was a pity for Waythorn's peace of mind that Haskett's very inoffensiveness shed a new light on the nature of those illusions. A man would rather think that his wife has been brutalized by her first husband than that the process has been reversed.

IV

"Mr. Waythorn, I don't like that French governess of Lily's."

Haskett, subdued and apologetic, stood before Waythorn in the library, revolving his shabby hat in his hand.

Waythorn, surprised in his armchair over the evening paper, stared back perplexedly at his visitor.

"You'll excuse my asking to see you," Haskett continued. "But this is my last visit, and I thought if I could have a word with you it would be a better way than writing to Mrs. Waythorn's lawyer."

Waythorn rose uneasily. He did not like the French governess either; but that was irrelevant.

"I am not so sure of that," he returned stiffly; "but since you wish it I will give your message to—my wife." He always hesitated over the possessive pronoun in addressing Haskett.

The latter sighed. "I don't know as that will help much. She didn't like it when I spoke to her."

Waythorn turned red. "When did you see her?" he asked.

"Not since the first day I came to see Lily—right after she was taken sick. I remarked to her then that I didn't like the governess."

Waythorn made no answer. He remembered distinctly that, after that first visit, he had asked his wife if she had seen Haskett. She had lied to him then, but she had respected his wishes since; and the incident cast a curious light on her character. He was sure she would not have seen Haskett that first day if she had divined that Waythorn would object, and the fact that she did not divine it was almost as disagreeable to the latter as the discovery that she had lied to him.

"I don't like the woman," Haskett was repeating with mild persistency. "She ain't straight, Mr. Waythorn—she'll teach the child to be underhand. I've noticed a change in Lily—she's too anxious to please—and she don't always tell the truth. She used to be the straightest child. Mr. Waythorn—" He broke off, his voice a little thick. "Not but what I want her to have a stylish education," he ended.

Waythorn was touched. "I'm sorry, Mr. Haskett; but frankly, I don't quite see what I can do."

Haskett hesitated. Then he laid his hat on the table, and advanced to the hearthrug, on which Waythorn was standing. There was nothing aggressive in his manner, but he had the solemnity of a timid man resolved on a decisive measure.

"There's just one thing you can do, Mr. Waythorn," he said. "You can remind Mrs. Waythorn that, by the decree of the courts, I am entitled to have a voice in Lily's bringing-up." He paused, and went on more deprecatingly: "I am not the kind to talk about enforcing my rights, Mr. Waythorn. I don't know as I think a man is entitled to rights he hasn't known how to hold on to; but this business of the child is different. I've never let go there—and I never mean to."

The scene left Waythorn deeply shaken. Shamefacedly, in indirect ways, he had been finding out about Haskett; and all that he had learned was favorable. The little man, in order to be near his daughter, had sold out his share in a profitable business in Utica, and accepted a modest clerkship in a New York manufacturing house. He boarded in a shabby street and had few acquaintances. His passion for Lily filled his life. Waythorn felt that this exploration of Haskett was like groping about with a dark lantern in his wife's past; but he saw now that there were recesses his lantern had not explored. He had never inquired into the exact circumstances of his wife's first matrimonial rupture. On the surface all had been fair. It was she who had obtained the divorce, and the court had given her the child. But Waythorn knew how many ambiguities such a verdict might cover. The mere fact that Haskett retained a right over his daughter implied an unsuspected compromise. Waythorn was an idealist. He always refused to recognize unpleasant contingencies till he found himself confronted with them, and then he saw them followed by a spectral train of consequences. His next days were thus haunted, and he determined to try to lay the ghosts by conjuring them up in his wife's presence.

When he repeated Haskett's request a flame of anger passed over her face; but she subdued it instantly and spoke with a slight quiver of outraged motherhood.

"It is very ungentlemanly of him," she said.

The word grated on Waythorn. "That is neither here nor there. It's a bare question of rights."

She murmured: "It's not as if he could ever be a help to Lily—"

Waythorn flushed. This was even less to his taste. "The question is," he repeated, "what authority has he over her?"

She looked downward, twisting herself a little in her seat. "I am willing to see him—I thought you objected," she faltered.

In a flash he understood that she knew the extent of Haskett's claims. Perhaps it was not the first time she had resisted them.

"My objecting has nothing to do with it," he said coldly; "if Haskett has a right to be consulted you must consult him."

She burst into tears, and he saw that she expected him to regard her as a victim.

Haskett did not abuse his rights. Waythorn had felt miserably sure that he would not. But the governess was dismissed, and from time to time the little man demanded an interview with Alice. After the first outburst she accepted the situation with her usual adaptability. Haskett had once reminded Waythorn of the piano tuner, and Mrs. Waythorn, after a month or two, appeared to class him with that domestic familiar. Waythorn could not but respect the father's tenacity. At first he had tried to cultivate the suspicion that Haskett might be "up to" something, that he had an object in securing a foothold in the house. But in his heart Waythorn was sure of Haskett's single-mindedness: he even guessed in the latter a mild contempt for such advantages as his relation with the Waythorns might offer. Haskett's sincerity of purpose made him invulnerable, and his successor had to accept him as a lien on the property.

Mr. Sellers was sent to Europe to recover from his gout, and Varick's affairs hung on Waythorn's hands. The negotiations were prolonged and complicated; they necessitated frequent conferences between the two men, and the interests of the firm forbade Waythorn's suggesting that his client should transfer his business to another office.

Varick appeared well in the transaction. In moments of relaxation his coarse streak appeared, and Waythorn dreaded his geniality: but in the office he was concise and clear-headed, with a flattering deference to Waythorn's judgment. Their business relations being so affably established, it would have been absurd for the two men to ignore each other in society. The first time they met in a drawing room, Varick took up their intercourse in the same easy key, and his hostess' grateful glance obliged Waythorn to respond to it. After that they ran across each other frequently, and one evening at a ball Waythorn, wandering through the remoter rooms, came upon Varick seated beside his wife. She colored a little, and faltered in what she was saying; but Varick nodded to Waythorn without rising, and the latter strolled on.

In the carriage, on the way home, he broke out nervously: "I didn't know you spoke to Varick."

Her voice trembled a little. "It's the first time—he happened to be standing near⁻ me; I didn't know what to do. It's so awkward, meeting everywhere—and he said you had been very kind about some business."

"That's different," said Waythorn.

She paused a moment. "I'll do just as you wish," she returned pliantly. "I thought it would be less awkward to speak to him when we meet."

Her pliancy was beginning to sicken him. Had she really no will of her own—no theory about her relation to these men? She had accepted Haskett—did she mean to accept Varick? It was "less awkward," as she had said, and her instinct was to evade difficulties or to circumvent them. With sudden vividness Waythorn saw how the instinct had developed. She was "as easy as an old shoe"—a shoe that too many feet had worn. Her elasticity was the result of tension in too many different directions. Alice Haskett—Alice Varick—Alice Waythorn—she had been each in turn, and had left hanging to each name a little of her privacy, a little of her personality, a little of the inmost self where the unknown god abides.

"Yes—it's better to speak to Varick," said Waythorn wearily.

V

The winter wore on, and society took advantage of the Waythorns' acceptance of Varick. Harassed hostesses were grateful to them for bridging over a social difficulty, and Mrs. Waythorn was held up as a miracle of good taste. Some experimental spirits could not resist the diversion of throwing Varick and his former wife together, and there were those who thought he found a zest in the propinquity. But Mrs. Waythorn's conduct remained irreproachable. She neither avoided Varick nor sought him out. Even Waythorn could not but admit that she had discovered the solution of the newest social problem.

He had married her without giving much thought to that problem. He had fancied that a woman can shed her past like a man. But now he saw that Alice was bound to hers both by the circumstances which forced her into continued relation with it, and by the traces it had left on her nature. With grim irony Waythorn compared himself to a member of a syndicate. He held so many shares in his wife's personality and his predecessors were his partners in the business. If there had been any element of passion in the transaction he would have felt less deteriorated by it. The fact that Alice took her change of husbands like a change of weather reduced the situation to mediocrity. He could have forgiven her for blunders, for excesses: for resisting Haskett, for yielding to Varick; for anything but her acquiescence and her tact. She reminded him of a juggler tossing knives; but the knives were blunt and she knew they would never cut her.

And then, gradually, habit formed a protecting surface for his sensibilities. If he paid for each day's comfort with the small change of his illusions, he grew daily to value the comfort more and set less store upon the coin. He had drifted into a dulling propinquity with Haskett and Varick and he took refuge in the cheap revenge of satirizing the situation. He even began to reckon up the advantages which accrued from it, to ask himself if it were not better to own a third of a wife who knew how to make a man happy than a whole one who had lacked opportunity to acquire the art. For it *was* an art, and made up, like all others, of concessions, eliminations and embellishments: of lights judiciously thrown and shadows skillfully softened. His wife knew exactly how to manage the lights, and he knew exactly to what training she owed her skill. He even tried to trace the source of his obligations, to discriminate between the influences which had combined to produce his domestic happiness: he perceived that Haskett's commonness had made Alice worship good breeding, while Varick's liberal construction of the marriage bond had taught her to value the conjugal virtues; so that he was directly indebted to his predecessors for the devotion which made his life easy if not inspiring.

From this phase he passed into that of complete acceptance. He ceased to satirize himself because time dulled the irony of the situation and the joke lost its humor with its sting. Even the sight of Haskett's hat on the hall table had ceased to touch the springs of epigram. The hat was often seen there now, for it had been decided that it was better for Lily's father to visit her than for the little girl to go to his boardinghouse. Waythorn, having acquiesced in this arrangement, had been surprised to find how little difference it made. Haskett was never obtrusive, and the few visitors who met him on the stairs were unaware of his identity. Waythorn did not know how often he saw Alice, but with himself Haskett was seldom in contact.

One afternoon, however, he learned on entering that Lily's father was waiting to see him. In the library he found Haskett occupying a chair in his usual provisional way. Waythorn always felt grateful to him for not leaning back.

"I hope you'll excuse me, Mr. Waythorn," he said rising. "I wanted to see Mrs. Waythorn about Lily, and your man asked me to wait here till she came in."

"Of course," said Waythorn, remembering that a sudden leak had that morning given over the drawing room to the plumbers.

He opened his cigar case and held it out to his visitor, and Haskett's acceptance seemed to mark a fresh stage in their intercourse. The spring evening was chilly, and Waythorn invited his guest to draw up his chair to the fire. He meant to find an excuse to leave Haskett in a moment; but he was tired and cold, and after all the little man no longer jarred on him.

The two were enclosed in the intimacy of their blended cigar smoke when the door opened and Varick walked into the room. Waythorn rose abruptly. It was the first time that Varick had come to the house, and the surprise of seeing him, combined with the singular inopportuneness of his arrival, gave a new edge to Waythorn's blunted sensibilities. He stared at his visitor without speaking.

Varick seemed too preoccupied to notice his host's embarrassment. "My dear fellow," he exclaimed in his most expansive tone, "I must apologize for tumbling in on you in this way, but I was too late to catch you downtown, and so I thought—"

He stopped short, catching sight of Haskett, and his sanguine color deepened to a flush which spread vividly under his scant blond hair. But in a moment he recovered himself and nodded slightly. Haskett returned the bow in silence, and Waythorn was still groping for speech when the footman came in carrying a tea table.

The intrusion offered a welcome vent to Waythorn's nerves. "What the deuce are you bringing this here for?" he said sharply.

"I beg your pardon, sir, but the plumbers are still in the drawing room, and Mrs. Waythorn said she would have tea in the library." The footman's perfectly respectful tone implied a reflection on Waythorn's reasonableness.

"Oh, very well," said the latter resignedly, and the footman proceeded to open the folding tea table and set out its complicated appointments. While this interminable process continued the three men stood motionless, watching it with a fascinated stare, till Waythorn, to break the silence, said to Varick, "Won't you have a cigar?"

He held out the case he had just tendered to Haskett, and Varick helped himself with a smile. Waythorn looked about for a match, and finding none, proffered a light from his own cigar. Haskett, in the background, held his ground mildly, examining his cigar tip now and then, and stepping forward at the right moment to knock its ashes into the fire.

The footman at last withdrew, and Varick immediately began: "If I could just say half a word to you about this business—"

"Certainly," stammered Waythorn; "in the dining room—" But as he placed his hand on the door it opened from without, and his wife appeared on the threshold.

She came in fresh and smiling, in her street dress and hat, shedding a fragrance from the boa which she loosened in advancing.

"Shall we have tea in here, dear?" she began; and then she caught sight of Varick. Her smile deepened, veiling a slight tremor of surprise.

"Why, how do you do?" she said with a distinct note of pleasure.

As she shook hands with Varick she saw Haskett standing behind him. Her smile faded for a moment, but she recalled it quickly, with a scarcely perceptible side glance at Waythorn.

"How do you do, Mr. Haskett?" she said, and shook hands with him a shade less cordially.

The three men stood awkwardly before her, till Varick, always the most self-possessed, dashed into an explanatory phrase.

"We—I had to see Waythorn a moment on business," he stammered, brick-red from chin to nape.

Haskett stepped forward with his air of mild obstinacy. "I am sorry to intrude; but you appointed five o'clock—" he directed his resigned glance to the timepiece on the mantel.

She swept aside their embarrassment with a charming gesture of hospitality.

"I'm so sorry—I'm always late: but the afternoon was so lovely." She stood drawing off her gloves, propitiatory and graceful, diffusing about her a sense of ease and familiarity in which the situation lost its grotesqueness. "But before talking business," she added brightly, "I'm sure everyone wants a cup of tea."

She dropped into her low chair by the tea table, and the two visitors, as if drawn by her smile, advanced to receive the cups she held out.

She glanced about for Waythorn, and he took the third cup with a laugh.

BY COURIER (1906)

O. Henry

*O. Henry was the pen name of William Sydney Porter (1862–1910). His short stories were so distinctive and influential in popular literary fiction that "O. Henry stories" became a by-word for a genre of narratives containing overly clever trick endings (*not present here in "By Courier"). When the author moved to New York from Texas in 1902, he began a productive period of writing a story a week in a Sunday newspaper magazine. In the next several years, he published 381 short stories and two book collections; his work* The Four Million *(1906) focuses on the inhabitants of New York City.*

IT WAS NEITHER the season nor the hour when the Park had frequenters; and it is likely that the young lady, who was seated on one of the benches at the side of the walk, had merely obeyed a sudden impulse to sit for a while and enjoy a foretaste of coming Spring.

She rested there, pensive and still. A certain melancholy that touched her countenance must have been of recent birth, for it had not yet altered the fine and youthful contours of her cheek, nor subdued the arch though resolute curve of her lips.

A tall young man came striding through the park along the path near which she sat. Behind him tagged a boy carrying a suit-case. At sight of the young lady, the man's face changed to red and back to pale again. He watched her countenance as he drew nearer, with hope and anxiety mingled on his own. He passed within a few yards of her, but he saw no evidence that she was aware of his presence or existence.

Some fifty yards further on he suddenly stopped and sat on a bench at one side. The boy dropped the suit-case and stared at him with wondering, shrewd eyes. The young man took out his handkerchief and wiped his brow. It was a good handkerchief, a good brow, and the young man was good to look at. He said to the boy:

"I want you to take a message to that young lady on that bench. Tell her I am on my way to the station, to leave for San Francisco, where I shall join that Alaska moose-hunting expedition. Tell her that, since she has commanded me neither to speak nor to write to her, I take this means of making one last appeal to her sense of justice, for the sake of what has been. Tell her that to condemn and discard one who has not deserved such treatment, without giving him her reasons or a chance to explain is contrary to her nature as I believe it to be. Tell her that I have thus, to a certain degree, disobeyed her injunctions, in the hope that she may yet be inclined to see justice done. Go, and tell her that."

The young man dropped a half-dollar into the boy's hand. The boy looked at him for a moment with bright, canny eyes out of a dirty, intelligent face, and then set off at a run. He approached the lady on the bench a little doubtfully, but unembarrassed. He touched the brim of the old plaid bicycle cap perched on the back of his head. The lady looked at him coolly, without prejudice or favour.

"Lady," he said, "dat gent on de oder bench sent yer a song and dance by me. If yer don't know de guy, and he's tryin' to do de Johnny act, say de word, and I'll call a cop in t'ree minutes. If yer does know him, and he's on de square, w'y I'll spiel yer de bunch of hot air he sent yer."

The young lady betrayed a faint interest.

"A song and dance!" she said, in a deliberate, sweet voice that seemed to clothe her words in a diaphanous garment of impalpable irony. "A new idea—in the troubadour line, I suppose. I—used to know the gentleman who sent you, so I think it will hardly be necessary to call the police. You may execute your song and dance, but do not sing too loudly. It is a little early yet for open-air vaude-ville, and we might attract attention."

"Awe," said the boy, with a shrug down the length of him, "yer know what I mean, lady. 'Tain't a turn, it's wind. He told me to tell yer he's got his collars and cuffs in dat grip for a scoot clean out to 'Frisco. Den he's goin' to shoot snow-birds in de Klondike. He says yer told him not to send 'round no more pink notes nor come hangin' over de garden gate, and he takes dis means of puttin' yer wise. He says yer refereed him out like a has-been, and never give him no chance to kick at de decision. He says yer swiped him, and never said why."

The slightly awakened interest in the young lady's eyes did not abate. Perhaps it was caused by either the originality or the audacity of the snow-bird hunter, in thus circumventing her express commands against the ordinary modes of communication. She fixed her eye on a statue standing disconsolate in the dishevelled park, and spoke into the transmitter:

"Tell the gentleman that I need not repeat to him a description of my ideals. He knows what they have been and what they still are. So far as they touch on this case, absolute loyalty and truth are the ones paramount. Tell him that I have studied my own heart as well as one can, and I know its weakness as well as I do its needs. That is why I decline to hear his pleas, whatever they may be. I did not condemn him through hearsay or doubtful evidence, and that is why I made no charge. But, since he persists in hearing what he already well knows, you may convey the matter.

"Tell him that I entered the conservatory that evening from the rear, to cut a rose for my mother. Tell him I saw him and Miss Ashburton beneath the pink oleander. The tableau was pretty, but the pose and juxtaposition were too eloquent and evident to require explanation. I left the conservatory, and, at the same time, the rose and my ideal. You may carry that song and dance to your impresario."

"I'm shy on one word, lady. Jux—jar—put me wise on dat, will yer? "

"Juxtaposition—or you may call it propinquity—or, if you like, being rather too near for one maintaining the position of an ideal."

The gravel spun from beneath the boy's feet. He stood by the other bench. The man's eyes interrogated him, hungrily. The boy's were shining with the impersonal zeal of the translator.

"De lady says dat she's on to de fact dat gals is dead easy when a feller comes spielin' ghost stories and tryin' to make up, and dat's why she won't listen to no soft-soap. She says she caught yer dead to rights, huggin' a bunch o' calico in de hot-house. She sidestepped in to pull some posies and yer was squeezin' de oder gal to beat de band. She says it looked cute, all right all right, but it made her sick. She says yer better git busy, and make a sneak for de train."

The young man gave a low whistle and his eyes flashed with a sudden thought. His hand flew to the inside pocket of his coat, and drew out a handful of letters. Selecting one, he handed it to the boy, following it with a silver dollar from his vest-pocket.

"Give that letter to the lady," he said, "and ask her to read it. Tell her that it should explain the situation. Tell her that, if she had mingled a little trust with her conception of the ideal, much heart-ache might have been avoided. Tell her that the loyalty she prizes so much has never wavered. Tell her I am waiting for an answer."

The messenger stood before the lady.

"De gent says he's had de ski-bunk put on him widout no cause. He says he's no bum guy; and, lady, yer read dat letter, and I'll bet yer he's a white sport, all right."

The young lady unfolded the letter, somewhat doubtfully, and read it.

DEAR DR. ARNOLD: I want to thank you for your most kind and opportune aid to my daughter last Friday evening, when she was overcome by an attack of her old heart-trouble in the conservatory at Mrs. Waldron's reception. Had you not been near to catch her as she fell and to render proper attention, we might have lost her. I would be glad if you would call and undertake the treatment of her case.

Gratefully yours,
ROBERT ASHBURTON.

The young lady refolded the letter, and handed it to the boy.

"De gent wants an answer," said the messenger. "Wot's de word?"

The lady's eyes suddenly flashed on him, bright, smiling and wet.

"Tell that guy on the other bench," she said, with a happy, tremulous laugh, "that his girl wants him."

THE AUNT AND THE SLUGGARD (1916)

P. G. Wodehouse

For several decades, P. G. Wodehouse (1881–1975), an Englishman, was a master of comic fiction. A frequent visitor to New York City, in 1915 he began writing for Broadway, and simultaneously created for his stories characters who would become his most famous heroes: the bumbling British aristocrat Bertie Wooster and Bertie's brilliant servant Jeeves. In "The Aunt and the Sluggard," Bertie's reclusive friend, Rockmetteller ("Rocky"), must learn to live it up and report on his high life to his rich aunt. "To have to come and live in New York! To have to leave my little cottage and take a stuffy, smelly, over-heated hole of an apartment in this Heaven-forsaken, festering Gehenna," declares the sluggard. "To have to mix night after night with a mob who think that life is a sort of St. Vitus's dance," continues Rocky, "and imagine that they're having a good time because they're making enough noise for six and drinking too much for ten. I loathe New York, Bertie. . . ." Jeeves, ever on hand to unknot Bertie's social and legal tangles, lends his precise knowledge of New York's hot spots to the decidedly withdrawn Rocky.

Now THAT IT's all over, I may as well admit that there was a time during the rather rummy affair of Rockmetteller Todd when I thought that Jeeves was going to let me down. The man had the appearance of being baffled.

Jeeves is my man, you know. Officially he pulls in his weekly wage for pressing my clothes, and all that sort of thing; but actually he's more like what the poet Johnnie called some bird of his acquaintance who was apt to rally round him in times of need—a guide, don't you know; philosopher, if I remember rightly, and—I rather fancy—friend. I rely on him at every turn.

So naturally, when Rocky Todd told me about his aunt, I didn't hesitate. Jeeves was in on the thing from the start.

The affair of Rocky Todd broke loose early one morning in spring. I was in bed, restoring the good old tissues with about nine hours of the dreamless, when the door flew open and somebody prodded me in the lower ribs and began to shake the bedclothes. After blinking a bit and generally pulling myself together, I located Rocky, and my first impression was that it was some horrid dream.

Rocky, you see, lived down on Long Island somewhere, miles away from New York; and not only that, but he had told me himself more than once that he never got up before twelve, and seldom earlier than one. Constitutionally the laziest young devil in America, he had hit on a walk in life which enabled him to go the limit in that direction. He was a poet. At least, he wrote poems when he did anything; but most of his time, as far as I could make out, he spent in a sort of trance. He told me once that he could sit on a fence, watching a worm and wondering what on earth it was up to, for hours at a stretch.

He had his scheme of life worked out to a fine point. About once a month he would take three days writing a few poems; the other three hundred and twenty-nine days of the year he rested. I didn't know there was enough money in poetry to support a chappie, even in the way in which Rocky lived; but it seems that, if you stick to exhortations to young men to lead the strenuous life and don't shove in any rhymes, American editors fight for the stuff. Rocky showed me one of his things once. It began:—

> Be!
> Be!
>> The past is dead.
>> To-morrow is not born.
>>> Be to-day!
>> To-day!
>> Be with every nerve,
>> With every muscle,
>>> With every drop of your red blood!
> Be!

It was printed opposite the frontispiece of a magazine with a sort of scroll round it, and a picture in the middle of a fairly nude chappie, with bulging muscles, giving the rising sun the glad eye. Rocky said they gave him a hundred dollars for it, and he stayed in bed till four in the afternoon for over a month.

As regarded the future he was pretty solid, owing to the fact that he had a moneyed aunt tucked away somewhere in Illinois; and, as he had been named Rockmetteller after her, and was her only nephew, his position was pretty sound. He told me that when he did come into the money he meant to do no work at all, except perhaps an occasional poem recommending the young man with life opening out before him, with all its splendid possibilities, to light a pipe and shove his feet upon the mantelpiece.

And this was the man who was prodding me in the ribs in the grey dawn!

"Read this, Bertie!" I could just see that he was waving a letter or something equally foul in my face. "Wake up and read this!"

I can't read before I've had my morning tea and a cigarette. I groped for the bell.

Jeeves came in, looking as fresh as a dewy violet. It's a mystery to me how he does it.

"Tea, Jeeves."

"Very good, sir."

He flowed silently out of the room—he always gives you the impression of being some liquid substance when he moves; and I found that Rocky was surging round with his beastly letter again.

"What is it?" I said. "What on earth's the matter?"

"Read it!"

"I can't. I haven't had my tea."

"Well, listen then."

"Who's it from?"

"My aunt."

At this point I fell asleep again. I woke to hear him saying: —

"So what on earth am I to do?"

Jeeves trickled in with the tray, like some silent stream meandering over its mossy bed; and I saw daylight.

"Read it again, Rocky, old top," I said. "I want Jeeves to hear it. Mr. Todd's aunt has written him a rather rummy letter, Jeeves, and we want your advice."

"Very good, sir."

He stood in the middle of the room, registering devotion to the cause, and Rocky started again: —

MY DEAR ROCKMETTELLER, —

I have been thinking things over for a long while, and I have come to the conclusion that I have been very thoughtless to wait so long before doing what I have made up my mind to do now.

"What do you make of that, Jeeves?"

"It seems a little obscure at present, sir, but no doubt it becomes clearer at a later point in the communication."

"It becomes as clear as mud!" said Rocky.

"Proceed, old scout," I said, champing my bread and butter.

You know how all my life I have longed to visit New York and see for myself the wonderful gay life of which I have read so much. I fear that now it will be impossible for me to fulfil my dream. I am old and worn out. I seem to have no strength left in me.

"Sad, Jeeves, what?"

"Extremely, sir."

"Sad nothing!" said Rocky. "It's sheer laziness. I went to see her last Christmas and she was bursting with health. Her doctor told me himself that there was nothing wrong with her whatever. But she will insist that she's a hopeless invalid, so he has to agree with her. She's got a fixed idea that the trip to New York would kill her; so, though it's been her ambition all her life to come here, she stays where she is."

"Rather like the chappie whose heart was 'in the Highlands a-chasing of the deer,' Jeeves?"

"The cases are in some respects parallel, sir."

"Carry on, Rocky, dear boy."

So I have decided that, if I cannot enjoy all the marvels of the city myself, I can at least enjoy them through you. I suddenly thought of this yesterday after reading a beautiful poem in the Sunday paper about a young man who had longed all his life for a certain thing and won it in the end only when he was too old to enjoy it. It was very sad, and it touched me.

"A thing," interpolated Rocky, bitterly, "that I've not been able to do in ten years."

As you know, you will have my money when I am gone; but until now I have never been able to see my way to giving you an allowance. I have now decided to do so—on one condition. I have written to a firm of lawyers in New York, giving them instructions to pay you quite a substantial sum each month. My one condition is that you live in New York and enjoy yourself as I have always wished to do. I want you to be my representative, to spend this money for me as I should do myself. I want you to plunge into the gay, prismatic life of New York. I want you to be the life and soul of brilliant supper parties.

Above all, I want you—indeed, I insist on this—to write me letters at least once a week, giving me a full description of all you are doing and all that is going on in the city, so that I may enjoy at secondhand what my wretched health prevents my enjoying for myself. Remember that I shall expect full details, and that no detail is too trivial to interest

Your affectionate Aunt,
ISABEL ROCKMETTELLER.

"What about it?" said Rocky.

"What about it?" I said.

"Yes. What on earth am I going to do?"

It was only then that I really got on to the extremely rummy attitude of the chappie, in view of the fact that a quite unexpected mess of the right stuff had suddenly descended on him from a blue sky. To my mind it was an occasion for the beaming smile and the joyous whoop; yet here the man was, looking and talking as if Fate had swung on his solar plexus. It amazed me.

"Aren't you bucked?" I said.

"Bucked!"

"If I were in your place I should be frightfully braced. I consider this pretty soft for you."

He gave a kind of yelp, stared at me for a moment, and then began to talk of New York in a way that reminded me of Jimmy Mundy, the reformer chappie. Jimmy had just come to New York on a hit-the-trail campaign, and I had popped in at the Garden a couple of days before, for half an hour or so, to hear him. He had certainly told New York some pretty straight things about itself, having apparently taken a dislike to the place, but, by Jove, you know, dear old Rocky made him look like a publicity agent for the old metrop!

"Pretty soft!" he cried. "To have to come and live in New York! To have to leave my little cottage and take a stuffy, smelly, overheated hole of an apartment in this Heaven-forsaken, festering Gehenna. To have to mix night after night with a mob who think that life is a sort of St. Vitus's dance, and imagine that they're having a good time because they're making enough noise for six and drinking too much for ten. I loathe New York, Bertie. I wouldn't come near the place if I hadn't got to see editors occasionally. There's a blight on it. It's got moral delirium tremens. It's the limit. The very thought of staying more than a day in it makes me sick. And you call this thing pretty soft for me!"

I felt rather like Lot's friends must have done when they dropped in for a quiet chat and their genial host began to criticize the Cities of the Plain. I had no idea old Rocky could be so eloquent.

"It would kill me to have to live in New York," he went on. "To have to share the air with six million people! To have to wear stiff collars and decent clothes all the time! To——" He started. "Good Lord! I suppose I should have to dress for dinner in the evenings. What a ghastly notion!"

I was shocked, absolutely shocked.

"My dear chap!" I said, reproachfully.

"Do you dress for dinner every night, Bertie?"

"Jeeves," I said, coldly. The man was still standing like a statue by the door. "How many suits of evening clothes have I?"

"We have three suits full of evening dress, sir; two dinner jackets——"

"Three."

"For practical purposes two only, sir. If you remember, we cannot wear the third. We have also seven white waistcoats."

"And shirts?"

"Four dozen, sir."

"And white ties?"

"The first two shallow shelves in the chest of drawers are completely filled with our white ties, sir."

I turned to Rocky.

"You see?"

The chappie writhed like an electric fan.

"I won't do it! I can't do it! I'll be hanged if I'll do it! How on earth can I dress up like that? Do you realize that most days I don't get out of my pyjamas till five in the afternoon, and then I just put on an old sweater?"

I saw Jeeves wince, poor chap! This sort of revelation shocked his finest feelings.

"Then, what are you going to do about it?" I said.

"That's what I want to know."

"You might write and explain to your aunt."

"I might—if I wanted her to get round to her lawyer's in two rapid leaps and cut me out of her will."

I saw his point.

"What do you suggest, Jeeves?" I said.

Jeeves cleared his throat respectfully.

"The crux of the matter would appear to be, sir, that Mr. Todd is obliged by the conditions under which the money is delivered into his possession to write Miss Rockmetteller long and detailed letters relating to his movements, and the only method by which this can be accomplished, if Mr. Todd adheres to his expressed intention of remaining in the country, is for Mr. Todd to induce some second party to gather the actual experiences which Miss Rockmetteller wishes reported to her, and to convey these to him in the shape of a careful report, on which it would be possible for him, with the aid of his imagination, to base the suggested correspondence."

Having got which off the old diaphragm, Jeeves was silent. Rocky looked at me in a helpless sort of way. He hasn't been brought up on Jeeves as I have, and he isn't on to his curves.

"Could he put it a little clearer, Bertie?" he said. "I thought at the start it was going to make sense, but it kind of flickered. What's the idea?"

"My dear old man, perfectly simple. I knew we could stand on Jeeves. All you've got to do is to get somebody to go round the town for you and take a few notes, and then you work the notes up into letters. That's it, isn't it, Jeeves?"

"Precisely, sir."

The light of hope gleamed in Rocky's eyes. He looked at Jeeves in a startled way, dazed by the man's vast intellect.

"But who would do it?" he said. "It would have to be a pretty smart sort of man, a man who would notice things."

"Jeeves!" I said. "Let Jeeves do it."

"But would he?"

"You would do it, wouldn't you, Jeeves?"

For the first time in our long connection I observed Jeeves almost smile. The corner of his mouth curved quite a quarter of an inch, and for a moment his eye ceased to look like a meditative fish's.

"I should be delighted to oblige, sir. As a matter of fact, I have already visited some of New York's places of interest on my evening out, and it would be most enjoyable to make a practice of the pursuit."

"Fine! I know exactly what your aunt wants to hear about, Rocky. She wants an earful of cabaret stuff. The place you ought to go to first, Jeeves, is Reigelheimer's. It's on Forty-second Street. Anybody will show you the way."

Jeeves shook his head.

"Pardon me, sir. People are no longer going to Reigelheimer's. The place at the moment is Frolics on the Roof."

"You see?" I said to Rocky. "Leave it to Jeeves. He knows."

It isn't often that you find an entire group of your fellow-humans happy in this world; but our little circle was certainly an example of the fact that it can be done. We were all full of beans. Everything went absolutely right from the start.

Jeeves was happy, partly because he loves to exercise his giant brain, and partly because he was having a corking time among the bright lights. I saw him one night at the Midnight Revels. He was sitting at a table on the edge of the dancing floor, doing himself remarkably well with a fat cigar and a bottle of the best. I'd never imagined he could look so nearly human. His face wore an expression of austere benevolence, and he was making notes in a small book.

As for the rest of us, I was feeling pretty good, because I was fond of old Rocky and glad to be able to do him a good turn. Rocky was perfectly contented, because he was still able to sit on fences in his pyjamas and watch worms. And, as for the aunt, she seemed tickled to death. She was getting Broadway at pretty long range, but it seemed to be hitting her just right. I read one of her letters to Rocky, and it was full of life.

But then Rocky's letters, based on Jeeves's notes, were enough to buck anybody up. It was rummy when you came to think of it. There was I, loving the life, while the mere mention of it gave Rocky a tired feeling; yet here is a letter I wrote home to a pal of mine in London: —

Dear Freddie, —

Well, here I am in New York. It's not a bad place. I'm not having a bad time. Everything's pretty all right. The cabarets aren't

bad. Don't know when I shall be back. How's everybody?
Cheer-o! —

Yours,
BERTIE.

P.S. — Seen old Ted lately?

Not that I cared about old Ted; but if I hadn't dragged him in I
couldn't have got the confounded thing on to the second page.
Now here's old Rocky on exactly the same subject: —

DEAREST AUNT ISABEL, —

How can I ever thank you enough for giving me the opportunity to live in this astounding city! New York seems more wonderful every day.

Fifth Avenue is at its best, of course, just now. The dresses are
magnificent!

Wads of stuff about the dresses. I didn't know Jeeves was such an
authority.

I was out with some of the crowd at the Midnight Revels the other
night. We took in a show first, after a little dinner at a new place
on Forty-third Street. We were quite a gay party. Georgie Cohan
looked in about midnight and got off a good one about Willie
Collier. Fred Stone could only stay a minute, but Doug Fairbanks
did all sorts of stunts and made us roar. Diamond Jim Brady was
there, as usual, and Laurette Taylor showed up with a party. The
show at the Revels is quite good. I am enclosing a programme.

Last night a few of us went round to Frolics on the Roof——

And so on and so forth, yards of it. I suppose it's the artistic
temperament or something. What I mean is, it's easier for a chappie
who's used to writing poems and that sort of tosh to put a bit of a
punch into a letter than it is for a chappie like me. Anyway, there's
no doubt that Rocky's correspondence was hot stuff. I called Jeeves
in and congratulated him.

"Jeeves, you're a wonder!"

"Thank you, sir."

"How you notice everything at these places beats me. I couldn't
tell you a thing about them, except that I've had a good time."

"It's just a knack, sir."

"Well, Mr. Todd's letters ought to brace Miss Rockmetteller all right, what?"

"Undoubtedly, sir," agreed Jeeves.

And, by Jove, they did! They certainly did, by George! What I mean to say is, I was sitting in the apartment one afternoon, about a month after the thing had started, smoking a cigarette and resting the old bean, when the door opened and the voice of Jeeves burst the silence like a bomb.

It wasn't that he spoke loud. He has one of those soft, soothing voices that slide through the atmosphere like the note of a far-off sheep. It was what he said that made me leap like a young gazelle.

"Miss Rockmetteller!"

And in came a large, solid female.

The situation floored me. I'm not denying it. Hamlet must have felt much as I did when his father's ghost bobbed up in the fairway. I'd come to look on Rocky's aunt as such a permanency at her own home that it didn't seem possible that she could really be here in New York. I stared at her. Then I looked at Jeeves. He was standing there in an attitude of dignified detachment, the chump, when, if ever he should have been rallying round the young master, it was now.

Rocky's aunt looked less like an invalid than any one I've ever seen, except my Aunt Agatha. She had a good deal of Aunt Agatha about her, as a matter of fact. She looked as if she might be deucedly dangerous if put upon; and something seemed to tell me that she would certainly regard herself as put upon if she ever found out the game which poor old Rocky had been pulling on her.

"Good afternoon," I managed to say.

"How do you do?" she said. "Mr. Cohan?"

"Er—no."

"Mr. Fred Stone?"

"Not absolutely. As a matter of fact, my name's Wooster—Bertie Wooster."

She seemed disappointed. The fine old name of Wooster appeared to mean nothing in her life.

"Isn't Rockmetteller home?" she said. "Where is he?"

She had me with the first shot. I couldn't think of anything to say. I couldn't tell her that Rocky was down in the country, watching worms.

There was me faintest flutter of sound in the background. It was the respectful cough with which Jeeves announces that he is about to speak without having been spoken to.

"If you remember, sir, Mr. Todd went out in the automobile with a party earlier in the afternoon."

"So he did, Jeeves; so he did," I said, looking at my watch. "Did he say when he would be back?"

"He gave me to understand, sir, that he would be somewhat late in returning."

He vanished; and the aunt took the chair which I'd forgotten to offer her. She looked at me in rather a rummy way. It was a nasty look. It made me feel as if I were something the dog had brought in and intended to bury later on, when he had time. My own Aunt Agatha, back in England, has looked at me in exactly the same way many a time, and it never fails to make my spine curl.

"You seem very much at home here, young man. Are you a great friend of Rockmetteller's?"

"Oh, yes, rather!"

She frowned as if she had expected better things of old Rocky.

"Well, you need to be," she said, "the way you treat his flat as your own!"

I give you my word, this quite unforeseen slam simply robbed me of the power of speech. I'd been looking on myself in the light of the dashing host, and suddenly to be treated as an intruder jarred me. It wasn't, mark you, as if she had spoken in a way to suggest that she considered my presence in the place as an ordinary social call. She obviously looked on me as a cross between a burglar and the plumber's man come to fix the leak in the bathroom. It hurt her—my being there.

At this juncture, with the conversation showing every sign of being about to die in awful agonies, an idea came to me. Tea—the good old stand-by.

"Would you care for a cup of tea?" I said

"Tea?"

She spoke as if she had never heard of the stuff.

"Nothing like a cup after a journey," I said. "Bucks you up! Puts a bit of zip into you. What I mean is, restores you, and so on, don't you know. I'll go and tell Jeeves."

I tottered down the passage to Jeeves's lair. The man was reading the evening paper as if he hadn't a care in the world.

"Jeeves," I said, "we want some tea."

"Very good, sir."

"I say, Jeeves, this is a bit thick, what?"

I wanted sympathy, don't you know—sympathy and kindness. The old nerve centres had had the deuce of a shock.

"She's got the idea this place belongs to Mr. Todd. What on earth put that into her head?"

Jeeves filled the kettle with a restrained dignity.

"No doubt because of Mr. Todd's letters, sir," he said. "It was my suggestion, sir, if you remember, that they should be addressed from this apartment in order that Mr. Todd should appear to possess a good central residence in the city."

I remembered. We had thought it a brainy scheme at the time.

"Well, it's bally awkward, you know, Jeeves. She looks on me as an intruder. By Jove! I suppose she thinks I'm some one who hangs about here, touching Mr. Todd for free meals and borrowing his shirts."

"Yes, sir."

"It's pretty rotten, you know."

"Most disturbing, sir."

"And there's another thing: What are we to do about Mr. Todd? We've got to get him up here as soon as ever we can. When you have brought the tea you had better go out and send him a telegram, telling him to come up by the next train."

"I have already done so, sir. I took the liberty of writing the message and dispatching it by the lift attendant."

"By Jove, you think of everything, Jeeves!"

"Thank you, sir. A little buttered toast with the tea? Just so, sir. Thank you."

I went back to the sitting-room. She hadn't moved an inch. She was still bolt upright on the edge of her chair, gripping her umbrella like a hammer-thrower. She gave me another of those looks as I came in. There was no doubt about it; for some reason she had taken a dislike to me. I suppose because I wasn't George M. Cohan. It was a bit hard on a chap.

"This is a surprise, what?" I said, after about five minutes' restful silence, trying to crank the conversation up again.

"What is a surprise?"

"Your coming here, don't you know, and so on."

She raised her eyebrows and drank me in a bit more through her glasses.

"Why is it surprising that I should visit my only nephew?" she said.

Put like that, of course, it did seem reasonable.

"Oh, rather," I said. "Of course! Certainly. What I mean is——"

Jeeves projected himself into the room with the tea. I was jolly glad to see him. There's nothing like having a bit of business arranged for one when one isn't certain of one's lines. With the teapot to fool about with I felt happier.

"Tea, tea, tea—what? What?" I said.

It wasn't what I had meant to say. My idea had been to be a good deal more formal, and so on. Still, it covered the situation. I poured her out a cup. She sipped it and put the cup down with a shudder.

"Do you mean to say, young man," she said, frostily, "that you expect me to drink this stuff?"

"Rather! Bucks you up, you know."

"What do you mean by the expression 'Bucks you up'?"

"Well, makes you full of beans, you know. Makes you fizz."

"I don't understand a word you say. You're English, aren't you?"

I admitted it. She didn't say a word. And somehow she did it in a way that made it worse than if she had spoken for hours. Somehow it was brought home to me that she didn't like Englishmen, and that if she had had to meet an Englishman I was the one she'd have chosen last.

Conversation languished again after that.

Then I tried again. I was becoming more convinced every moment that you can't make a real lively *salon* with a couple of people, especially if one of them lets it go a word at a time.

"Are you comfortable at your hotel?" I said.

"At which hotel?"

"The hotel you're staying at."

"I am not staying at an hotel."

"Stopping with friends—what?"

"I am naturally stopping with my nephew."

I didn't get it for the moment; then it hit me.

"What! Here?" I gurgled.

"Certainly! Where else should I go?"

The full horror of the situation rolled over me like a wave. I couldn't see what on earth I was to do. I couldn't explain that this wasn't Rocky's flat without giving the poor old chap away hopelessly, because she would then ask me where he did live, and then he would be right in the soup. I was trying to induce the old bean to recover from the shock and produce some results when she spoke again.

"Will you kindly tell my nephew's manservant to prepare my room? I wish to lie down."

"Your nephew's manservant?"

"The man you call Jeeves. If Rockmetteller has gone for an automobile ride there is no need for you to wait for him. He will naturally wish to be alone with me when he returns."

I found myself tottering out of the room. The thing was too much for me. I crept into Jeeves's den.

"Jeeves!" I whispered.

"Sir?"

"Mix me a b.-and-s., Jeeves. I feel weak."

"Very good, sir."

"This is getting thicker every minute, Jeeves."

"Sir?"

"She thinks you're Mr. Todd's man. She thinks the whole place is his, and everything in it. I don't see what you're to do, except stay on and keep it up. We can't say anything or she'll get on to the whole thing, and I don't want to let Mr. Todd down. By the way, Jeeves, she wants you to prepare her bed."

He looked wounded.

"It is hardly my place, sir——"

"I know—I know. But do it as a personal favour to me. If you come to that, it's hardly my place to be flung out of the flat like this and have to go to an hotel, what?"

"Is it your intention to go to an hotel, sir? What will you do for clothes?"

"Good Lord! I hadn't thought of that. Can you put a few things in a bag when she isn't looking, and sneak them down to me at the St. Aurea?"

"I will endeavour to do so, sir."

"Well, I don't think there's anything more, is there? Tell Mr. Todd where I am when he gets here."

"Very good, sir."

I looked round the place. The moment of parting had come. I felt sad. The whole thing reminded me of one of those melodramas where they drive chappies out of the old homestead into the snow.

"Good-bye, Jeeves," I said.

"Good-bye, sir."

And I staggered out.

You know, I rather think I agree with those poet-and-philosopher Johnnies who insist that a fellow ought to be devilish pleased if he has a bit of trouble. All that stuff about being refined by suffering, you know. Suffering does give a chap a sort of broader and more sympathetic outlook. It helps you to understand other people's misfortunes if you've been through the same thing yourself.

As I stood in my lonely bedroom at the hotel, trying to tie my white tie myself, it struck me for the first time that there must be whole squads of chappies in the world who had to get along without a man to look after them. I'd always thought of Jeeves as a kind of natural phenomenon; but, by Jove! of course, when you come to think of it, there must be quite a lot of fellows who have to press their own clothes themselves, and haven't got anybody to bring them tea in the morning, and so on. It was rather a solemn thought, don't you know, I mean to say, ever since then I've been able to appreciate the frightful privations the poor have to stick.

I got dressed somehow. Jeeves hadn't forgotten a thing in his packing. Everything was there, down to the final stud. I'm not sure this didn't make me feel worse. It kind of deepened the pathos. It was like what somebody or other wrote about the touch of a vanished hand.

I had a bit of dinner somewhere and went to a show of some kind; but nothing seemed to make any difference. I simply hadn't the heart to go on to supper anywhere. I just sucked down a whisky-and-soda in the hotel smoking-room and went straight up to bed. I don't know when I've felt so rotten. Somehow I found myself moving about the room softly, as if there had been a death in the family. If I had had anybody to talk to I should have talked in a whisper; in fact, when the telephone-bell rang I answered in such a sad, hushed voice that the fellow at the other end of the wire said "Halloa!" five times, thinking he hadn't got me.

It was Rocky. The poor old scout was deeply agitated.

"Bertie! Is that you, Bertie? Oh, gosh! I'm having a time!"

"Where are you speaking from?"

"The Midnight Revels. We've been here an hour, and I think we're a fixture for the night. I've told Aunt Isabel I've gone out to call up a friend to join us. She's glued to a chair, with this-is-the-life written all over her, taking it in through the pores. She loves it, and I'm nearly crazy."

"Tell me all, old top," I said.

"A little more of this," he said, "and I shall sneak quietly off to the river and end it all. Do you mean to say you go through this sort of thing every night, Bertie, and enjoy it? It's simply infernal! I was just snatching a wink of sleep behind the bill of fare just now when about a million yelling girls swooped down, with toy balloons. There are two orchestras here, each trying to see if it can't play louder than the other. I'm a mental and physical wreck. When your telegram arrived I was just lying down for a quiet pipe, with a sense of absolute peace stealing over me. I had to get dressed and sprint two miles to catch the train. It nearly gave me heart failure; and on top of that I almost got brain fever inventing lies to tell Aunt Isabel. And then I had to cram myself into these confounded evening clothes of yours."

I gave a sharp wail of agony. It hadn't struck me till then that Rocky was depending on my wardrobe to see him through.

"You'll ruin them!"

"I hope so," said Rocky, in the most unpleasant way. His troubles seemed to have had the worst effect on his character. "I should like to get back at them somehow; they've given me a bad enough time. They're about three sizes too small, and something's apt to give at any moment. I wish to goodness it would, and give me a chance to breathe. I haven't breathed since half-past seven. Thank Heaven, Jeeves managed to get out and buy me a collar that fitted, or I should be a strangled corpse by now! It was touch and go till the stud broke. Bertie, this is pure Hades! Aunt Isabel keeps on urging me to dance. How on earth can I dance when I don't know a soul to dance with? And how the deuce could I, even if I knew every girl in the place? It's taking big chances even to move in these trousers. I had to tell her I've hurt my ankle. She keeps asking me when Cohan and Stone are going to turn up; and it's simply a question of time before she discovers that Stone is sitting two tables away. Something's got to be done, Bertie! You've got to think up some way of getting me out of this mess. It was you who got me into it."

"Me! What do you mean?"

"Well, Jeeves, then. It's all the same. It was you who suggested leaving it to Jeeves. It was those letters I wrote from his notes that did the mischief. I made them too good! My aunt's just been telling me about it. She says she had resigned herself to ending her life where she was, and then my letters began to arrive, describing the joys of New York; and they stimulated her to such an extent that she pulled herself together and made the trip. She seems to think she's had some miraculous kind of faith cure. I tell you I can't stand it, Bertie! It's got to end!"

"Can't Jeeves think of anything?"

"No. He just hangs round, saying: 'Most disturbing, sir!' A fat lot of help that is!"

"Well, old lad," I said, "after all, it's far worse for me than it is for you. You've got a comfortable home and Jeeves. And you're saving a lot of money."

"Saving money? What do you mean—saving money?"

"Why, the allowance your aunt was giving you. I suppose she's paying all the expenses now, isn't she?"

"Certainly she is; but she's stopped the allowance. She wrote the lawyers to-night. She says that, now she's in New York, there is no necessity for it to go on, as we shall always be together, and it's simpler for her to look after that end of it. I tell you, Bertie, I've examined the darned cloud with a microscope, and if it's got a silver lining it's some little dissembler!"

"But, Rocky, old top, it's too bally awful! You've no notion of what I'm going through in this beastly hotel, without Jeeves. I must get back to the flat."

"Don't come near the flat!"

"But it's my own flat."

"I can't help that. Aunt Isabel doesn't like you. She asked me what you did for a living. And when I told her you didn't do anything she said she thought as much, and that you were a typical specimen of a useless and decaying aristocracy. So if you think you have made a hit, forget it. Now I must be going back, or she'll be coming out here after me. Good-bye."

Next morning Jeeves came round. It was all so home-like when he floated noiselessly into the room that I nearly broke down.

"Good morning, sir," he said. "I have brought a few more of your personal belongings."

He began to unstrap the suit-case he was carrying.

"Did you have any trouble sneaking them away?"

"It was not easy, sir. I had to watch my chance. Miss Rockmetteller is a remarkably alert lady."

'You know, Jeeves, say what you like—this *is* a bit thick, isn't it?"

"The situation is certainly one that has never before come under my notice, sir. I have brought the heather-mixture suit, as the climatic conditions are congenial. To-morrow, if not prevented, I will endeavour to add the brown lounge with the faint green twill."

"It can't go on—this sort of thing—Jeeves."

"We must hope for the best, sir."

"Can't you think of anything to do?"

"I have been giving the matter considerable thought, sir, but so far without success. I am placing three silk shirts—the dove-coloured, the light blue, and the mauve—in the first long drawer, sir."

"You don't mean to say you can't think of anything, Jeeves?"

"For the moment, sir, no. You will find a dozen handkerchiefs and the tan socks in the upper drawer on the left." He strapped the suit-case and put it on a chair. "A curious lady. Miss Rockmetteller, sir."

"You understate it, Jeeves."

He gazed meditatively out of the window.

"In many ways, sir, Miss Rockmetteller reminds me of an aunt of mine who resides in the south-east portion of London. Their temperaments are much alike. My aunt has the same taste for the pleasures of the great city. It is a passion with her to ride in hansom cabs, sir. Whenever the family take their eyes off her she escapes from the house and spends the day riding about in cabs. On several occasions she has broken into the children's savings bank to secure the means to enable her to gratify this desire."

"I love to have these little chats with you about your female relatives, Jeeves," I said, coldly, for I felt that the man had let me down, and I was fed up with him. "But I don't see what all this has got to do with my trouble."

"I beg your pardon, sir. I am leaving a small assortment of your neckties on the mantelpiece, sir, for you to select according to your preference. I should recommend the blue with the red domino pattern, sir."

Then he streamed imperceptibly toward the door and flowed silently out.

I've often heard that chappies, after some great shock or loss, have a habit, after they've been on the floor for a while wondering what hit them, of picking themselves up and piecing themselves together, and sort of taking a whirl at beginning a new life. Time, the great healer, and Nature, adjusting itself, and so on and so forth. There's a lot in it. I know, because in my own case, after a day or two of what you might call prostration, I began to recover. The frightful loss of Jeeves made any thought of pleasure more or less a mockery, but at least I found that I was able to have a dash at enjoying life again. What I mean is, I braced up to the extent of going round the cabarets once more, so as to try to forget, if only for the moment.

New York's a small place when it comes to the part of it that wakes up just as the rest is going to bed, and it wasn't long before my tracks began to cross old Rocky's. I saw him once at Peale's, and again at Frolics on the Roof. There wasn't anybody with him either time except the aunt, and, though he was trying to look as if he had struck the ideal life, it wasn't difficult for me, knowing the circumstances, to see that beneath the mask the poor chap was suffering. My heart bled for the fellow. At least, what there was of it that wasn't bleeding for myself bled for him. He had the air of one who was about to crack under the strain.

It seemed to me that the aunt was looking slightly upset also. I took it that she was beginning to wonder when the celebrities were going to surge round, and what had suddenly become of all those wild, careless spirits Rocky used to mix with in his letters. I didn't blame her. I had only read a couple of his letters, but they certainly gave the impression that poor old Rocky was by way of being the hub of New York night life, and that, if by any chance he failed to show up at a cabaret, the management said, "What's the use?" and put up the shutters.

The next two nights I didn't come across them, but the night after that I was sitting by myself at the Maison Pierre when somebody tapped me on the shoulder-blade, and I found Rocky standing beside me, with a sort of mixed expression of wistfulness and apoplexy on his face. How the chappie had contrived to wear my evening clothes so many times without disaster was a mystery to me. He confided later that early in the proceedings he had slit the waistcoat up the back and that that had helped a bit.

For a moment I had the idea that he had managed to get away from his aunt for the evening; but, looking past him, I saw that she was in again. She was at a table over by the wall, looking at me as if I were something the management ought to be complained to about.

"Bertie, old scout," said Rocky, in a quiet, sort of crushed voice, "we've always been pals, haven't we? I mean, you know I'd do you a good turn if you asked me."

"My dear old lad," I said. The man had moved me.

'Then, for Heaven's sake, come over and sit at our table for the rest of the evening."

Well, you know, there are limits to the sacred claims of friendship.

"My dear chap," I said, "you know I'd do anything in reason; but—"

"You must come, Bertie. You've got to. Something's got to be done to divert her mind. She's brooding about something. She's been like that for the last two days. I think she's beginning to suspect. She can't understand why we never seem to meet any one I know at these joints. A few nights ago I happened to run into two newspaper men I used to know fairly well. That kept me going for a while. I introduced them to Aunt Isabel as David Belasco and Jim Corbett, and it went well. But the effect has worn off now, and she's beginning to wonder again. Something's got to be done, or she will find out everything, and if she does I'd take a nickel for my chance of getting a cent from her later on. So, for the love of Mike, come across to our table and help things along."

I went along. One has to rally round a pal in distress. Aunt Isabel was sitting bolt upright, as usual. It certainly did seem as if she had lost a bit of the zest with which she had started out to explore Broadway. She looked as if she had been thinking a good deal about rather unpleasant things.

"You've met Bertie Wooster, Aunt Isabel?" said Rocky.

"I have."

There was something in her eye that seemed to say: —

"Out of a city of six million people, why did you pick on me?"

"Take a seat, Bertie. What'll you have?" said Rocky.

And so the merry party began. It was one of those jolly, happy, bread-crumbling parties where you cough twice before you speak, and then decide not to say it after all. After we had had an hour of this wild dissipation, Aunt Isabel said she wanted to go home. In the light of what Rocky had been telling me, this struck me as sinister. I had gathered that at the beginning of her visit she had had to be dragged home with ropes.

It must have hit Rocky the same way, for he gave me a pleading look.

"You'll come along, won't you, Bertie, and have a drink at the flat?"

I had a feeling that this wasn't in the contract, but there wasn't anything to be done. It seemed brutal to leave the poor chap alone with the woman, so I went along.

Right from the start, from the moment we stepped into the taxi, the feeling began to grow that something was about to break loose. A massive silence prevailed in the corner where the aunt sat, and, though Rocky, balancing himself on the little seat in front, did his best to supply dialogue, we weren't a chatty party.

I had a glimpse of Jeeves as we went into the flat, sitting in his lair, and I wished I could have called to him to rally round. Something told me that I was about to need him.

The stuff was on the table in the sitting-room. Rocky took up the decanter.

"Say when, Bertie."

"Stop!" barked the aunt, and he dropped it.

I caught Rocky's eye as he stooped to pick up the ruins. It was the eye of one who sees it coming.

"Leave it there, Rockmetteller!" said Aunt Isabel; and Rocky left it there.

"The time has come to speak," she said. "I cannot stand idly by and see a young man going to perdition!"

Poor old Rocky gave a sort of gurgle, a kind of sound rather like the whisky had made running out of the decanter on to my carpet.

"Eh?" he said, blinking.

The aunt proceeded.

"The fault," she said, "was mine. I had not then seen the light. But now my eyes are open. I see the hideous mistake I have made. I shudder at the thought of the wrong I did you, Rockmetteller, by urging you into contact with this wicked city."

I saw Rocky grope feebly for the table. His fingers touched it, and a look of relief came into the poor chappie's face. I understood his feelings.

"But when I wrote you that letter, Rockmetteller, instructing you to go to the city and live its life, I had not had the privilege of hearing Mr. Mundy speak on the subject of New York."

"Jimmy Mundy!" I cried.

You know how it is sometimes when everything seems all mixed up and you suddenly get a clue. When she mentioned Jimmy Mundy I began to understand more or less what had happened. I'd seen it happen before. I remember, back in England, the man I had before Jeeves sneaked off to a meeting on his evening out and came back and denounced me in front of a crowd of chappies I was giving a bit of supper to as a moral leper.

The aunt gave me a withering up and down.

"Yes; Jimmy Mundy!" she said. "I am surprised at a man of your stamp having heard of him. There is no music, there are no drunken, dancing men, no shameless, flaunting women at his meetings; so for you they would have no attraction. But for others, less dead in sin, he has his message. He has come to save New York from itself; to force it—in his picturesque phrase—to hit the trail. It was three days ago, Rockmetteller, that I first heard him. It was an accident that took me to his meeting. How often in this life a mere accident may shape our whole future!

"You had been called away by that telephone message from Mr. Belasco; so you could not take me to the Hippodrome, as we had arranged. I asked your man-servant, Jeeves, to take me there. The man has very little intelligence. He seems to have misunderstood me. I am thankful that he did. He took me to what I subsequently learned was Madison Square Garden, where Mr. Mundy is holding his meetings. He escorted me to a seat and then left me. And it was not till the meeting had begun that I discovered the mistake which had been made. My seat was in the middle of a row. I could not leave without inconveniencing a great many people, so I remained."

She gulped.

"Rockmetteller, I have never been so thankful for anything else. Mr. Mundy was wonderful! He was like some prophet of old, scourging the sins of the people. He leaped about in a frenzy of inspiration till I feared he would do himself an injury. Sometimes he expressed himself in a somewhat odd manner, but every word carried conviction. He showed me New York in its true colours. He showed me the vanity and wickedness of sitting in gilded haunts of vice, eating lobster when decent people should be in bed.

"He said that the tango and the fox-trot were devices of the devil to drag people down into the Bottomless Pit. He said that there was more sin in ten minutes with a negro banjo orchestra than in all the ancient revels of Nineveh and Babylon. And when he stood on one leg and pointed right at where I was sitting and shouted 'This means you!' I could have sunk through the floor. I came away a changed woman. Surely you must have noticed the change in me, Rockmetteller? You must have seen that I was no longer the careless, thoughtless person who had urged you to dance in those places of wickedness?"

Rocky was holding on to the table as if it was his only friend.

"Y-yes," he stammered; "I — I thought something was wrong."

"Wrong? Something was right! Everything was right! Rockmetteller, it is not too late for you to be saved. You have only sipped of the evil cup. You have not drained it. It will be hard at first, but you will find that you can do it if you fight with a stout heart against the glamour and fascination of this dreadful city. Won't you, for my sake, try, Rockmetteller? Won't you go back to the country to-morrow and begin the struggle? Little by little, if you use your will—"

I can't help thinking it must have been that word "will" that roused dear old Rocky like a trumpet call. It must have brought home to him the realization that a miracle had come off and saved him from being cut out of Aunt Isabel's. At any rate, as she said it he perked up, let go of the table, and faced her with gleaming eyes.

"Do you want me to go back to the country, Aunt Isabel?"

"Yes."

"Not to live in the country?"

"Yes, Rockmetteller."

"Stay in the country all the time, do you mean? Never come to New York?"

'Yes, Rockmetteller; I mean just that. It is the only way. Only there can you be safe from temptation. Will you do it, Rockmetteller? Will you—for my sake?"

Rocky grabbed the table again. He seemed to draw a lot of encouragement from that table.

"I will!" he said.

"Jeeves," I said. It was next day, and I was back in the old flat, lying in the old arm-chair, with my feet upon the good old table. I had just come from seeing dear old Rocky off to his country cottage, and an hour before he had seen his aunt off to whatever hamlet it was that she was the curse of; so we were alone at last. "Jeeves, there's no place like home—what?"

"Very true, sir."

"The jolly old roof-tree, and all that sort of thing—what?"

"Precisely, sir."

I lit another cigarette.

"Jeeves."

"Sir?"

"Do you know, at one point in the business I really thought you were baffled."

"Indeed, sir?"

"When did you get the idea of taking Miss Rockmetteller to the meeting? It was pure genius!"

"Thank you, sir. It came to me a little suddenly, one morning when I was thinking of my aunt, sir."

"Your aunt? The hansom cab one?"

"Yes, sir. I recollected that, whenever we observed one of her attacks coming on, we used to send for the clergyman of the parish. We always found that if he talked to her a while of higher things it diverted her mind from hansom cabs. It occurred to me that the same treatment might prove efficacious in the case of Miss Rockmetteller."

I was stunned by the man's resource.

"It's brain," I said; "pure brain! What do you do to get like that, Jeeves? I believe you must eat a lot of fish, or something. Do you eat a lot of fish, Jeeves?"

"No, sir."

"Oh, well, then, it's just a gift, I take it; and if you aren't born that way there's no use worrying."

"Precisely, sir," said Jeeves. "If I might make the suggestion, sir, I should not continue to wear your present tie. The green shade gives you a slightly bilious air. I should strongly advocate the blue with the red domino pattern instead, sir."

"All right, Jeeves," I said, humbly. "You know!"

ARDESSA (1919)

Willa Cather

Willa Cather (1873–1947) moved from Pittsburgh to New York City in 1906; she was already a well-regarded journalist and writer of short stories (she published her first story in 1892). Cather became the managing editor of McClure's *magazine in 1908 but left that job in 1912 to have more time to write. Her famous Nebraska novels followed:* O Pioneers! *(1913) and* My Ántonia *(1918). In "Arabella," Cather describes the routines of self-satisfied, clever Arabella, who has mastered her job with that type of mastery that allows one to coast. Arabella's protégé, Becky, seems to be a predecessor of the actress America Ferrera's TV character in* Ugly Betty: *a plucky, competent, honest, hard-working outsider. Cather and her partner, Edith Lewis, lived in Greenwich Village from 1912 to 1927.*

THE GRAND-MANNERED OLD man who sat at a desk in the reception-room of "The Outcry" offices to receive visitors and incidentally to keep the time-book of the employees, looked up as Miss Devine entered at ten minutes past ten and condescendingly wished him good morning. He bowed profoundly as she minced past his desk, and with an indifferent air took her course down the corridor that led to the editorial offices. Mechanically he opened the flat, black book at his elbow and placed his finger on D, running his eye along the line of figures after the name Devine. "It's banker's hours she keeps, indeed," he muttered. What was the use of entering so capricious a record? Nevertheless, with his usual preliminary flourish he wrote 10:10 under this, the fourth day of May.

The employee who kept banker's hours rustled on down the corridor to her private room, hung up her lavender jacket and her trim spring hat, and readjusted her side combs by the mirror inside her closet door. Glancing at her desk, she rang for an office boy, and reproved him because he had not dusted more carefully and because there were lumps in her paste. When he disappeared with the paste-jar, she sat down to decide which of her employer's letters he should see and which he should not.

Ardessa was not young and she was certainly not handsome. The coquettish angle at which she carried her head was a mannerism surviving from a time when it was more becoming. She shuddered at the cold candor of the new business woman, and was insinuatingly feminine.

Ardessa's employer, like young Lochinvar, had come out of the West, and he had done a great many contradictory things before he became proprietor and editor of "The Outcry." Before he decided to go to New York and make the East take notice of him, O'Mally had acquired a punctual, reliable silver-mine in South Dakota. This silent friend in the background made his journalistic success comparatively easy. He had figured out, when he was a rich nobody in Nevada, that the quickest way to cut into the known world was through the printing-press. He arrived in New York, bought a highly respectable publication, and turned it into a red-hot magazine of protest, which he called "The Outcry." He knew what the West wanted, and it proved to be what everybody secretly wanted. In six years he had done the thing that had hitherto seemed impossible: built up a national weekly, out on the news-stands the same day in New York and San Francisco; a magazine the people howled for, a moving-picture film of their real tastes and interests.

O'Mally bought "The Outcry" to make a stir, not to make a career, but he had got built into the thing more than he ever intended. It had made him a public man and put him into politics. He found the publicity game diverting, and it held him longer than any other game had ever done. He had built up about him an organization of which he was somewhat afraid and with which he was vastly bored. On his staff there were five famous men, and he had made every one of them. At first it amused him to manufacture celebrities. He found he could take an average reporter from the daily press, give him a "line" to follow, a trust to fight, a vice to expose,—this was all in that good time when people were eager to read about their own wickedness,—and in two years the reporter would be recognized as an authority. Other people—Napoleon, Disraeli, Sarah Bernhardt—had discovered that advertising would go a long way; but Marcus O'Mally discovered that in America it would go all the way—as far as you wished to pay its passage. Any human countenance, plastered in three-sheet posters from sea to sea, would be revered by the American people. The strangest thing was that the owners of these grave countenances, staring at their own faces on news-stands and billboards, fell to venerating themselves; and even he, O'Mally, was more or less constrained by these reputations that he had created out of cheap paper and cheap ink.

Constraint was the last thing O'Mally liked. The most engaging and unusual thing about the man was that he couldn't be fooled by the success of his own methods, and no amount of "recognition" could make a stuffed shirt of him. No matter how much he was advertised as a great medicine-man in the councils of the nation, he knew that he was a born gambler and a soldier of fortune. He left his dignified office to take care of itself for a good many months of the year while he played about on the outskirts of social order. He liked being a great man from the East in rough-and-tumble Western cities where he had once been merely an unconsidered spender.

O'Mally's long absences constituted one of the supreme advantages of Ardessa Devine's position. When he was at his post her duties were not heavy, but when he was giving balls in Goldfield, Nevada, she lived an ideal life. She came to the office every day, indeed, to forward such of O'Mally's letters as she thought best, to attend to his club notices and tradesmen's bills, and to taste the sense of her high connections. The great men of the staff were all about her, as contemplative as Buddhas in their private offices, each meditating upon the particular trust or form of vice confided to his care. Thus surrounded, Ardessa had a pleasant sense of being at the heart of things. It was like a mental message, exercise without exertion. She read and she embroidered. Her room was pleasant, and she liked to be seen at ladylike tasks and to feel herself a graceful contrast to the crude girls in the advertising and circulation departments across the hall. The younger stenographers, who had to get through with the enormous office correspondence, and who rushed about from one editor to another with wire baskets full of letters, made faces as they passed Ardessa's door and saw her cool and cloistered, daintily plying her needle. But no matter how hard the other stenographers were driven, no one, not even one of the five oracles of the staff, dared dictate so much as a letter to Ardessa. Like a sultan's bride, she was inviolate in her lord's absence; she had to be kept for him.

Naturally the other young women employed in "The Outcry" offices disliked Miss Devine. They were all competent girls, trained in the exacting methods of modern business, and they had to make good every day in the week, had to get through with a great deal of work or lose their position. O'Mally's private secretary was a mystery to them. Her exemptions and privileges, her patronizing remarks, formed an exhaustless subject of conversation at the lunchhour. Ardessa had, indeed, as they knew she must have, a kind of "purchase" on her employer.

When O'Mally first came to New York to break into publicity, he engaged Miss Devine upon the recommendation of the editor whose ailing publication he bought and rechristened. That editor was a conservative, scholarly gentleman of the old school, who was retiring because he felt out of place in the world of brighter, breezier magazines that had been flowering since the new century came in. He believed that in this vehement world young O'Mally would make himself heard and that Miss Devine's training in an editorial office would be of use to him.

When O'Mally first sat down at a desk to be an editor, all the cards that were brought in looked pretty much alike to him. Ardessa was at his elbow. She had long been steeped in literary distinctions and in the social distinctions which used to count for much more than they do now. She knew all the great men, all the nephews and clients of great men. She knew which must be seen, which must be made welcome, and which could safely be sent away. She could give O'Mally on the instant the former rating in magazine offices of nearly every name that was brought in to him. She could give him an idea of the man's connections, of the price his work commanded, and insinuate whether he ought to be met with the old punctiliousness or with the new joviality. She was useful in explaining to her employer the significance of various invitations, and the standing of clubs and associations. At first she was virtually the social mentor of the bullet-headed young Westerner who wanted to break into everything, the solitary person about the office of the humming new magazine who knew anything about the editorial traditions of the eighties and nineties which, antiquated as they now were, gave an editor, as O'Mally said, a background.

Despite her indolence, Ardessa was useful to O'Mally as a social reminder. She was the card catalogue of his ever-changing personal relations. O'Mally went in for everything and got tired of everything; that was why he made a good editor. After he was through with people, Ardessa was very skilful in covering his retreat. She read and answered the letters of admirers who had begun to bore him. When great authors, who had been dined and fêted the month before, were suddenly left to cool their heels in the reception-room, thrown upon the suave hospitality of the grand old man at the desk, it was Ardessa who went out and made soothing and plausible explanations as to why the editor could not see them. She was the brake that checked the too-eager neophyte, the emollient that eased the severing of relationships, the gentle extinguisher of the lights that failed. When there were no longer messages of hope and cheer to be sent to ardent young writers and reformers, Ardessa delivered, as sweetly as possible, whatever messages were left.

In handling these people with whom O'Mally was quite through, Ardessa had gradually developed an industry which was immensely gratifying to her own vanity. Not only did she not crush them; she even fostered them a little. She continued to advise them in the reception-room and "personally" received their manuscripts long after O'Mally had declared that he would never read another line they wrote. She let them outline their plans for stories and articles to her, promising to bring these suggestions to the editor's attention. She denied herself to nobody, was gracious even to the Shakespere-Bacon man, the perpetual-motion man, the travel-article man, the ghosts which haunt every magazine office. The writers who had had their happy hour of O'Mally's favor kept feeling that Ardessa might reinstate them. She answered their letters of inquiry in her most polished and elegant style, and even gave them hints as to the subjects in which the restless editor was or was not interested at the moment: she feared it would be useless to send him an article on "How to Trap Lions," because he had just bought an article on "Elephant-Shooting in Majuba Land," etc.

So when O'Mally plunged into his office at 11:30 on this, the fourth day of May, having just got back from three-days' fishing, he found Ardessa in the reception-room, surrounded by a little court of discards. This was annoying, for he always wanted his stenographer at once. Telling the office boy to give her a hint that she was needed, he threw off his hat and top-coat and began to race through the pile of letters Ardessa had put on his desk. When she entered, he did not wait for her polite inquiries about his trip, but broke in at once.

"What is that fellow who writes about phossy jaw still hanging round here for? I don't want any articles on phossy jaw, and if I did, I wouldn't want his."

"He has just sold an article on the match industry to 'The New Age,' Mr. O'Mally," Ardessa replied as she took her seat at the editor's right.

"Why does he have to come and tell us about it? We've nothing to do with 'The New Age.' And that prison-reform guy, what's he loafing about for?"

Ardessa bridled.

"You remember, Mr. O'Mally, he brought letters of introduction from Governor Harper, the reform Governor of Mississippi."

O'Mally jumped up, kicking over his waste-basket in his impatience.

"That was months ago. I went through his letters and went through him, too. He hasn't got anything we want. I've been through with Governor Harper a long while. We're asleep at the switch in here. And let me tell you, if I catch sight of that causes-of-blindness-in-babies woman around here again. I'll do something violent. Clear them out, Miss Devine! Clear them out! We need a traffic policeman in this office. Have you got that article on 'Stealing Our National Water Power' ready for me?"

"Mr. Gerrard took it back to make modifications. He gave it to me at noon on Saturday, just before the office closed. I will have it ready for you to-morrow morning, Mr. O'Mally, if you have not too many letters for me this afternoon," Ardessa replied pointedly.

"Holy Mike!" muttered O'Mally, "we need a traffic policeman for the staff, too. Gerrard's modified that thing half a dozen times already. Why don't they get accurate information in the first place?"

He began to dictate his morning mail, walking briskly up and down the floor by way of giving his stenographer an energetic example. Her indolence and her ladylike deportment weighed on him. He wanted to take her by the elbows and run her around the block. He didn't mind that she loafed when he was away, but it was becoming harder and harder to speed her up when he was on the spot. He knew his correspondence was not enough to keep her busy, so when he was in town he made her type his own breezy editorials and various articles by members of his staff.

Transcribing editorial copy is always laborious, and the only way to make it easy is to farm it out. This Ardessa was usually clever enough to do. When she returned to her own room after O'Mally had gone out to lunch, Ardessa rang for an office boy and said languidly, "James, call Becky, please."

In a moment a thin, tense-faced Hebrew girl of eighteen or nineteen came rushing in, carrying a wire basket full of typewritten sheets. She was as gaunt as a plucked spring chicken, and her cheap, gaudy clothes might have been thrown on her. She looked as if she were running to catch a train and in mortal dread of missing it. While Miss Devine examined the pages in the basket, Becky stood with her shoulders drawn up and her elbows drawn in, apparently trying to hide herself in her insufficient open-work waist. Her wild, black eyes followed Miss Devine's hands desperately. Ardessa sighed.

"This seems to be very smeary copy again, Becky. You don't keep your mind on your work, and so you have to erase continually."

Becky spoke up in wailing self-vindication.

"It ain't that, Miss Devine. It's so many hard words he uses that I have to be at the dictionary all the time. Look! Look!" She produced a bunch of manuscript faintly scrawled in pencil, and thrust it under Ardessa's eyes. "He don't write out the words at all. He just begins a word, and then makes waves for you to guess."

"I see you haven't always guessed correctly, Becky," said Ardessa, with a weary smile. "There are a great many words here that would surprise Mr. Gerrard, I am afraid."

"And the inserts," Becky persisted. "How is anybody to tell where they go, Miss Devine? It's mostly inserts; see, all over the top and sides and back."

Ardessa turned her head away.

"Don't claw the pages like that, Becky. You make me nervous. Mr. Gerrard has not time to dot his i's and cross his t's. That is what we keep copyists for. I will correct these sheets for you,—it would be terrible if Mr. O'Mally saw them,—and then you can copy them over again. It must be done by to-morrow morning, so you may have to work late. See that your hands are clean and dry, and then you will not smear it."

"Yes, ma'am. Thank you, Miss Devine. Will you tell the janitor, please, it's all right if I have to stay? He was cross because I was here Saturday afternoon doing this. He said it was a holiday, and when everybody else was gone I ought to—"

"That will do, Becky. Yes, I will speak to the janitor for you. You may go to lunch now."

Becky turned on one heel and then swung back.

"Miss Devine," she said anxiously, "will it be all right if I get white shoes for now?"

Ardessa gave her kind consideration.

"For office wear, you mean? No, Becky. With only one pair, you could not keep them properly clean; and black shoes are much less conspicuous. Tan, if you prefer."

Becky looked down at her feet. They were too large, and her skirt was as much too short as her legs were too long.

"Nearly all the girls I know wear white shoes to business," she pleaded.

"They are probably little girls who work in factories or department stores, and that is quite another matter. Since you raise the question, Becky, I ought to speak to you about your new waist. Don't wear it to the office again, please. Those cheap open-work waists are not appropriate in an office like this. They are all very well for little chorus girls."

"But Miss Kalski wears expensive waists to business more open than this, and jewelry—"

Ardessa interrupted. Her face grew hard.

"Miss Kalski," she said coldly, "works for the business department. You are employed in the editorial offices. There is a great difference. You see, Becky, I might have to call you in here at any time when a scientist or a great writer or the president of a university is here talking over editorial matters, and such clothes as you have on to-day would make a bad impression. Nearly all our connections are with important people of that kind, and we ought to be well, but quietly, dressed."

"Yes, Miss Devine. Thank you," Becky gasped and disappeared. Heaven knew she had no need to be further impressed with the greatness of "The Outcry" office. During the year and a half she had been there she had never ceased to tremble. She knew the prices all the authors got as well as Miss Devine did, and everything seemed to her to be done on a magnificent scale. She hadn't a good memory for long technical words, but she never forgot dates or prices or initials or telephone numbers.

Becky felt that her job depended on Miss Devine, and she was so glad to have it that she scarcely realized she was being bullied. Besides, she was grateful for all that she had learned from Ardessa; Ardessa had taught her to do most of the things that she was supposed to do herself. Becky wanted to learn, she had to learn; that was the train she was always running for. Her father, Isaac Tietelbaum, the tailor, who pressed Miss Devine's skirts and kept her ladylike suits in order, had come to his client two years ago and told her he had a bright girl just out of a commercial high school. He implored Ardessa to find some office position for his daughter. Ardessa told an appealing story to O'Mally, and brought Becky into the office, at a salary of six dollars a week, to help with the copying and to learn business routine. When Becky first came she was as ignorant as a young savage. She was rapid at her shorthand and typing, but a Kafir girl would have known as much about the English language. Nobody ever wanted to learn more than Becky. She fairly wore the dictionary out. She dug up her old school grammar and worked over it at night. She faithfully mastered Miss Devine's fussy system of punctuation.

There were eight children at home, younger than Becky, and they were all eager to learn. They wanted to get their mother out of the three dark rooms behind the tailor shop and to move into a flat upstairs, where they could, as Becky said, "live private." The young Tietelbaums doubted their father's ability to bring this change about, for the more things he declared himself ready to do in his window placards, the fewer were brought to him to be done. "Dyeing, Cleaning, Ladies' Furs Remodeled"—it did no good.

Rebecca was out to "improve herself," as her father had told her she must. Ardessa had easy way with her. It was one of those rare relationships from which both persons profit. The more Becky could learn from Ardessa, the happier she was; and the more Ardessa could unload on Becky, the greater was her contentment. She easily broke Becky of the gum-chewing habit, taught her to walk quietly, to efface herself at the proper moment, and to hold her tongue. Becky had been raised to eight dollars a week; but she didn't care half so much about that as she did about her own increasing efficiency. The more work Miss Devine handed over to her the happier she was, and the faster she was able to eat it up. She tested and tried herself in every possible way. She now had full confidence that she would surely one day be a high-priced stenographer, a real "business woman."

Becky would have corrupted a really industrious person, but a bilious temperament like Ardessa's couldn't make even a feeble stand against such willingness. Ardessa had grown soft and had lost the knack of turning out work. Sometimes, in her importance and serenity, she shivered. What if O'Mally should die, and she were thrust out into the world to work in competition with the brazen, competent young women she saw about her everywhere? She believed herself indispensable, but she knew that in such a mischanceful world as this the very powers of darkness might rise to separate her from this pearl among jobs.

When Becky came in from lunch she went down the long hall to the wash-room, where all the little girls who worked in the advertising and circulation departments kept their hats and jackets. There were shelves and shelves of bright spring hats, piled on top of one another, all as stiff as sheet-iron and trimmed with gay flowers. At the marble wash-stand stood Rena Kalski, the right bower of the business manager, polishing her diamond rings with a nail-brush.

"Hullo, kid," she called over her shoulder to Becky. "I've got a ticket for you for Thursday afternoon."

Becky's black eyes glowed, but the strained look on her face drew tighter than ever.

"I'll never ask her, Miss Kalski," she said rapidly. "I don't dare. I have to stay late tonight again; and I know she'd be hard to please after, if I was to try to get off on a weekday. I thank you, Miss Kalski, but I'd better not."

Miss Kalski laughed. She was a slender young Hebrew, handsome in an impudent, Tenderloin sort of way, with a small head, reddish-brown almond eyes, a trifle tilted, a rapacious mouth, and a beautiful chin.

"Ain't you under that woman's thumb, though! Call her bluff. She isn't half the prima donna she thinks she is. On my side of the hall we know who's who about this place."

The business and editorial departments of "The Outcry" were separated by a long corridor and a great contempt. Miss Kalski dried her rings with tissue-paper and studied them with an appraising eye.

"Well, since you're such a 'fraidy-calf,'" she went on, "maybe I can get a rise out of her myself. Now I've got you a ticket out of that shirt-front, I want you to go. I'll drop in on Devine this afternoon."

When Miss Kalski went back to her desk in the business manager's private office, she turned to him familiarly, but not impertinently.

"Mr. Henderson, I want to send a kid over in the editorial stenographers' to the Palace Thursday afternoon. She's a nice kid, only she's scared out of her skin all the time. Miss Devine's her boss, and she'll be just mean enough not to let the young one off. Would you say a word to her?"

The business manager lit a cigar.

"I'm not saying words to any of the high-brows over there. Try it out with Devine yourself. You're not bashful."

Miss Kalski shrugged her shoulders and smiled.

"Oh, very well." She serpentined out of the room and crossed the Rubicon into the editorial offices. She found Ardessa typing O'Mally's letters and wearing a pained expression.

"Good afternoon, Miss Devine," she said carelessly. "Can we borrow Becky over there for Thursday afternoon? We're short."

Miss Devine looked piqued and tilted her head.

"I don't think it's customary, Miss Kalski, for the business department to use our people. We never have girls enough here to do the work. Of course if Mr. Henderson feels justified—"

"Thanks awfully, Miss Devine,"—Miss Kalski interrupted her with the perfectly smooth, good-natured tone which never betrayed a hint of the scorn every line of her sinuous figure expressed,—"I will tell Mr. Henderson. Perhaps we can do something for you some day." Whether this was a threat, a kind wish, or an insinuation, no mortal could have told. Miss Kalski's face was always suggesting insolence without being quite insolent. As she returned to her own domain she met the cashier's head clerk in the hall. "That Devine woman's a crime," she murmured. The head clerk laughed tolerantly.

That afternoon as Miss Kalski was leaving the office at 5:15, on her way down the corridor she heard a typewriter clicking away in the empty, echoing editorial offices. She looked in, and found Becky bending forward over the machine as if she were about to swallow it.

"Hello, kid. Do you sleep with that?" she called. She walked up to Becky and glanced at her copy. "What do you let 'em keep you up nights over that stuff for?" she asked contemptuously. "The world wouldn't suffer if that stuff never got printed."

Rebecca looked up wildly. Not even Miss Kalski's French pansy hat or her ear-rings and landscape veil could loosen Becky's tenacious mind from Mr. Gerrard's article on water power. She scarcely knew what Miss Kalski had said to her, certainly not what she meant.

"But I must make progress already, Miss Kalski," she panted.

Miss Kalski gave her low, siren laugh.

"I should say you must!" she ejaculated.

Ardessa decided to take her vacation in June, and she arranged that Miss Milligan should do O'Mally's work while she was away. Miss Milligan was blunt and noisy, rapid and inaccurate. It would be just as well for O'Mally to work with a coarse instrument for a time; he would be more appreciative, perhaps, of certain qualities to which he had seemed insensible of late. Ardessa was to leave for East Hampton on Sunday, and she spent Saturday morning instructing her substitute as to the state of the correspondence. At noon O'Mally burst into her room. All the morning he had been closeted with a new writer of mystery-stories just over from England.

"Can you stay and take my letters this afternoon, Miss Devine? You're not leaving until tomorrow."

Ardessa pouted, and tilted her head at the angle he was tired of.

"I'm sorry, Mr. O'Mally, but I've left all my shopping for this afternoon. I think Becky Tietelbaum could do them for you. I will tell her to be careful."

"Oh, all right." O'Mally bounced out with a reflection of Ardessa's disdainful expression on his face. Saturday afternoon was always a half-holiday, to be sure, but since she had weeks of freedom when he was away—However—

At two o'clock Becky Tietelbaum appeared at his door, clad in the sober office suit which Miss Devine insisted she should wear, her note-book in her hand, and so frightened that her fingers were cold and her lips were pale. She had never taken dictation from the editor before. It was a great and terrifying occasion.

"Sit down," he said encouragingly. He began dictating while he shook from his bag the manuscripts he had snatched away from the amazed English author that morning. Presently he looked up.

"Do I go too fast?"

"No, sir," Becky found strength to say.

At the end of an hour he told her to go and type as many of the letters as she could while he went over the bunch of stuff he had torn from the Englishman. He was with the Hindu detective in an opium den in Shanghai when Becky returned and placed a pile of papers on his desk.

"How many?" he asked, without looking up.

"All you gave me, sir."

"All, so soon? Wait a minute and let me see how many mistakes." He went over the letters rapidly, signing them as he read. "They seem to be all right. I thought you were the girl that made so many mistakes."

Rebecca was never too frightened to vindicate herself.

"Mr. O'Mally, sir, I don't make mistakes with letters. It's only copying the articles that have so many long words, and when the writing isn't plain, like Mr. Gerrard's. I never make many mistakes with Mr. Johnson's articles, or with yours I don't."

O'Mally wheeled round in his chair, looked with curiosity at her long, tense face, her black eyes, and straight brows.

"Oh, so you sometimes copy articles, do you? How does that happen?"

"Yes, sir. Always Miss Devine gives me the articles to do. It's good practice for me."

"I see." O'Mally shrugged his shoulders. He was thinking that he could get a rise out of the whole American public any day easier than he could get a rise out of Ardessa. "What editorials of mine have you copied lately, for instance?"

Rebecca blazed out at him, reciting rapidly:

"Oh, 'A Word about the Rosenbaums,' 'Useless Navy-Yards,' 'Who Killed Cock Robin'—"

"Wait a minute." O'Mally checked her flow. "What was that one about—Cock Robin?"

"It was all about why the secretary of the interior dismissed—"

"All right, all right. Copy those letters, and put them down the chute as you go out. Come in here for a minute on Monday morning."

Becky hurried home to tell her father that she had taken the editor's letters and had made no mistakes. On Monday she learned that she was to do O'Mally's work for a few days. He disliked Miss Milligan, and he was annoyed with Ardessa for trying to put her over on him when there was better material at hand. With Rebecca he got on very well; she was impersonal, unreproachful, and she fairly panted for work. Everything was done almost before he told her what he wanted. She raced ahead with him; it was like riding a good modern bicycle after pumping along on an old hard tire.

On the day before Miss Devine's return O'Mally strolled over for a chat with the business office.

"Henderson, your people are taking vacations now, I suppose? Could you use an extra girl?"

"If it's that thin black one, I can."

O'Mally gave him a wise smile.

"It isn't. To be honest, I want to put one over on you. I want you to take Miss Devine over here for a while and speed her up. I can't do anything. She's got the upper hand of me. I don't want to fire her, you understand, but she makes my life too difficult. It's my fault, of course. I've pampered her. Give her a chance over here; maybe she'll come back. You can be firm with 'em, can't you?"

Henderson glanced toward the desk where Miss Kalski's lightning eye was skimming over the printing-house bills that he was supposed to verify himself.

"Well, if I can't, I know who can," he replied, with a chuckle.

"Exactly," O'Mally agreed. "I'm counting on the force of Miss Kalski's example. Miss Devine's all right, Miss Kalski, but she needs regular exercise. She owes it to her complexion. I can't discipline people."

Miss Kalski's only reply was a low, indulgent laugh.

O'Mally braced himself on the morning of Ardessa's return. He told the waiter at his club to bring him a second pot of coffee and to bring it hot. He was really afraid of her. When she presented herself at his office at 10:30 he complimented her upon her tan and asked about her vacation. Then he broke the news to her.

"We want to make a few temporary changes about here, Miss Devine, for the summer months. The business department is short of help. Henderson is going to put Miss Kalski on the books for a while to figure out some economies for him, and he is going to take you over. Meantime I'll get Becky broken in so that she could take your work if you were sick or anything."

Ardessa drew herself up.

"I've not been accustomed to commercial work, Mr. O'Mally. I've no interest in it, and I don't care to brush up in it."

"Brushing up is just what we need, Miss Devine." O'Mally began tramping about his room expansively. "I'm going to brush everybody up. I'm going to brush a few people out; but I want you

to stay with us, of course. You belong here. Don't be hasty now.
Go to your room and think it over."

Ardessa was beginning to cry, and O'Mally was afraid he would
lose his nerve. He looked out of the window at a new sky-scraper
that was building, while she retired without a word.

At her own desk Ardessa sat down breathless and trembling. The
one thing she had never doubted was her unique value to O'Mally.
She had, as she told herself, taught him everything. She would say
a few things to Becky Tietelbaum, and to that pigeon-breasted
tailor, her father, too! The worst of it was that Ardessa had herself
brought it all about; she could see that clearly now. She had carefully trained and qualified her successor. Why had she ever civilized
Becky? Why had she taught her manners and deportment, broken
her of the gum-chewing habit, and made her presentable? In her
original state O'Mally would never have put up with her, no matter what her ability.

Ardessa told herself that O'Mally was notoriously fickle; Becky
amused him, but he would soon find out her limitations. The wise
thing, she knew, was to humor him: but it seemed to her that she
could not swallow her pride. Ardessa grew yellower within the
hour. Over and over in her mind she bade O'Mally a cold adieu
and minced out past the grand old man at the desk for the last time.
But each exit she rehearsed made her feel sorrier for herself. She
thought over all the offices she knew, but she realized that she
could never meet their inexorable standards of efficiency.

While she was bitterly deliberating, O'Mally himself wandered
in, rattling his keys nervously in his pocket. He shut the door
behind him.

"Now, you're going to come through with this all right, aren't
you, Miss Devine? I want Henderson to get over the notion that
my people over here are stuck up and think the business department
are old shoes. That's where we get our money from, as he often
reminds me. You'll be the best-paid girl over there; no reduction,
of course. You don't want to go wandering off to some new office
where personality doesn't count for anything." He sat down confi-
dentially on the edge of her desk. "Do you, now, Miss Devine?"

Ardessa simpered tearfully as she replied.

"Mr. O'Mally," she brought out, "you'll soon find that Becky is
not the sort of girl to meet people for you when you are away. I
don't see how you can think of letting her."

"That's one thing I want to change, Miss Devine. You're too soft-handed with the has-beens and the never-was-ers. You're too much of a lady for this rough game. Nearly everybody who comes in here wants to sell us a gold-brick, and you treat them as if they were bringing in wedding presents. Becky is as rough as sandpaper, and she'll clear out a lot of dead wood." O'Mally rose, and tapped Ardessa's shrinking shoulder. "Now, be a sport and go through with it, Miss Devine. I'll see that you don't lose. Henderson thinks you'll refuse to do his work, so I want you to get moved in there before he comes back from lunch. I've had a desk put in his office for you. Miss Kalski is in the bookkeeper's room half the time now."

Rena Kalski was amazed that afternoon when a line of office boys entered, carrying Miss Devine's effects, and when Ardessa herself coldly followed them. After Ardessa had arranged her desk, Miss Kalski went over to her and told her about some matters of routine very good-naturedly. Ardessa looked pretty badly shaken up, and Rena bore no grudges.

"When you want the dope on the correspondence with the paper men, don't bother to look it up. I've got it all in my head, and I can save time for you. If he wants you to go over the printing bills every week, you'd better let me help you with that for a while. I can stay almost any afternoon. It's quite a trick to figure out the plates and over-time charges till you get used to it. I've worked out a quick method that saves trouble."

When Henderson came in at three he found Ardessa, chilly, but civil, awaiting his instructions. He knew she disapproved of his tastes and his manners, but he didn't mind. What interested and amused him was that Rena Kalski, whom he had always thought as cold-blooded as an adding-machine, seemed to be making a hair-mattress of herself to break Ardessa's fall.

At five o'clock, when Ardessa rose to go, the business manager said breezily:

"See you at nine in the morning. Miss Devine. We begin on the stroke."

Ardessa faded out of the door, and Miss Kalski's slender back squirmed with amusement.

"I never thought to hear such words spoken," she admitted; "but I guess she'll limber up all right. The atmosphere is bad over there. They get moldy."

After the next monthly luncheon of the heads of departments, O'Mally said to Henderson, as he feed the coat-boy:

"By the way, how are you making it with the bartered bride?"

Henderson smashed on his Panama as he said:

"Any time you want her back, don't be delicate."

But O'Mally shook his red head and laughed.

"Oh, I'm no Indian giver!"

WINGS (1920)

Anzia Yezierska

Sentimental but thoroughly touching, "Wings" recounts the hard luck of a 22-year-old Jewish immigrant. Working as a janitor for her uncle on the Lower East Side, Shenah Pessah dreams of improving her lot and is inspired by love to strive for education. Anzia Yezierska (c. 1885–1970) was probably less naïve and certainly not an orphan, as is her plucky heroine. Yezierska and her parents arrived in America in the 1890s (her precise birth and arrival dates are unknown). Her father devoted himself to the study of the Torah and did not encourage Anzia's career ambitions; nevertheless, she enrolled at Columbia University's Teachers College. She graduated and was a grammar school teacher before becoming a celebrated writer of fiction. "Wings" is the first story in her Hungry Hearts *collection (1920). Her most famous work, the novel* Bread Givers, *was published in 1925. Yezierska spent much of her long life advocating for Lower East Side immigrant groups, including those from Puerto Rico.*

"My heart chokes in me like in a prison! I'm dying for a little love and I got nobody—nobody!" wailed Shenah Pessah, as she looked out of the dismal basement window.

It was a bright Sunday afternoon in May, and into the gray, cheerless, janitor's basement a timid ray of sunlight announced the dawn of spring.

"Oi weh! Light!" breathed Shenah Pessah, excitedly, throwing open the sash. "A little light in the room for the first time!" And she stretched out her hands hungrily for the warming bit of sun.

The happy laughter of the shopgirls standing on the stoop with their beaux and the sight of the young mothers with their husbands and babies fanned anew the consuming fire in her breast.

"I'm not jealous!" she gasped, chokingly. "My heart hurts too deep to want to tear from them their luck to happiness. But why should they live and enjoy life and why must I only *look on* how they are happy?"

She clutched at her throat like one stifled for want of air. "What is the matter with you? Are you going out of your head? For what is your crying? Who will listen to you? Who gives a care what's going to become from you?"

Crushed by her loneliness, she sank into a chair. For a long time she sat motionless, finding drear fascination in the mocking faces traced in the patches of the torn plaster. Gradually, she became aware of a tingling warmth playing upon her cheeks. And with a revived breath, she drank in the miracle of the sunlit wall.

"Ach!" she sighed. "Once a year the sun comes to light up even this dark cellar, so why shouldn't the High One send on me too a little brightness?"

This new wave of hope swept aside the fact that she was the "greenhorn" janitress, that she was twenty-two and dowryless, and, according to the traditions of her people, condemned to be shelved aside as an unmated thing—a creature of pity and ridicule.

"I can't help it how old I am or how poor I am!" she burst out to the deaf and dumb air. "I want a little life! I want a little joy!"

The bell rang sharply, and as she turned to answer the call, she saw a young man at the doorway—a framed picture of her innermost dreams.

The stranger spoke.

Shenah Pessah did not hear the words, she heard only the music of his voice. She gazed fascinated at his clothes—the loose Scotch tweeds, the pongee shirt, a bit open at the neck, but she did not see him or the things he wore. She only felt an irresistible presence seize her soul. It was as though the god of her innermost longings had suddenly taken shape in human form and lifted her in mid-air.

"Does the janitor live here?" the stranger repeated.

Shenah Pessah nodded.

"Can you show me the room to let?"

"Yes, right away, but wait only a minute," stammered Shenah Pessah, fumbling for the key on the shelf.

"Don't fly into the air!" She tried to reason with her wild, throbbing heart, as she walked upstairs with him. In an effort to down the chaos of emotion that shook her she began to talk nervously: "Mrs. Stein who rents out the room ain't going to be back till the evening, but I can tell you the price and anything you want to know. She's a grand cook and you can eat by her your breakfast and dinner—" She did not have the slightest notion of what she was saying, but talked on in a breathless stream lest he should hear the loud beating of her heart.

"Could I have a drop-light put in here?" the man asked, as he looked about the room.

Shenah Pessah stole a quick, shy glance at him. "Are you maybe a teacher or a writing man?"

"Yes, sometimes I teach," he said, studying her, drawn by the struggling soul of her that cried aloud to him out of her eyes.

"I could tell right away that you must be some kind of a somebody," she said, looking up with wistful worship in her eyes. "Ach, how grand it must be to live only for learning and thinking."

"Is this your home?"

"I never had a home since I was eight years old. I was living by strangers even in Russia."

"Russia?" he repeated with quickened attention. So he was in their midst, the people he had come to study. The girl with her hungry eyes and intense eagerness now held a new interest for him.

John Barnes, the youngest instructor of sociology in his university, congratulated himself at his good fortune in encountering such a splendid type for his research. He was preparing his thesis on the "Educational Problems of the Russian Jews," and in order to get into closer touch with his subject, he had determined to live on the East Side during his spring and summer vacation.

He went on questioning her, unconsciously using all the compelling power that made people open their hearts to him. "And how long have you been here?"

"Two years already."

"You seem to be fond of study. I suppose you go to night-school?"

"I never yet stepped into a night-school since I came to America. From where could I get the time? My uncle is such an old man he can't do much and he got already used to leave the whole house on me."

"You stay with your uncle, then?"

"Yes, my uncle sent for me the ticket for America when my aunt was yet living. She got herself sick. And what could an old man like him do with only two hands?"

"Was that sufficient reason for you to leave your homeland?"

"What did I have out there in Savel that I should be afraid to lose? The cows that I used to milk had it better than me. They got at least enough to eat and me slaving from morning till night went around hungry."

"You poor child!" broke from the heart of the man, the scientific inquisition of the sociologist momentarily swept away by his human sympathy.

Who had ever said "poor child" to her—and in such a voice? Tears gathered in Shenah Pessah's eyes. For the first time she mustered the courage to look straight at him. The man's face, his voice, his bearing, so different from any one she had ever known, and yet what was there about him that made her so strangely at ease with him? She went on talking, led irresistibly by the friendly glow in his eyes.

"I got yet a lot of luck. I learned myself English from a Jewish English reader, and one of the boarders left me a grand book. When I only begin to read, I forget I'm on this world. It lifts me on wings with high thoughts." Her whole face and figure lit up with animation as she poured herself out to him.

"So even in the midst of these sordid surroundings were 'wings' and 'high thoughts,'" he mused. Again the gleam of the visionary— the eternal desire to reach out and up, which was the predominant racial trait of the Russian immigrant.

"What is the name of your book?" he continued, taking advantage of this providential encounter.

"The book is 'Dreams,' by Olive Schreiner."

"H—m," he reflected. "So these are the 'wings' and 'high thoughts.' No wonder the blushes—the tremulousness. What an opportunity for a psychological test-case, and at the same time I could help her by pointing the way out of her nebulous emotionalism and place her feet firmly on earth." He made a quick, mental note of certain books that he would place in her hands and wondered how she would respond to them.

"Do you belong to a library?"

"Library? How? Where?"

Her lack of contact with Americanizing agencies appalled him.

"I'll have to introduce you to the library when I come to live here," he said.

"Ci–i! You really like it, the room?" Shenah Pessah clapped her hands in a burst of uncontrollable delight.

"I like the room very much, and I shall be glad to take it if you can get it ready for me by next week."

Shenah Pessah looked up at the man. "Do you mean it? You really want to come and live here, in this place? The sky is falling to the earth!"

"Live here?" Most decidedly he would live here. He became suddenly enthusiastic. But it was the enthusiasm of the scientist for the specimen of his experimentation—of the sculptor for the clay that would take form under his touch.

"I'm coming here to live—" He was surprised at the eager note in his voice, the sudden leaven of joy that surged through his veins. "And I'm going to teach you to read sensible books, the kind that will help you more than your dream book."

Shenah Pessah drank in his words with a joy that struck back as fear lest this man—the visible sign of her answered prayer—would any moment be snatched up and disappear in the heavens where he belonged. With a quick leap toward him she seized his hand in both her own. "Oi, mister! Would you like to learn me English lessons too? I'll wash for you your shirts for it. If you would even only talk to me, it would be more to me than all the books in the world."

He instinctively recoiled at this outburst of demonstrativeness. His eyes narrowed and his answer was deliberate. "Yes, you ought to learn English," he said, resuming his professional tone, but the girl was too overwrought to notice the change in his manner.

"There it is," he thought to himself on his way out. "The whole gamut of the Russian Jew—the pendulum swinging from abject servility to boldest aggressiveness."

Shenah Pessah remained standing and smiling to herself after Mr. Barnes left. She did not remember a thing she had said. She only felt herself whirling in space, millions of miles beyond the earth. The god of dreams had arrived and nothing on earth could any longer hold her down.

Then she hurried back to the basement and took up the broken piece of mirror that stood on the shelf over the sink and gazed at her face trying to see herself through his eyes. "Was it only pity that made him stop to talk to me? Or can it be that he saw what's inside me?"

Her eyes looked inward as she continued to talk to herself in the mirror.

"God from the world!" she prayed. "I'm nothing and nobody now, but ach! How beautiful I would become if only the light from his eyes would fall on me!"

Covering her flushed face with her hands as if to push back the tumult of desire that surged within her, she leaned against the wall. "Who are you to want such a man?" she sobbed.

"But no one is too low to love God, the Highest One. There is no high in love and there is no low in love. Then why am I too low to love him?"

"Shenah Pessah!" called her uncle angrily. "What are you standing there like a yok, dreaming in the air? Don't you hear the tenants knocking on the pipes? They are hollering for the hot water. You let the fire go out."

At the sound of her uncle's voice all her "high thoughts" fled. The mere reminder of the furnace with its ashes and cinders smothered her buoyant spirits and again she was weighed down by the strangling yoke of her hateful, daily round.

It was evening when she got through with her work. To her surprise she did not feel any of the old weariness. It was as if her feet danced under her. Then from the open doorway of their kitchen she overheard Mrs. Melker, the matchmaker, talking to her uncle.

"Motkeh, the fish-peddler, is looking for a wife to cook him his eating and take care on his children," she was saying in her shrill, grating voice. "So I thought to myself this is a golden chance for Shenah Pessah to grab. You know a girl in her years and without money, a single man wouldn't give a look on her."

Shenah Pessah shuddered. She wanted to run away from the branding torture of their low talk, but an unreasoning curiosity drew her to listen.

"Living is so high," went on Mrs. Melker, "that single men don't want to marry themselves even to *young* girls, except if they can get themselves into a family with money to start them up in business. It is Shenah Pessah's luck yet that Motkeh likes good eating and he can't stand it any more the meals in a restaurant. He heard from people what a good cook and housekeeper Shenah Pessah is, so he sent me around to tell you he would take her as she stands without a cent."

Mrs. Melker dramatically beat her breast. "I swear I shouldn't live to go away from here alive, I shouldn't live to see my own children married if I'm taking this match for the few dollars that Motkeh will pay me for it, but because I want to do something for a poor orphan. I'm a mother, and it weeps in me my heart to see a girl in her years and not married."

"And who'll cook for me my eating, if I'll let her go?" broke out her uncle angrily. "And who'll do me my work? Didn't I spend fifty dollars to send for her the ticket to America? Oughtn't I have a little use from her for so many dollars I laid out on her?"

"Think on God!" remonstrated Mrs. Melker. "The girl is an orphan and time is pushing itself on her. Do you want her to sit till her braids grow gray, before you'll let her get herself a man? It stands in the Talmud that a man should take the last bite away from his mouth to help an orphan get married. You'd beg yourself out a place in heaven in the next world—"

"In America a person can't live on hopes for the next world. In America everybody got to look out for himself. I'd have to give up the janitor's work to let her go, and then where would I be?"

"You lived already your life. Give her also a chance to lift up her head in the world. Couldn't you get yourself in an old man's home?"

"These times you got to have money even in an old man's home. You know how they say, if you oil the wheels you can ride. With dry hands you can't get nothing in America."

"So you got no pity on an orphan and your own relation? All her young years she choked herself in darkness and now comes already a little light for her, a man that can make a good living wants her—"

"And who'll have pity on me if I'll let her out from my hands? Who is this Motkeh, anyway? Is he good off? Would I also have a place where to lay my old head? Where stands he out with his pushcart?"

"On Essex Street near Delancey."

"Oi-i! You mean Motkeh Pelz? Why, I know him yet from years ago. They say his wife died him from hunger. She had to chew the earth before she could beg herself out a cent from him. By me Shenah Pessah has at least enough to eat and shoes on her feet. I ask you only is it worth already to grab a man if you got to die from hunger for it?"

Shenah Pessah could listen no longer.

"Don't you worry yourself for me," she commanded, charging into the room. "Don't take pity on my years. I'm living in America, not in Russia. I'm not hanging on anybody's neck to support me. In America, if a girl earns her living, she can be fifty years old and without a man, and nobody pities her."

Seizing her shawl, she ran out into the street. She did not know where her feet carried her. She had only one desire—to get away. A fierce rebellion against everything and everybody raged within her and goaded her on until she felt herself choked with hate.

All at once she visioned a face and heard a voice. The blacker, the more stifling the ugliness of her prison, the more luminous became the light of the miraculous stranger who had stopped for a moment to talk to her. It was as though inside a pit of darkness the heavens opened and hidden hopes began to sing.

Her uncle was asleep when she returned. In the dim gaslight she looked at his yellow, care-crushed face with new compassion in her heart. "Poor old man!" she thought, as she turned to her room. "Nothing beautiful never happened to him. What did he have in life outside the worry for bread and rent? Who knows, maybe if such a god of men would have shined on him—" She fell asleep and she awoke with visions opening upon visions of new, gleaming worlds of joy and hope. She leaped out of bed singing a song she had not heard since she was a little child in her mother's home.

Several times during the day, she found herself at the broken mirror, arranging and rearranging her dark mass of unkempt hair with fumbling fingers. She was all a-tremble with breathless excitement to imitate the fluffy style of the much-courted landlady's daughter.

For the first time she realized how shabby and impossible her clothes were. "Oi weh!" she wrung her hands. "I'd give away everything in the world only to have something pretty to wear for him. My whole life hangs on how I'll look in his eyes. I got to have a hat and a new dress. I can't no more wear my 'greenhorn' shawl going out with an American.

"But from where can I get the money for new clothes? Oi weh! How bitter it is not to have the dollar! Woe is me! No mother, no friend, nobody to help me lift myself out of my greenhorn rags."

"Why not pawn the feather bed your mother left you?" She jumped at the thought.

"What? Have you no heart? No feelings? Pawn the only one thing left from your dead mother?"

"Why not? Nothing is too dear for him. If your mother could stand up from her grave, she'd cut herself in pieces, she'd tear the sun and stars out from the sky to make you beautiful for him."

Late one evening Zaretsky sat in his pawnshop, absorbed in counting the money of his day's sales, when Shenah Pessah, with a shawl over her head and a huge bundle over her shoulder, edged her way hesitantly into the store. Laying her sacrifice down on the counter, she stood dumbly and nervously fingering the fringes of her shawl.

The pawnbroker lifted his miserly face from the cash-box and shot a quick glance at the girl's trembling figure.

"Nu?" said Zaretsky, in his cracked voice, cutting the twine from the bundle and unfolding a feather bed. His appraising hand felt that it was of the finest down. "How much ask you for it?"

The fiendish gleam of his shrewd eyes paralyzed her with terror. A lump came in her throat and she wavered speechless.

"I'll give you five dollars," said Zaretsky.

"Five dollars?" gasped Shenah Pessah. Her hands rushed back anxiously to the feather bed and her fingers clung to it as if it were a living thing. She gazed panic-stricken at the gloomy interior of the pawnshop with its tawdry jewels in the cases; the stacks of second-hand clothing hanging overhead, back to the grisly face of the pawnbroker. The weird tickings that came from the cheap clocks on the shelves behind Zaretsky, seemed to her like the smothered heart-beats of people who like herself had been driven to barter their last precious belongings for a few dollars.

"Is it for yourself that you come?" he asked, strangely stirred by the mute anguish in the girl's eyes. This morgue of dead belongings had taken its toll of many a pitiful victim of want. But never before had Zaretsky been so affected. People bargained and rebelled and struggled with him on his own plane. But the dumb helplessness of this girl and her coming to him at such a late hour touched the man's heart.

"Is it for yourself?" he repeated, in a softened tone.

The new note of feeling in his voice made her look up. The hard, crafty expression on his face had given place to a look of sympathy.

"Yes, it's mine, from my mother," she stammered, brokenly. "The last memory from Russia. How many winters it took my mother to pick together the feathers. She began it when I was yet a little baby in the cradle—and—" She covered her face with her shawl and sobbed.

"Any one sick? Why do you got to pawn it?"

She raised her tear-stained face and mutely looked at him. How could she explain and how could he possibly understand her sudden savage desire for clothes?

Zaretsky, feeling that he had been clumsy and tactless, hastened to add, "Nu—I'll give you—a—a—a—ten dollars," he finished with a motion of his hand, as if driving from him the onrush of generosity that seized him.

"Oi, mister!" cried Shenah Pessah, as the man handed her the bill. "You're saving me my life! God will pay you for this goodness." And crumpling the money in her hand, she hurried back home elated.

The following evening, as soon as her work was over, Shenah Pessah scurried through the ghetto streets, seeking in the myriad-colored shop windows the one hat and the one dress that would voice the desire of her innermost self. At last she espied a shining straw with cherries so red, so luscious, that they cried out to her, "Bite me!" That was the hat she bought.

The magic of those cherries on her hat brought back to her the green fields and orchards of her native Russia. Yes, a green dress was what she craved. And she picked out the greenest, crispest organdie.

That night, as she put on her beloved colors, she vainly tried to see herself from head to foot, but the broken bit of a mirror that she owned could only show her glorious parts of her. Her clothes seemed to enfold her in flames of desire leaping upon desire. "Only to be beautiful! Only to be beautiful!" she murmured breathlessly. "Not for myself, but only for him."

Time stood still for Shenah Pessah as she counted the days, the hours, and the minutes for the arrival of John Barnes. At last, through her basement window, she saw him walk up the front steps. She longed to go over to him and fling herself at his feet and cry out to him with what hunger of heart she awaited his coming. But the very intensity of her longing left her faint and dumb.

He passed to his room. Later, she saw him walk out without even stopping to look at her. The next day and the day after, she watched him from her hidden corner pass in and out of the house, but still he did not come to her.

Oh, how sweet it was to suffer the very hurt of his oblivion of her! She gloried in his great height that made him so utterly unaware of her existence. It was enough for her worshiping eyes just to glimpse him from afar. What was she to him? Could she expect him to greet the stairs on which he stepped? Or take notice of the door that swung open for him? After all, she was nothing but part of the house. So why should he take notice of her? She was the steps on which he walked. She was the door that swung open for him. And he did not know it.

For four evenings in succession, ever since John Barnes had come to live in the house, Shenah Pessah arrayed herself in her new things and waited. Was it not a miracle that he came the first time when she did not even dream that he was on earth? So why shouldn't the miracle happen again? This evening, however, she was so spent with the hopelessness of her longing that she had no energy left to put on her adornments.

All at once she was startled out of her apathy by a quick tap on her window-pane. "How about going to the library, to-morrow evening?" asked John Barnes.

"Oi-i-i! Yes! Thanks!—" she stammered in confusion.

"Well, to-morrow night, then, at seven. Thank you." He hurried out embarrassed by the grateful look that shone to him out of her eyes. The gaze haunted him and hurt him. It was the beseeching look of a homeless dog, begging to be noticed. "Poor little immigrant," he thought, "how lonely she must be!"

"So he didn't forget," rejoiced Shenah Pessah. "How only the sound from his voice opens the sky in my heart! How the deadness and emptiness in me flames up into life! Ach! The sun is beginning to shine!"

An hour before the appointed time Shenah Pessah dressed herself in all her finery for John Barnes. She swung open the door and stood in full readiness watching the little clock on the mantel-shelf. The ticking thing seemed to throb with the unutterable hopes compressed in her heart, all the mute years of her stifled life. Each little thud of time sang a wild song of released joy—the joy of his coming nearer.

For the tenth time Shenah Pessah went over in her mind what she would say to him when he'd come.

"It was so kind from you to take from your dear time—to—"

"No—that sounds not good. I'll begin like this—Mr. Barnes! I can't give it out in words your kindness, to stop from your high thoughts to—to—"

"No—no! Oi weh! God from the world! Why should it be so hard for me to say to him what I mean? Why shouldn't I be able to say to him plain out—Mr. Barnes! You are an angel from the sky! You are saving me my life to let me only give a look on you! I'm happier than a bird in the air when I think only that such goodness like you—"

The sudden ring of the bell shattered all her carefully rehearsed phrases and she met his greeting in a flutter of confusion.

"My! Haven't you blossomed out since last night!" exclaimed Mr. Barnes, startled by Shenah Pessah's sudden display of color.

"Yes," she flushed, raising to him her radiant face. "I'm through for always with old women's shawls. This is my first American dress-up."

"Splendid! So you want to be an American! The next step will be to take up some work that will bring you in touch with American people."

"Yes. You'll help me? Yes?" Her eyes sought his with an appeal of unquestioning reliance.

"Have you ever thought what kind of work you would like to take up?" he asked, when they got out into the street.

"No—I want only to get away from the basement. I'm crazy for people."

"Would you like to learn a trade in a factory?"

"Anything—anything! I'm burning to learn. Give me only an advice. What?"

"What can you do best with your hands?"

"With the hands the best? It's all the same what I do with the hands. Think you not maybe now, I could begin already something with the head? Yes?"

"We'll soon talk this over together, after you have read a book that will tell you how to find what you are best fitted for."

When they entered the library, Shenah Pessah halted in awe. "What a stillness full from thinking! So beautiful, it comes on me like music!"

"Yes. This is quite a place," he acquiesced, seeing again the public library in a new light through her eyes. "Some of the best minds have worked to give us just this."

"How the book-ladies look so quiet like the things."

"Yes," he replied, with a tell-tale glance at her. "I too like to see a woman's face above her clothes."

The approach of the librarian cut off further comment. As Mr. Barnes filled out the application card, Shenah Pessah noted the librarian's simple attire. "What means he a woman's face above her clothes?" she wondered. And the first shadow of a doubt crossed her mind as to whether her dearly bought apparel was pleasing to his eyes. In the few brief words that passed between Mr. Barnes and the librarian, Shenah Pessah sensed that these two were of the same world and that she was different. Her first contact with him in a well-lighted room made her aware that "there were other things to the person besides the dress-up." She had noticed their well-kept hands on the desk and she became aware that her own were calloused and rough. That is why she felt her dirty finger-nails curl in awkwardly to hide themselves as she held the pen to sign her name.

When they were out in the street again, he turned to her and said, "If you don't mind, I'd prefer to walk back. The night is so fine and I've been in the stuffy office all day."

"I don't mind"—the words echoed within her. If he only knew how above all else she wanted this walk.

"It was grand in there, but the electric lights are like so many eyes looking you over. In the street it is easier for me. The dark covers you up so good."

He laughed, refreshed by her unconscious self-revelation.

"As long as you feel in your element let's walk on to the pier."

"Like for a holiday, it feels itself in me," she bubbled, as he took her arm in crossing the street. "Now I see America for the first time!"

It was all so wonderful to Barnes that in the dirt and noise of the overcrowded ghetto, this erstwhile drudge could be transfigured into such a vibrant creature of joy. Even her clothes that had seemed so bold and garish awhile ago, were now inexplicably in keeping with the carnival spirit that he felt steal over him.

As they neared the pier, he reflected strangely upon the fact that out of the thousands of needy, immigrant girls whom he might have befriended, this eager young being at his side was ordained by some peculiar providence to come under his personal protection.

"How long did you say you have been in this country, Shenah Pessah?"

"How long?" She echoed his words as though waking from a dream. "It's two years already. But that didn't count life. From now on I live."

"And you mean to tell me that in all this time, no one has taken you by the hand and shown you the ways of our country? The pity of it!"

"I never had nothing, nor nobody. But now—it dances under me the whole earth! It feels in me grander than dreams!"

He drank in the pure joy out of her eyes. For the moment, the girl beside him was the living flame of incarnate Spring.

"He feels for me," she rejoiced, as they walked on in silence. The tenderness of his sympathy enfolded her like some blessed warmth.

When they reached the end of the pier, they paused and watched the moonlight playing on the water. In the shelter of a truck they felt benignly screened from any stray glances of the loiterers near by.

How big seemed his strength as he stood silhouetted against the blue night! For the first time Shenah Pessah noticed the splendid straightness of his shoulders. The clean glowing youth of him drew her like a spell.

"Ach! Only to keep always inside my heart the kindness, the gentlemanness that shines from his face," thought Shenah Pessah, instinctively nestling closer.

"Poor little immigrant!" murmured John Barnes. "How lonely, how barren your life must have been till—" In an impulse of compassion, his arms opened and Shenah Pessah felt her soul swoon in ecstasy as he drew her toward him.

It was three days since the eventful evening on the pier and Shenah Pessah had not seen John Barnes since. He had vanished like a dream, and yet he was not a dream. He was the only real thing in the unreal emptiness of her unlived life. She closed her eyes and she saw again his face with its joy-giving smile. She heard again his voice and felt again his arms around her as he kissed her lips. Then in the midst of her sweetest visioning a gnawing emptiness seized her and the cruel ache of withheld love sucked dry all those beautiful feelings his presence inspired. Sometimes there flashed across her fevered senses the memory of his compassionate endearments: "Poor lonely little immigrant!" And she felt his sweet words smite her flesh with their cruel mockery.

She went about her work with restlessness. At each step, at each sound, she started, "Maybe it's him! Maybe!" She could not fall asleep at night, but sat up in bed writing and tearing up letters to him. The only lull to the storm that uprooted her being was in trying to tell him how every throb within her clamored for him, but the most heart-piercing cry that she could utter only stabbed her heart with the futility of words.

In the course of the week it was Shenah Pessah's duty to clean Mrs. Stein's floor. This brought her to Mr. Barnes's den in his absence. She gazed about her, calling up his presence at the sight of his belongings.

"How fine to the touch is the feel from everything his," she sighed, tenderly resting her cheek on his dressing-gown. With a timid hand she picked up a slipper that stood beside his bed and she pressed it to her heart reverently. "I wish I was this leather thing only to hold his feet!" The she turned to his dresser and passed her hands caressingly over the ivory things on it. "Ach! You lucky brush—smoothing his hair every day!"

All at once she heard footsteps, and before she could collect her thoughts, he entered. Her whole being lit up with the joy of his coming. But one glance at him revealed to her the changed expression that darkened his face. His arms hung limply at his side—the arms she expected to stretch out to her and enfold her. As if struck in the face by his heartless rebuff, she rushed out blindly.

"Just a minute, please," he managed to detain her. "As a gentleman, I owe you an apology. That night—it was a passing moment of forgetfulness. It's not to happen again—"

Before he had finished, she had run out scorched with shame by his words.

"Good lord!" he ejaculated, when he found he was alone. "Who'd ever think that she would take it so? I suppose there is no use trying to explain to her."

For some time he sat on his bed, staring ruefully. Then, springing to his feet, he threw his things together in a valise. "You'd be a cad if you did not clear out of here at once," he muttered to himself. "No matter how valuable the scientific inquiry might prove to be, you can't let the girl run away with herself."

Shenah Pessah was at the window when she saw John Barnes go out with his suitcases.

"In God's name, don't leave me!" she longed to cry out. "You are the only bit of light that I ever had, and now it will be darker and emptier for my eyes than ever before!" But no voice could rise out of her parched lips. She felt a faintness stunning her senses, as though some one had cut open the arteries of her wrists and all the blood rushed out of her body.

"Oi weh!" she moaned. "Then it was all nothing to him. Why did he make bitter to me the little sweetness that was dearer to me than my life? What means he a gentleman?

"Why did he make me to shame telling me he didn't mean nothing? It is because I'm not a lady alike to him? Is a gentleman only a make-believe man?"

With a defiant resolve she seized hold of herself and rose to her feet. "Show him what's in you. If it takes a year, or a million years, you got to show him you're a person. From now on, you got why to live. You got to work not with the strength of one body and one brain, but with the strength of a million bodies and a million brains. By day and by night, you got to push, push yourself up till you get to him and can look him in his face eye to eye."

Spent by the fervor of this new exaltation, she sat with her head in her hands in a dull stupor. Little by little the darkness cleared from her soul and a wistful serenity crept over her. She raised her face toward the solitary ray of sunlight that stole into her basement room.

"After all, he done for you more than you could do for him. You owe it to him the deepest, the highest he waked up in you. He opened the wings of your soul."

O RUSSET WITCH! (1921)

F. Scott Fitzgerald

F. Scott Fitzgerald (1896–1940) is admired for his dazzling prose. No one ever doubted his talent at spinning gorgeous sentences and popular short stories and novels about the Jazz Age. Fitzgerald, born in Saint Paul, Minnesota, and a graduate of Princeton, lived at various times in New York City; he made his name as the author of the novel This Side of Paradise *(1920) before he was twenty-five. This light-hearted romantic tale concerns a book-store employee with a magical name who is bewitched by a temptress named Caroline.*

Chapter I

Merlin Grainger was employed by the Moonlight Quill Bookshop, which you may have visited, just around the corner from the Ritz-Carlton on Forty-seventh Street. The Moonlight Quill is, or rather was, a very romantic little store, considered radical and admitted dark. It was spotted interiorly with red and orange posters of breathless exotic intent, and lit no less by the shiny reflecting bindings of special editions than by the great squat lamp of crimson satin that, lighted through all the day, swung overhead. It was truly a mellow bookshop. The words "Moonlight Quill" were worked over the door in a sort of serpentine embroidery. The windows seemed always full of something that had passed the literary censors with little to spare; volumes with covers of deep orange which offer their titles on little white paper squares. And over all there was the smell of the musk, which the clever, inscrutable Mr. Moonlight Quill ordered to be sprinkled about—the smell half of a curiosity shop in Dickens' London and half of a coffee-house on the warm shores of the Bosphorus.

From nine until five-thirty Merlin Grainger asked bored old ladies in black and young men with dark circles under their eyes if they "cared for this fellow" or were interested in first editions. Did they buy novels with Arabs on the cover, or books which gave Shakespeare's newest sonnets as dictated psychically to Miss Sutton of South Dakota? he sniffed. As a matter of fact, his own taste ran to these latter, but as an employee at the Moonlight Quill he assumed for the working day the attitude of a disillusioned connoisseur.

After he had crawled over the window display to pull down the front shade at five-thirty every afternoon, and said good-bye to the mysterious Mr. Moonlight Quill and the lady clerk, Miss McCracken, and the lady stenographer, Miss Masters, he went home to the girl, Caroline. He did not eat supper with Caroline. It is unbelievable that Caroline would have considered eating off his bureau with the collar buttons dangerously near the cottage cheese, and the ends of Merlin's necktie just missing his glass of milk—he had never asked her to eat with him. He ate alone. He went into Braegdort's delicatessen on Sixth Avenue and bought a box of crackers, a tube of anchovy paste, and some oranges, or else a little jar of sausages and some potato salad and a bottled soft drink, and with these in a brown package he went to his room at Fifty-something West Fifty-eighth Street and ate his supper and saw Caroline.

Caroline was a very young and gay person who lived with some older lady and was possibly nineteen. She was like a ghost in that she never existed until evening. She sprang into life when the lights went on in her apartment at about six, and she disappeared, at the latest, about midnight. Her apartment was a nice one, in a nice building with a white stone front, opposite the south side of Central Park. The back of her apartment faced the single window of the single room occupied by the single Mr. Grainger.

He called her Caroline because there was a picture that looked like her on the jacket of a book of that name down at the Moonlight Quill.

Now, Merlin Grainger was a thin young man of twenty-five, with dark hair and no mustache or beard or anything like that, but Caroline was dazzling and light, with a shimmering morass of russet waves to take the place of hair, and the sort of features that remind you of kisses—the sort of features you thought belonged to your first love, but know, when you come across an old picture, didn't.

She dressed in pink or blue usually, but of late she had sometimes put on a slender black gown that was evidently her especial pride, for whenever she wore it she would stand regarding a certain place on the wall, which Merlin thought must be a mirror. She sat usually in the profile chair near the window, but sometimes honored the *chaise longue* by the lamp, and often she leaned 'way back and smoked a cigarette with posturings of her arms and hands that Merlin considered very graceful.

At another time she had come to the window and stood in it magnificently, and looked out because the moon had lost its way and was dripping the strangest and most transforming brilliance into the areaway between, turning the motif of ash-cans and clothes-lines into a vivid impressionism of silver casks and gigantic gossamer cobwebs. Merlin was sitting in plain sight, eating cottage cheese with sugar and milk on it; and so quickly did he reach out for the window cord that he tipped the cottage cheese into his lap with his free hand—and the milk was cold and the sugar made spots on his trousers, and he was sure that she had seen him after all.

Sometimes there were callers—men in dinner coats, who stood and bowed, hat in hand and coat on arm, as they talked to Caroline; then bowed some more and followed her out of the light, obviously bound for a play or for a dance. Other young men came and sat and smoked cigarettes, and seemed trying to tell Caroline something—she sitting either in the profile chair and watching them with eager intentness or else in the *chaise longue* by the lamp, looking very lovely and youthfully inscrutable indeed.

Merlin enjoyed these calls. Of some of the men he approved. Others won only his grudging toleration, one or two he loathed—especially the most frequent caller, a man with black hair and a black goatee and a pitch-dark soul, who seemed to Merlin vaguely familiar, but whom he was never quite able to recognize.

Now, Merlin's whole life was not "bound up with this romance he had constructed"; it was not "the happiest hour of his day." He never arrived in time to rescue Caroline from "clutches"; nor did he even marry her. A much stranger thing happened than any of these, and it is this strange thing that will presently be set down here. It began one October afternoon when she walked briskly into the mellow interior of the Moonlight Quill.

It was a dark afternoon, threatening rain and the end of the world, and done in that particularly gloomy gray in which only

New York afternoons indulge. A breeze was crying down the streets, whisking along battered newspapers and pieces of things, and little lights were pricking out all the windows—it was so desolate that one was sorry for the tops of sky-scrapers lost up there in the dark green and gray heaven, and felt that now surely the farce was to close, and presently all the buildings would collapse like card houses, and pile up in a dusty, sardonic heap upon all the millions who presumed to wind in and out of them.

At least these were the sort of musings that lay heavily upon the soul of Merlin Grainger, as he stood by the window putting a dozen books back in a row after a cyclonic visit by a lady with ermine trimmings. He looked out of the window full of the most distressing thoughts—of the early novels of H. G. Wells, of the book of Genesis, of how Thomas Edison had said that in thirty years there would be no dwelling-houses upon the island, but only a vast and turbulent bazaar; and then he set the last book right side up, turned—and Caroline walked coolly into the shop.

She was dressed in a jaunty but conventional walking costume— he remembered this when he thought about it later. Her skirt was plaid, pleated like a concertina; her jacket was a soft but brisk tan; her shoes and spats were brown and her hat, small and trim, completed her like the top of a very expensive and beautifully filled candy box.

Merlin, breathless and startled, advanced nervously toward her.

"Good-afternoon—" he said, and then stopped—why, he did not know, except that it came to him that something very portentous in his life was about to occur, and that it would need no furbishing but silence, and the proper amount of expectant attention. And in that minute before the thing began to happen he had the sense of a breathless second hanging suspended in time: he saw through the glass partition that bounded off the little office the malevolent conical head of his employer, Mr. Moonlight Quill, bent over his correspondence. He saw Miss McCracken and Miss Masters as two patches of hair drooping over piles of paper; he saw the crimson lamp overhead, and noticed with a touch of pleasure how really pleasant and romantic it made the book-store seem.

Then the thing happened, or rather it began to happen. Caroline picked up a volume of poems lying loose upon a pile, fingered it absently with her slender white hand, and suddenly, with an easy gesture, tossed it upward toward the ceiling where it disappeared in the crimson lamp and lodged there, seen through the illuminated silk as a dark, bulging rectangle. This pleased her—she broke into young, contagious laughter, in which Merlin found himself presently joining.

"It stayed up!" she cried merrily. "It stayed up, didn't it?" To both of them this seemed the height of brilliant absurdity. Their laughter mingled, filled the bookshop, and Merlin was glad to find that her voice was rich and full of sorcery.

"Try another," he found himself suggesting—"try a red one."

At this her laughter increased, and she had to rest her hands upon the stack to steady herself.

"Try another," she managed to articulate between spasms of mirth. "Oh, golly, try another!"

"Try two."

"Yes, try two. Oh, I'll choke if I don't stop laughing. Here it goes."

Suiting her action to the word, she picked up a red book and sent it in a gentle hyperbola toward the ceiling, where it sank into the lamp beside the first. It was a few minutes before either of them could do more than rock back and forth in helpless glee; but then by mutual agreement they took up the sport anew, this time in unison. Merlin seized a large, specially bound French classic and whirled it upward. Applauding his own accuracy, he took a bestseller in one hand and a book on barnacles in the other, and waited breathlessly while she made her shot. Then the business waxed fast and furious—sometimes they alternated, and, watching, he found how supple she was in every movement; sometimes one of them made shot after shot, picking up the nearest book, sending it off, merely taking time to follow it with a glance before reaching for another. Within three minutes they had cleared a little place on the table, and the lamp of crimson satin was so bulging with books that it was near breaking.

"Silly game, basket-ball," she cried scornfully as a book left her hand. "High-school girls play it in hideous bloomers."

"Idiotic," he agreed.

She paused in the act of tossing a book, and replaced it suddenly in its position on the table.

"I think we've got room to sit down now," she said gravely.

They had; they had cleared an ample space for two. With a faint touch of nervousness Merlin glanced toward Mr. Moonlight Quill's glass partition, but the three heads were still bent earnestly over their work, and it was evident that they had not seen what had gone on in the shop. So when Caroline put her hands on the table and hoisted herself up Merlin calmly imitated her, and they sat side by side looking very earnestly at each other.

"I had to see you," she began, with a rather pathetic expression in her brown eyes.

"I know."

"It was that last time," she continued, her voice trembling a little, though she tried to keep it steady. "I was frightened. I don't like you to eat off the dresser. I'm so afraid you'll—you'll swallow a collar button."

"I did once—almost," he confessed reluctantly, "but it's not so easy, you know. I mean you can swallow the flat part easy enough or else the other part—that is, separately—but for a whole collar button you'd have to have a specially made throat." He was astonishing himself by the debonnaire appropriateness of his remarks. Words seemed for the first time in his life to run at him shrieking to be used, gathering themselves into carefully arranged squads and platoons, and being presented to him by punctilious adjutants of paragraphs.

"That's what scared me," she said. "I knew you had to have a specially made throat—and I knew, at least I felt sure, that you didn't have one."

He nodded frankly.

"I haven't. It costs money to have one—more money unfortunately than I possess."

He felt no shame in saying this—rather a delight in making the admission—he knew that nothing he could say or do would be beyond her comprehension; least of all his poverty, and the practical impossibility of ever extricating himself from it.

Caroline looked down at her wrist watch, and with a little cry slid from the table to her feet.

"It's after five," she cried. "I didn't realize. I have to be at the Ritz at five-thirty. Let's hurry and get this done. I've got a bet on it."

With one accord they set to work. Caroline began the matter by seizing a book on insects and sending it whizzing, and finally crashing through the glass partition that housed Mr. Moonlight Quill. The proprietor glanced up with a wild look, brushed a few pieces of glass from his desk, and went on with his letters. Miss McCracken gave no sign of having heard—only Miss Masters started and gave a little frightened scream before she bent to her task again.

But to Merlin and Caroline it didn't matter. In a perfect orgy of energy they were hurling book after book in all directions until sometimes three or four were in the air at once, smashing against shelves, cracking the glass of pictures on the walls, falling in bruised and torn heaps upon the floor. It was fortunate that no customers happened to come in, for it is certain they would never have come in again—the noise was too tremendous, a noise of smashing and ripping and tearing, mixed now and then with the tinkling of glass, the quick breathing of the two throwers, and the intermittent outbursts of laughter to which both of them periodically surrendered.

At five-thirty Caroline tossed a last book at the lamp, and gave the final impetus to the load it carried. The weakened silk tore and dropped its cargo in one vast splattering of white and color to the already littered floor. Then with a sigh of relief she turned to Merlin and held out her hand.

"Good-by," she said simply.

"Are you going?" He knew she was. His question was simply a lingering will to detain her and extract for another moment that dazzling essence of light he drew from her presence, to continue his enormous satisfaction in her features, which were like kisses and, he thought, like the features of a girl he had known back in 1910. For a minute he pressed the softness of her hand—then she smiled and withdrew it and, before he could spring to open the door, she had done it herself and was gone out into the turbid and ominous twilight that brooded narrowly over Forty-seventh Street.

I would like to tell you how Merlin, having seen how beauty regards the wisdom of the years, walked into the little partition of Mr. Moonlight Quill and gave up his job then and there; thence issuing out into the street a much finer and nobler and increasingly ironic man. But the truth is much more commonplace. Merlin Grainger stood up and surveyed the wreck of the bookshop, the ruined volumes, the torn silk remnants of the once beautiful crimson lamp, the crystalline sprinkling of broken glass which lay in iridescent dust over the whole interior—and then he went to a corner where a broom was kept and began cleaning up and rearranging and, as far as he was able, restoring the shop to its former condition. He found that, though some few of the books were uninjured, most of them had suffered in varying extents. The backs were off some, the pages were torn from others, still others were just slightly cracked in the front, which, as all careless book return- ers know, makes a book unsalable, and therefore second-hand.

Nevertheless by six o'clock he had done much to repair the damage. He had returned the books to their original places, swept the floor, and put new lights in the sockets overhead. The red shade itself was ruined beyond redemption, and Merlin thought in some trepidation that the money to replace it might have to come out of his salary. At six, therefore, having done the best he could, he crawled over the front window display to pull down the blind. As he was treading delicately back, he saw Mr. Moonlight Quill rise from his desk, put on his overcoat and hat, and emerge into the shop. He nodded mysteriously at Merlin and went toward the door. With his hand on the knob he paused, turned around, and in a voice curiously compounded of ferocity and uncertainty, he said:

"If that girl comes in here again, you tell her to behave."

With that he opened the door, drowning Merlin's meek "Yessir" in its creak, and went out.

Merlin stood there for a moment, deciding wisely not to worry about what was for the present only a possible futurity, and then he went into the back of the shop and invited Miss Masters to have supper with him at Pulpat's French Restaurant, where one could still obtain red wine at dinner, despite the Great Federal Government. Miss Masters accepted.

"Wine makes me feel all tingly," she said.

Merlin laughed inwardly as he compared her to Caroline, or rather as he didn't compare her. There was no comparison.

GLORY IN THE DAYTIME (1933)

Dorothy Parker

"Glory in the Daytime" is about a "devoted wife" who meets, through a seductive intermediary, a famous Broadway actress. As is not unusual in Dorothy Parker's stories, the comedy, delivered with Parker's particularly sharp dialogue and tone, is colored with disillusionment. Parker (1893– 1967) grew up on the Upper West Side of Manhattan. As a young woman, she worked at Vanity Fair *and* Vogue. *She was a founding member of the Algonquin Round Table, an informal group of New York writers and entertainers who met at the Algonquin Hotel in Midtown Manhattan and were famous for their wit as well as their drinking. Parker published numerous reviews, poems, and stories in* The New Yorker *magazine.*

MR. MURDOCK WAS one who carried no enthusiasm whatever for plays and their players, and that was too bad, for they meant so much to little Mrs. Murdock. Always she had been in a state of devout excitement over the luminous, free, passionate elect who serve the theater. And always she had done her wistful worshiping, along with the multitudes, at the great public altars. It is true that once, when she was a particularly little girl, love had impelled her to write Miss Maude Adams a letter beginning "Dearest Peter," and she had received from Miss Adams a miniature thimble inscribed "A kiss from Peter Pan." (That was a day!) And once, when her mother had taken her holiday shopping, a limousine door was held open and there had passed her, as close as *that,* a wonder of sable and violets and round red curls that seemed to tinkle on the air; so, forever after, she was as good as certain that she had been not a foot away from Miss Billie Burke. But until some three years after her marriage, these had remained her only personal experiences with the people of the lights and the glory.

Then it turned out that Miss Noyes, new come to little Mrs. Murdock's own bridge club, knew an actress. She actually knew an actress; the way you and I know collectors of recipes and members of garden clubs and amateurs of needlepoint.

The name of the actress was Lily Wynton, and it was famous. She was tall and slow and silvery; often she appeared in the role of a duchess, or of a Lady Pam or an Honorable Moira. Critics recurrently referred to her as "that great lady of our stage." Mrs. Murdock had attended, over years, matinee performances of the Wynton successes. And she had no more thought that she would one day have opportunity to meet Lily Wynton face to face than she had thought—well, than she had thought of flying!

Yet it was not astounding that Miss Noyes should walk at ease among the glamorous. Miss Noyes was full of depths and mystery, and she could talk with a cigarette still between her lips. She was always doing something difficult, like designing her own pajamas, or reading Proust, or modeling torsos in plasticine. She played excellent bridge. She liked little Mrs. Murdock. "Tiny one," she called her.

"How's for coming to tea tomorrow, tiny one? Lily Wynton's going to drop up," she said, at a therefore memorable meeting of the bridge club. "You might like to meet her."

The words fell so easily that she could not have realized their weight. Lily Wynton was coming to tea. Mrs. Murdock might like to meet her. Little Mrs. Murdock walked home through the early dark, and stars sang in the sky above her.

Mr. Murdock was already at home when she arrived. It required but a glance to tell that for him there had been no singing stars that evening in the heavens. He sat with his newspaper opened at the financial page, and bitterness had its way with his soul. It was not the time to cry happily to him of the impending hospitalities of Miss Noyes; not the time, that is, if one anticipated exclamatory sympathy. Mr. Murdock did not like Miss Noyes. When pressed for a reason, he replied that he just plain didn't like her. Occasionally he added, with a sweep that might have commanded a certain admiration, that all those women made him sick. Usually, when she told him of the temperate activities of the bridge club meetings, Mrs. Murdock kept any mention of Miss Noyes's name from the accounts. She had found that this omission made for a more agreeable evening. But now she was caught in such a sparkling swirl of excitement that she had scarcely kissed him before she was off on her story.

"Oh, Jim," she cried. "Oh, what do you think! Hallie Noyes asked me to tea tomorrow to meet Lily Wynton!"

"Who's Lily Wynton?" he said.

"Ah, Jim," she said. "Ah, really, Jim. Who's Lily Wynton! Who's Greta Garbo, I suppose!"

"She some actress or something?" he said.

Mrs. Murdock's shoulders sagged. "Yes, Jim," she said. "Yes. Lily Wynton's an actress."

She picked up her purse and started slowly toward the door. But before she had taken three steps, she was again caught up in her sparkling swirl. She turned to him, and her eyes were shining.

"Honestly," she said, "it was the funniest thing you ever heard in your life. We'd just finished the last rubber—oh, I forgot to tell you, I won three dollars, isn't that pretty good for me?—and Hallie Noyes said to me, 'Come on in to tea tomorrow. Lily Wynton's going to drop up,' she said. Just like that, she said it. Just as if it was anybody."

"Drop up?" he said. "How can you drop *up*?"

"Honestly, I don't know what I said when she asked me," Mrs. Murdock said. "I suppose I said I'd love to—I guess I must have. But I was so simply—Well, you know how I've always felt about Lily Wynton. Why, when I was a little girl, I used to collect her pictures. And I've seen her in, oh, everything she's ever been in, I should think, and I've read every word about her, and interviews and all. Really and truly, when I think of *meeting* her—Oh, I'll simply die. What on earth shall I say to her?"

"You might ask her how she'd like to try dropping down, for a change," Mr. Murdock said.

"All right, Jim," Mrs. Murdock said. "If that's the way you want to be."

Wearily she went toward the door, and this time she reached it before she turned to him. There were no lights in her eyes.

"It—it isn't so awfully nice," she said, "to spoil somebody's pleasure in something. I was so thrilled about this. You don't see what it is to me, to meet Lily Wynton. To meet somebody like that, and see what they're like, and hear what they say, and maybe get to know them. People like that mean—well, they mean something different to me. They're not like this. They're not like me. Who do I ever see? What do I ever hear? All my whole life, I've wanted to know—I've almost prayed that some day I could meet—Well. All right, Jim."

She went out, and on to her bedroom.

Mr. Murdock was left with only his newspaper and his bitterness for company. But he spoke aloud.

"'Drop up!'" he said. "'Drop up,' for God's sake!"

The Murdocks dined, not in silence, but in pronounced quiet. There was something straitened about Mr. Murdock's stillness; but little Mrs. Murdock's was the sweet, far quiet of one given over to dreams. She had forgotten her weary words to her husband, she had passed through her excitement and her disappointment. Luxuriously she floated on innocent visions of days after the morrow. She heard her own voice in future conversations. . . .

I saw Lily Wynton at Hallie's the other day, and she was telling me all about her new play—no, I'm terribly sorry, but it's a secret, I promised her I wouldn't tell anyone the name of it. . . . Lily Wynton dropped up to tea yesterday, and we just got to talking, and she told me the most interesting things about her life; she said she'd never dreamed of telling them to anyone else. . . . Why, I'd love to come, but I promised to have lunch with Lily Wynton. . . . I had a long, long letter from Lily Wynton. . . . Lily Wynton called me up this morning. . . . Whenever I feel blue, I just go and have a talk with Lily Wynton, and then I'm all right again. . . . Lily Wynton told me . . . Lily Wynton and I. . . "Lily," I said to her. . .

The next morning, Mr. Murdock had left for his office before Mrs. Murdock rose. This had happened several times before, but not often. Mrs. Murdock felt a little queer about it. Then she told herself that it was probably just as well. Then she forgot all about it, and gave her mind to the selection of a costume suitable to the afternoon's event. Deeply she felt that her small wardrobe included no dress adequate to the occasion; for, of course, such an occasion had never before arisen. She finally decided upon a frock of dark blue serge with fluted white muslin about the neck and wrists. It was her style, that was the most she could say for it. And that was all she could say for herself. Blue serge and little white ruffles—that was she.

The very becomingness of the dress lowered her spirits. A nobody's frock, worn by a nobody. She blushed and went hot when she recalled the dreams she had woven the night before, the mad visions of intimacy, of equality with Lily Wynton. Timidity turned her heart liquid, and she thought of telephoning Miss Noyes and saying she had a bad cold and could not come. She steadied, when she planned a course of conduct to pursue at teatime. She would not try to say anything; if she stayed silent, she could not sound foolish. She would listen and watch and worship and then come home, stronger, braver, better for an hour she would remember proudly all her life.

Miss Noyes's living-room was done in the early modern period. There were a great many oblique lines and acute angles, zigzags of aluminum and horizontal stretches of mirror. The color scheme was sawdust and steel. No seat was more than twelve inches above the floor, no table was made of wood. It was, as has been said of larger places, all right for a visit.

Little Mrs. Murdock was the first arrival. She was glad of that: no, maybe it would have been better to have come after Lily Wynton; no, maybe this was right. The maid motioned her toward the living-room, and Miss Noyes greeted her in the cool voice and the warm words that were her special combination. She wore black velvet trousers, a red cummerbund, and a white silk shirt, opened at the throat. A cigarette clung to her lower lip, and her eyes, as was her habit, were held narrow against its near smoke.

"Come in, come in, tiny one," she said. "Bless its little heart. Take off its little coat. Good Lord, you look easily eleven years old in that dress. Sit ye doon, here beside of me. There'll be a spot of tea in a jiff."

Mrs. Murdock sat down on the vast, perilously low divan, and, because she was never good at reclining among cushions, held her back straight. There was room for six like her, between herself and her hostess. Miss Noyes lay back with one ankle flung upon the other knee, and looked at her.

"I'm a wreck," Miss Noyes announced. "I was modeling like a mad thing, all night long. It's taken everything out of me. I was like a thing bewitched."

"Oh, what were you making?" cried Mrs. Murdock.

"Oh, Eve," Miss Noyes said. "I always do Eve. What else is there to do? You must come pose for me some time, tiny one. You'd be nice to do. Ye-es, you'd be very nice to do. My tiny one."

"Why, I—" Mrs. Murdock said, and stopped. "Thank you very much, though," she said.

"I wonder where Lily is," Miss Noyes said. "She said she'd be here early—well, she always says that. You'll adore her, tiny one. She's really rare. She's a real person. And she's been through perfect hell. God, what a time she's had!"

"Ah, what's been the matter?" said Mrs. Murdock.

"Men," Miss Noyes said. "Men. She never had a man that wasn't a louse." Gloomily she stared at the toe of her flat-heeled patent leather pump. "A pack of lice, always. All of them. Leave her for the first little floozie that comes along."

"But—" Mrs. Murdock began. No, she couldn't have heard right. How could it be right? Lily Wynton was a great actress. A great actress meant romance. Romance meant Grand Dukes and Crown Princes and diplomats touched with gray at the temples and lean, bronzed, reckless Younger Sons. It meant pearls and emeralds and chinchilla and rubies red as the blood that was shed for them. It meant a grim-faced boy sitting in the fearful Indian midnight, beneath the dreary whirring of the *punkahs,* writing a letter to the lady he had seen but once; writing his poor heart out, before he turned to the service revolver that lay beside him on the table. It meant a golden-locked poet, floating face downward in the sea, and in his pocket his last great sonnet to the lady of ivory. It meant brave, beautiful men, living and dying for the lady who was the pale bride of art, whose eyes and heart were soft with only compassion for them.

A pack of lice. Crawling after little floozies; whom Mrs. Murdock swiftly and hazily pictured as rather like ants.

"But—" said little Mrs. Murdock.

"She gave them all her money," Miss Noyes said. "She always did. Or if she didn't, they took it anyway. Took every cent she had, and then spat in her face. Well, maybe I'm teaching her a little bit of sense now. Oh, there's the bell—that'll be Lily. No, sit ye doon, tiny one. You belong there." Miss Noyes rose and made for the archway that separated the living-room from the hall. As she passed Mrs. Murdock, she stooped suddenly, cupped her guest's round chin, and quickly, lightly kissed her mouth.

"Don't tell Lily," she murmured, very low.

Mrs. Murdock puzzled. Don't tell Lily what? Could Hallie Noyes think that she might babble to the Lily Wynton of these strange confidences about the actress's life? Or did she mean—But she had no more time for puzzling. Lily Wynton stood in the arch-way. There she stood, one hand resting on the wooden molding and her body swayed toward it, exactly as she stood for her third-act entrance of her latest play, and for a like half-minute.

You would have known her anywhere, Mrs. Murdock thought. Oh, yes, anywhere. Or at least you would have exclaimed, "That

woman looks something like Lily Wynton." For she was somehow
different in the daylight. Her figure looked heavier, thicker, and her
face—there was so much of her face that the surplus sagged from
the strong, fine bones. And her eyes, those famous dark, liquid eyes.
They were dark, yes, and certainly liquid, but they were set in little
hammocks of folded flesh, and seemed to be set but loosely, so
readily did they roll. Their whites, that were visible all around the
irises, were threaded with tiny scarlet veins.

"I suppose footlights are an awful strain on their eyes," thought
little Mrs. Murdock.

Lily Wynton wore, just as she should have, black satin and sables,
and long white gloves were wrinkled luxuriously about her wrists.
But there were delicate streaks of grime in the folds of her gloves,
and down the shining length of her gown there were small, irregu-
larly shaped dull patches; bits of food or drops of drink, or perhaps
both, sometime must have slipped their carriers and found brief
sanctuary there. Her hat—oh, her hat. It was romance, it was mystery, it was strange, sweet sorrow; it was Lily Wynton's hat, of all
the world, and no other could dare it. Black it was, and tilted, and
a great, soft plume drooped from it to follow her cheek and curl
across her throat.

Beneath it, her hair had the various hues of neglected brass. But,
oh, her hat.

"Darling!" cried Miss Noyes.

"Angel," said Lily Wynton. "My sweet."

It was that voice. It was that deep, soft, glowing voice. "Like
purple velvet," someone had written. Mrs. Murdock's heart beat
visibly.

Lily Wynton cast herself upon the steep bosom of her hostess,
and murmured there. Across Miss Noyes's shoulder she caught
sight of little Mrs. Murdock.

"And who is this?" she said. She disengaged herself.

"That's my tiny one," Miss Noyes said. "Mrs. Murdock."

"What a clever little face," said Lily Wynton. "Clever, clever
little face. What does she do, sweet Hallie? I'm sure she writes,
doesn't she? Yes, I can feel it. She writes beautiful, beautiful words.
Don't you, child?"

"Oh, no, really I—" Mrs. Murdock said.

"And you must write me a play," said Lily Wynton. "A beautiful, beautiful play. And I will play in it, over and over the world,

until I am a very, very old lady. And then I will die. But I will never be forgotten, because of the years I played in your beautiful, beautiful play."

She moved across the room. There was a slight hesitancy, a seeming insecurity, in her step, and when she would have sunk into a chair, she began to sink two inches, perhaps, to its right. But she swayed just in time in her descent, and was safe.

"To write," she said, smiling sadly at Mrs. Murdock, "to write. And such a little thing, for such a big gift. Oh, the privilege of it. But the anguish of it, too. The agony."

"But, you see, I—" said little Mrs. Murdock.

"Tiny one doesn't write, Lily," Miss Noyes said. She threw herself back upon the divan. "She's a museum piece. She's a devoted wife."

"A wife!" Lily Wynton said. "A wife. Your first marriage, child?"

"Oh, yes," said Mrs. Murdock.

"How sweet," Lily Wynton said. "How sweet, sweet, sweet. Tell me, child, do you love him very, very much?"

"Why, I—" said little Mrs. Murdock, and blushed. "I've been married for ages," she said.

"You love him," Lily Wynton said. "You love him. And is it sweet to go to bed with him?"

"Oh—" said Mrs. Murdock, and blushed till it hurt.

"The first marriage," Lily Wynton said. "Youth, youth. Yes, when I was your age I used to marry, too. Oh, treasure your love, child, guard it, live in it. Laugh and dance in the love of your man. Until you find out what he's really like."

There came a sudden visitation upon her. Her shoulders jerked upward, her cheeks puffed, her eyes sought to start from their hammocks. For a moment she sat thus, then slowly all subsided into place. She lay back in her chair, tenderly patting her chest. She shook her head sadly, and there was grieved wonder in the look with which she held Mrs. Murdock.

"Gas," said Lily Wynton, in the famous voice. "Gas. Nobody knows what I suffer from it."

"Oh. I'm so sorry." Mrs. Murdock said. "Is there anything—"

"Nothing," Lily Wynton said. "There is nothing. There is nothing that can be done for it. I've been everywhere."

"How's for a spot of tea, perhaps?" Miss Noyes said. "It might help." She turned her face toward the archway and lifted up her voice. "Mary! Where the hell's the tea?"

"You don't know," Lily Wynton said, with her grieved eyes fixed on Mrs. Murdock, "you don't know what stomach distress is. You can never, never know, unless you're a stomach sufferer yourself. I've been one for years. Years and years and years."

"I'm terribly sorry," Mrs. Murdock said.

"Nobody knows the anguish," Lily Wynton said. "The agony."

The maid appeared, bearing a triangular tray upon which was set an heroic-sized tea service of bright white china, each piece a hectagon. She set it down on a table within the long reach of Miss Noyes and retired, as she had come, bashfully.

"Sweet Hallie," Lily Wynton said, "my sweet. Tea—I adore it. I worship it. But my distress turns it to gall and wormwood in me. Gall and wormwood. For hours, I should have no peace. Let me have a little, tiny bit of your beautiful, beautiful brandy, instead."

"You really think you should, darling?" Miss Noyes said. "You know—"

"My angel," said Lily Wynton, "it's the only thing for acidity."

"Well," Miss Noyes said. "But do remember you've got a performance tonight." Again she hurled her voice at the archway. "Mary! Bring the brandy and a lot of soda and ice and things."

"Oh, no, my saint," Lily Wynton said. "No, no, sweet Hallie. Soda and ice are rank poison to me. Do you want to freeze my poor, weak stomach? Do you want to kill poor, poor Lily?"

"Mary!" roared Miss Noyes. "Just bring the brandy and a glass." She turned to little Mrs. Murdock. "How's for your tea, tiny one? Cream? Lemon?"

"Cream, if I may, please," Mrs. Murdock said. "And two lumps of sugar, please, if I may."

"Oh, youth, youth," Lily Wynton said. "Youth and love."

The maid returned with an octagonal tray supporting a decanter of brandy and a wide, squat, heavy glass. Her head twisted on her neck in a spasm of diffidence.

"Just pour it for me, will you, my dear?" said Lily Wynton. "Thank you. And leave the pretty, pretty decanter here, on this enchanting little table. Thank you. You're so good to me."

The maid vanished, fluttering. Lily Wynton lay back in her chair, holding in her gloved hand the wide, squat glass, colored brown to the brim. Little Mrs. Murdock lowered her eyes to her teacup, carefully carried it to her lips, sipped, and replaced it on its saucer.

When she raised her eyes, Lily Wynton lay back in her chair, holding in her gloved hand the wide, squat, colorless glass.

"My life," Lily Wynton said, slowly, "is a mess. A stinking mess. It always has been, and it always will be. Until I am a very, very old lady. Ah, little Clever-Face, you writers don't know what struggle is."

"But really I'm not—" said Mrs. Murdock.

"To write," Lily Wynton said. "To write. To set one word beautifully beside another word. The privilege of it. The blessed, blessed peace of it. Oh, for quiet, for rest. But do you think those cheap bastards would close that play while it's doing a nickel's worth of business? Oh, no. Tired as I am, sick as I am, I must drag along. Oh, child, child, guard your precious gift. Give thanks for it. It is the greatest thing of all. It is the only thing. To write."

"Darling, I told you tiny one doesn't write," said Miss Noyes. "How's for making more sense? She's a wife."

"Ah, yes, she told me. She told me she had perfect, passionate love," Lily Wynton said. "Young love. It is the greatest thing. It is the only thing." She grasped the decanter; and again the squat glass was brown to the brim.

"What time did you start today, darling?" said Miss Noyes.

"Oh, don't scold me, sweet love," Lily Wynton said. "Lily hasn't been naughty. Her wuzzunt naughty dirl 't all. I didn't get up until late, late, late. And though I parched, though I burned, I didn't have a drink until after my breakfast. 'It is for Hallie,' I said." She raised the glass to her mouth, tilted it, and brought it away, colorless.

"Good Lord, Lily," Miss Noyes said. "Watch yourself. You've got to walk on that stage tonight, my girl."

"All the world's a stage," said Lily Wynton. "And all the men and women merely players. They have their entrance and their exitses, and each man in his time plays many parts, his act being seven ages. At first, the infant, mewling and puking——"

"How's the play doing?" Miss Noyes said.

"Oh, lousily," Lily Wynton said. "Lousily, lousily, lousily. But what isn't? What isn't, in this terrible, terrible world? Answer me that." She reached for the decanter.

"Lily, listen," said Miss Noyes. "Stop that. Do you hear?"

"Please, sweet Hallie," Lily Wynton said. "Pretty please. Poor, poor Lily."

"Do you want me to do what I had to do last time?" Miss Noyes said. "Do you want me to strike you, in front of tiny one, here?"

Lily Wynton drew herself high. "You do not realize," she said, icily, "what acidity is." She filled the glass and held it, regarding it as though through a lorgnon. Suddenly her manner changed, and she looked up and smiled at little Mrs. Murdock.

"You must let me read it," she said. "You mustn't be so modest."

"Read——?" said little Mrs. Murdock.

"Your play," Lily Wynton said. "Your beautiful, beautiful play. Don't think I am too busy. I always have time. I have time for everything. Oh, my God, I have to go to the dentist tomorrow. Oh, the suffering I have gone through with my teeth. Look!" She set down her glass, inserted a gloved forefinger in the corner of her mouth, and dragged it to the side. "Oogh!" she insisted. "Oogh!"

Mrs. Murdock craned her neck shyly, and caught a glimpse of shining gold.

"Oh, I'm so sorry," she said.

"As wah ee id a me ass ime," Lily Wynton said. She took away her forefinger and let her mouth resume its shape. "That's what he did to me last time," she repeated. "The anguish of it. The agony. Do you suffer with your teeth, little Clever-Face?"

"Why, I'm afraid I've been awfully lucky," Mrs. Murdock said. "I——"

"You don't know," Lily Wynton said. "Nobody knows what it is. You writers—you don't know." She took up her glass, sighed over it, and drained it.

"Well," Miss Noyes said. "Go ahead and pass out, then, darling. You'll have time for a sleep before the theater."

"To sleep," Lily Wynton said. "To sleep, perchance to dream. The privilege of it. Oh, Hallie, sweet, sweet Hallie, poor Lily feels so terrible. Rub my head for me, angel. Help me."

"I'll go get the Eau de Cologne," Miss Noyes said. She left the room lightly patting Mrs. Murdock's knee as she passed her. Lily Wynton lay in her chair and closed her famous eyes.

"To sleep," she said. "To sleep, perchance to dream."

"I'm afraid," little Mrs. Murdock began. "I'm afraid," she said, "I really must be going home. I'm afraid I didn't realize how awfully late it was."

"Yes, go, child," Lily Wynton said. She did not open her eyes. "Go to him. Go to him, live in him, love him. Stay with him always. But when he starts bringing them into the house—get out."

"I'm afraid—I'm afraid I didn't quite understand," Mrs. Murdock said.

"When he starts bringing his fancy women into the house," Lily Wynton said. "You must have pride, then. You must go. I always did. But it was always too late then. They'd got all my money. That's all they want, marry them or not. They say it's love, but it isn't. Love is the only thing. Treasure your love, child. Go back to him. Go to bed with him. It's the only thing. And your beautiful, beautiful play."

"Oh, dear," said little Mrs. Murdock. "I—I'm afraid it's really terribly late."

There was only the sound of rhythmic breathing from the chair where Lily Wynton lay. The purple voice rolled along the air no longer.

Little Mrs. Murdock stole to the chair upon which she had left her coat. Carefully she smoothed her white muslin frills, so that they would be fresh beneath the jacket. She felt a tenderness for her frock; she wanted to protect it. Blue serge and little ruffles—they were her own.

When she reached the outer door of Miss Noyes's apartment, she stopped a moment and her manners conquered her. Bravely she called in the direction of Miss Noyes's bedroom.

"Good-by, Miss Noyes," she said. "I've simply got to run. I didn't realize it was so late. I had a lovely time—thank you ever so much."

"Oh, good-by, tiny one," Miss Noyes called. "Sorry Lily went by-by. Don't mind her—she's really a real person. I'll call you up, tiny one. I want to see you. Now where's that damned Cologne?"

"Thank you ever so much," Mrs. Murdock said. She let herself out of the apartment.

Little Mrs. Murdock walked homeward, through the clustering dark. Her mind was busy, but not with memories of Lily Wynton. She thought of Jim; Jim, who had left for his office before she had arisen that morning. Jim, whom she had not kissed good-by. Darling Jim. There were no others born like him. Funny Jim, stiff and cross and silent; but only because he knew so much. Only because he knew the silliness of seeking afar for the glamour and beauty and romance of living. When they were right at home all the time, she thought. Like the Blue Bird, thought little Mrs. Murdock.

Darling Jim. Mrs. Murdock turned in her course, and entered an enormous shop where the most delicate and esoteric of foods were sold for heavy sums. Jim liked red caviar. Mrs. Murdock bought a jar of the shiny, glutinous eggs. They would have cocktails that night, though they had no guests, and the red caviar would be served with them for a surprise, and it would be a little, secret party to celebrate her return to contentment with her Jim, a party to mark her happy renunciation of all the glory of the world. She bought, too, a large, foreign cheese. It would give a needed touch to dinner. Mrs. Murdock had not given much attention to ordering dinner, that morning. "Oh, anything you want, Signe," she had said to the maid. She did not want to think of that. She went on home with her packages.

Mr. Murdock was already there when she arrived. He was sitting with his newspaper opened to the financial page. Little Mrs. Murdock ran in to him with her eyes a-light. It is too bad that the light in a person's eyes is only the light in a person's eyes, and you cannot tell at a look what causes it. You do not know if it is excitement about you, or about something else. The evening before, Mrs. Murdock had run in to Mr. Murdock with her eyes a-light.

"Oh, hello," he said to her. He looked back at his paper, and kept his eyes there. "What did you do? Did you drop up to Hank Noyes's?"

Little Mrs. Murdock stopped right where she was.

"You know perfectly well, Jim," she said, "that Hallie Noyes's first name is Hallie."

"It's Hank to me," he said. "Hank or Bill. Did what's-her-name show up? I mean drop up. Pardon me."

"To whom are you referring?" said Mrs. Murdock, perfectly.

"What's-her-name," Mr. Murdock said. "The movie star."

"If you mean Lily Wynton," Mrs. Murdock said, "she is not a movie star. She is an actress. She is a great actress."

"Well, did she drop up?" he said.

Mrs. Murdock's shoulders sagged. "Yes," she said. "Yes, she was there, Jim."

"I suppose you're going on the stage now," he said.

"Ah, Jim," Mrs. Murdock said. "Ah, Jim, please. I'm not sorry at all I went to Hallie Noyes's today. It was—it was a real experience to meet Lily Wynton. Something I'll remember all my life."

"What did she do?" Mr. Murdock said. "Hang by her feet?"

"She did no such thing!" Mrs. Murdock said. "She recited Shakespeare, if you want to know."

"Oh, my God," Mr. Murdock said. "That must have been great."

"All right, Jim," Mrs. Murdock said. "If that's the way you want to be."

Wearily she left the room and went down the hall. She stopped at the pantry door, pushed it open, and spoke to the pleasant little maid.

"Oh, Signe," she said. "Oh, good evening, Signe. Put these things somewhere, will you? I got them on the way home. I thought we might have them some time."

Wearily little Mrs. Murdock went on down the hall to her bedroom.

MIDSUMMER MADNESS (1953)

Langston Hughes

The unnamed prim, educated Harlem resident who narrates "Midsummer Madness" is the recurring "partner" of Langston Hughes's recurring protagonist, Jesse B. Semple. Simple (as Semple is known) was born and raised in Virginia, but, like Hughes (who was born in Missouri), he found himself happiest in Harlem. During World War II, Hughes created the Simple character for a newspaper column and discovered that Simple's irreverent and comic voice cut quicker and deeper into issues of social justice and race than Hughes's own could. Hughes (1902–1967) moved to New York in 1921 to attend Columbia University, but soon abandoned his studies there for life as a writer in Harlem. One of the most important figures of the Harlem Renaissance, Hughes, for more than forty years, was the country's most persistent and enthusiastic advocate for black writers and artists.

PAVEMENT HOT AS a frying pan on Ma Frazier's griddle. Heat devils dancing in the air. Men in windows with no undershirts on—which is one thing ladies can't get by with if they lean out windows. Sunset. Stoops running over with people, curbs running over with kids. August in Harlem too hot to be August in hell. Beer is going up a nickel a glass, I hear, but I do not care. I would still be forced to say gimme a cool one.

"That bar's sign is lying—air cooled—which is why I'd just as well stay out here on the sidewalk. Girl, where did you get them baby-doll clothes? Wheee-ee-oooo!" The woman did not stop, but you could tell by the way she walked that she heard him. Simple whistled. "Hey, lawdy, Miss Claudy! Or might your name be Cleopatra?" No response. "Partner, she ig-ed me."

"She really ignored you," I said.

"Well, anyhow, every dog has its day—but the trouble is there arc more dogs than there are days, more people than there are houses, more roomers than there are rooms, and more babies than there are cribs."

"You're speaking philosophically this evening."

"I'm making up proverbs. For instance: 'A man with no legs don't need shoes.'"

"Like most proverbs, that states the obvious."

"It came right out of my own head—even if I did hear it before," insisted Simple. "Also I got another one for you based on experience: 'Don't get a woman that *you* love. Get a woman that loves YOU!'"

"Meaning, I take it, that if a woman loves *you,* she will take care of you, and you won't have to take care of her."

"Something like that," said Simple, "because if you love a woman you are subject to lay down your all before her, empty your heart and your pockets, and then have nothing left. I bet if I had been born with a silver spoon in my mouth, some woman would of had my spoon before I got to the breakfast table. I always was weak for women. In fact, womens is the cause of my being broke tonight. After I buy Joyce her summer ice cream and Zarita her summer beer, I cannot hardly buy myself a drink by the middle of the week. At dinner time all I can do is walk in a restaurant and say, 'Gimme an order of water—in a clean glass.'"

"I will repeat a proverb for *you,*" I said. "'It's a mighty poor chicken that can't scratch up his own food.'"

"I am a poor rooster," said Simple. "Womens have cleaned me to the bone. I may give out, but I'll never give up, though. Neither womens nor white folks are going to get Jesse B. down."

"Can't you ever keep race out of the conversation?" I said.

"I am race conscious," said Simple. "And I ain't ashamed of my race. I ain't like that woman that bought a watermelon and had it *wrapped* before she carried it out of the store. I am what I am. And what I say is: 'If you're corn bread, don't try to be an angel-food cake!' That's a mistake. . . . Look at that chick! Look at that de-light under the light! So round, so firm, so fully packed! But don't you be looking, too, partner. You might strain your neckbone."

"You had better take your own advice," I said, "or you might get your head cut off. A woman with a shape like that is bound to have a boy friend."

"One more boy friend would do her no harm," said Simple, "so it might as well be me. But you don't see me moving out of my tracks, do you? I have learned one thing just by observation: Midsummer madness brings winter sadness, so curb your badness. If you can't be good, be careful. In this hot weather with womens going around not only with bare back, but some of them with mighty near everything else bare, a man has got to watch his self. Look at them right here on the Avenue—play suits, sun suits, swim suits, practically no suits. I swear, if I didn't care for Joyce, I'd be turning my head every which-a-way, and looking every which-a-where. As it is, I done eye-balled a plenty. This is the hottest summer I ever seen—but the womens look cool. That is why a man has to be careful."

"Cool, too, you mean—controlled!"

"Also careful," said Simple. "I remember last summer seeing them boys around my stoop, also the mens on the corner jiving with them girls in the windows, and the young mens in the candy store buying ice cream for jail bait and beating bongos under be-bop windows. And along about the middle of the winter, or maybe it was spring, I heard a baby crying in the room underneath me, and another one gurgling in the third floor front. And this summer on the sidewalk I see *more* new baby carriages, and rattles being raised, and milk bottles being sucked. It is beautiful the way nature keeps right on producing Negroes. But the welfare has done garnished some of these men's wages. And the lady from the Domestic Relations Court has been upstairs in the front room investigating twice as to where Carlyle has gone. When he do come home he will meet up with a summons."

"I take it Carlyle is a young man who does not yet realize the responsibilities of parenthood."

"Carlyle is old enough to know a baby has to eat. And I do not give him credit for cutting out and leaving that girl with that child— except that they had a fight, and Carlyle left her a note which was writ: 'Him who fights and runs away, lives to fight some other day.' The girl said Carlyle learned that in high school when he ought to have been learning how to get a good job that pays more than thirty-two dollars a week. When their baby were born, it was the coldest day in March. And my big old fat landlady, what always said she did not want no children in the house, were mad when the Visiting Health Nurse came downstairs and told her to send some heat up.

"She said, 'You just go back upstairs and tell that Carlyle to send me some money down. He is two weeks behind now on his rent. I told him not to be setting on my stoop with that girl last summer. Instead of making hay while the sun were shining, he were using his time otherwise. Just go back upstairs and tell him what I said.'

"'All of which is no concern of mine,' says the Health Nurse. 'I am concerned with the welfare of mother and child. Your house is cold, except down here where you and your dog is at.'

"'Just leave Trixie out of this,' says the landlady. 'Trixie is an old dog and has rheumatism. I love this dog better than I love myself, and I intends to keep her warm.'

"'If you do not send some steam upstairs, I will advise your tenants to report you to the Board of Health,' says the Health Nurse.

"She were a real spunky little nurse. I love that nurse—because about every ten days she came by to see how them new babies was making out. And every time she came, that old landlady would steam up. So us roomers was warm some part of last winter, anyhow."

"Thanks especially to Carlyle and his midsummer madness," I said. "But where do you suppose the boy went when he left his wife?"

"To his mama's in the Bronx," said Simple. "He is just a young fellow what is not housebroke yet. I seen him last night on the corner of Lenox and 125th and he said he was coming back soon as he could find himself a good job. Fight or not fight, he says he loves that girl and is crazy about his baby, and all he wants is to find himself a Fifty or Sixty Dollar a week job so he can meet his responsibilities. I said, 'Boy, how much did you say you want to make a week?' And he repeated himself, Fifty to Sixty.

"So I said, 'You must want your baby to be in high school before you returns.'

"Carlyle said, 'I'm a man now, so I want to get paid like a man.'

"'You mean a white man,' I said.

"'I mean a *grown* man,' says Carlyle.

"By that time the Bronx bus come along and he got on it, so I did not get a chance to tell that boy that I knowed what he meant, but I did not know how it could come true. . . . Man, look at that chick going yonder, stacked up like the Queen Mary! . . . Wheee-ee-ooo! Baby, if you must walk away, walk straight—and don't shake your tail-gate."

"Watch yourself! Have you no respect for women?"

"I have nothing but respect for a figure like that," said Simple. "Miss, your mama must of been sweet sixteen when she borned you. Sixteen divided by two, you come out a figure 8! Can I have a date? Hey, Lawdy, Miss Claudy! You must be deaf—you done left! I'm standing here by myself.

"Come on, boy, let's go on in the bar and put that door between me and temptation. If the air cooler is working, the treat's on me. Let's investigate. Anyhow, I always did say if you can't be good, be careful. If you can't be nice, take advice. If you don't think once, you can't think twice."

NEW YORK DAY WOMEN

Edwidge Danticat

(from *Krik? Krak!*, 1996)

Born on January 19, 1969, in Port-au-Prince, Haiti, Edwidge Danticat is the author of novels, essays, and collections of stories that have focused primarily on the lives and trials of Haitians and Haitian-Americans. Raised for most of her childhood by her aunt and uncle after her parents immigrated to the United States, she moved to Brooklyn to rejoin her parents when she was twelve. Already an avid reader, she learned English and, though challenged by an unfamiliar culture in America, immediately took to expressing her discoveries of her new world and herself through writing. She graduated with a degree in French literature from Barnard College in New York City and earned a master's degree in creative writing at Brown University in 1993. She won a prestigious MacArthur Foundation Award in 2009. This story, "New York Day Women," comes from her second book and first short story collection, Krik? Krak!

TODAY, WALKING DOWN the street, I see my mother. She is strolling with a happy gait, her body thrust toward the DON'T WALK sign and the yellow taxicabs that make forty-five-degree turns on the corner of Madison and Fifty-seventh Street.

I have never seen her in this kind of neighborhood, peering into Chanel and Tiffany's and gawking at the jewels glowing in the Bulgari windows. My mother never shops outside of Brooklyn. She has never seen the advertising office where I work. She is afraid to take the subway, where you may meet those young black militant street preachers who curse black women for straightening their hair.

Yet, here she is, my mother, who I left at home that morning in her bathrobe, with pieces of newspapers twisted like rollers in her

hair. My mother, who accuses me of random offenses as I dash out
of the house.

**Would you get up and give an old lady like me your sub-
way seat? In this state of mind, I bet you don't even give
up your seat to a pregnant lady.**

My mother, who is often right about that. Sometimes I get up and
give my seat. Other times, I don't. It all depends on how pregnant
the woman is and whether or not she is with her boyfriend or husband and whether or not *he* is sitting down.

   As my mother stands in front of Carnegie Hall, one taxi driver
yells to another, "What do you think this is, a dance floor?"

   My mother waits patiently for this dispute to be settled before
crossing the street.

**In Haiti when you get hit by a car, the owner of the car
gets out and kicks you for getting blood on his bumper.**

My mother who laughs when she says this and shows a large gap in
her mouth where she lost three more molars to the dentist last
week. My mother, who at fifty-nine, says dentures are okay.

**You can take them out when they bother you. I'll like
them. I'll like them fine.**

Will it feel empty when Papa kisses you?

Oh no, he doesn't kiss me that way anymore.

My mother, who watches the lottery drawing every night on channel 11 without ever having played the numbers.

**A third of that money is all I would need. We would pay
the mortgage, and your father could stop driving that taxi-
cab all over Brooklyn.**

I follow my mother, mesmerized by the many possibilities of her
journey. Even in a flowered dress, she is lost in a sea of pinstripes

and gray suits, high heels and elegant short skirts, Reebok sneakers, dashing from building to building.

My mother, who won't go out to dinner with anyone.

If they want to eat with me, let them come to my house, even if I boil water and give it to them.

My mother, who talks to herself when she peels the skin off poultry.

Fat, you know, and cholesterol. Fat and cholesterol killed your aunt Hermine.

My mother, who makes jam with dried grapefruit peel and then puts in cinnamon bark that I always think is cockroaches in the jam. My mother, whom I have always bought household appliances for, on her birthday. A nice rice cooker, a blender.

I trail the red orchids in her dress and the heavy faux leather bag on her shoulders. Realizing the ferocious pace of my pursuit, I stop against a wall to rest. My mother keeps on walking as though she owns the sidewalk under her feet.

As she heads toward the Plaza Hotel, a bicycle messenger swings so close to her that I want to dash forward and rescue her, but she stands dead in her tracks and lets him ride around her and then goes on.

My mother stops at a corner hot-dog stand and asks for something. The vendor hands her a can of soda that she slips into her bag. She stops by another vendor selling sundresses for seven dollars each. I can tell that she is looking at an African print dress, contemplating my size. I think to myself, Please Ma, don't buy it. It would be just another thing that I would bury in the garage or give to Goodwill.

Why should we give to Goodwill when there are so many people back home who need clothes? We save our clothes for the relatives in Haiti.

Twenty years we have been saving all kinds of things for the relatives in Haiti. I need the place in the garage for an exercise bike.

You are pretty enough to be a stewardess. Only dogs like bones.

This mother of mine, she stops at another hot-dog vendor's and buys a frankfurter that she eats on the street. I never knew that she ate frankfurters. With her blood pressure, she shouldn't eat anything with sodium. She has to be careful with her heart, this day woman.

I cannot just swallow salt. Salt is heavier than a hundred bags of shame.

She is slowing her pace, and now I am too close. If she turns around, she might see me. I let her walk into the park before I start to follow again.

My mother walks toward the sandbox in the middle of the park. There a woman is waiting with a child. The woman is wearing a leotard with biker's shorts and has small weights in her hands. The woman kisses the child good-bye and surrenders him to my mother; then she bolts off, running on the cemented stretches in the park.

The child given to my mother has frizzy blond hair. His hand slips into hers easily, like he's known her for a long time. When he raises his face to look at my mother, it is as though he is looking at the sky.

My mother gives this child the soda that she bought from the vendor on the street corner. The child's face lights up as she puts in a straw in the can for him. This seems to be a conspiracy just between the two of them.

My mother and the child sit and watch the other children play in the sandbox. The child pulls out a comic book from a knapsack with Big Bird on the back. My mother peers into his comic book. My mother, who taught herself to read as a little girl in Haiti from the books that her brothers brought home from school.

My mother, who has now lost six of her seven sisters in Ville Rose and has never had the strength to return for their funerals.

Many graves to kiss when I go back. Many graves to kiss.

She throws away the empty soda can when the child is done with it. I wait and watch from a corner until the woman in the leotard and biker's shorts returns, sweaty and breathless, an hour later. My mother gives the woman back her child and strolls farther into the park.

I turn around and start to walk out of the park before my mother can see me. My lunch hour is long since gone. I have to hurry back to work. I walk through a cluster of joggers, then race to a *Sweden Tours* bus. I stand behind the bus and take a peek at my mother in the park. She is standing in a circle, chatting with a group of women who are taking other people's children on an afternoon outing. They look like a Third World Parent-Teacher Association meeting.

I quickly jump into a cab heading back to the office. Would Ma have said hello had she been the one to see me first?

As the cab races away from the park, it occurs to me that perhaps one day I would chase an old woman down a street by mistake and that old woman would be somebody else's mother, who I would have mistaken for mine.

Day women come out when nobody expects them.

Tonight on the subway, I will get up and give my seat to a pregnant woman or a lady about Ma's age.
My mother, who stuffs thimbles in her mouth and then blows up her cheeks like Dizzy Gillespie while sewing yet another Raggedy Ann doll that she names Suzette after me.

I will have all these little Suzettes in case you never have any babies, which looks more and more like it is going to happen.

My mother who had me when she was thirty-three—*l'âge du Christ*—at the age that Christ died on the cross.

That's a blessing, believe you me, even if American doctors say by that time you can make retarded babies.

My mother, who sews lace collars on my company softball T-shirts when she does my laundry.

Why, you can't you look like a lady playing softball?

My mother, who never went to any of my Parent-Teacher Association meetings when I was in school.

You're so good anyway. What are they going to tell me? I don't want to make you ashamed of this day woman. Shame is heavier than a hundred bags of salt.

NEGOCIOS (1996)

Junot Díaz

"Negocios" is the story of the narrator Yunior's father, Ramon, an immigrant from the Dominican Republic who makes his way to New York City: "Nueva York was the city of jobs." Yunior imagines and investigates those several years that Papi spent in New York before he finally returned to Santo Domingo to fetch his wife and children. "Negocios" is the last story in Drown *(1996), Díaz's first book. Junot Díaz (born in 1968) lives in Cambridge, Massachusetts, where he teaches writing at the Massachusetts Institute of Technology, as well as in New York City.*

MY FATHER, RAMÓN de las Casas, left Santo Domingo just before my fourth birthday. Papi had been planning to leave for months, hustling and borrowing from his friends, from anyone he could put the bite on. In the end it was just plain luck that got his visa processed when it did. The last of his luck on the Island, considering that Mami had recently discovered he was keeping with an overweight puta he had met while breaking up a fight on her street in Los Millonitos. Mami learned this from a friend of hers, a nurse and a neighbor of the puta. The nurse couldn't understand what Papi was doing loafing around her street when he was supposed to be on patrol.

The initial fights, with Mami throwing our silverware into wild orbits, lasted a week. After a fork pierced him in the cheek, Papi decided to move out, just until things cooled down. He took a small bag of clothes and broke out early in the morning. On his second night away from the house, with the puta asleep at his side, Papi had a dream that the money Mami's father had promised him was spiraling away in the wind like bright bright birds. The dream blew him out of bed like a gunshot. Are you OK? the puta asked and he shook his head. I think I have to go somewhere, he said. He borrowed a clean mustard-colored guayabera from a friend, put himself in a concho and paid our abuelo a visit.

Abuelo had his rocking chair in his usual place, out on the sidewalk where he could see everyone and everything. He had fashioned that chair as a thirtieth-birthday present to himself and twice had to replace the wicker screens that his ass and shoulders had worn out. If you were to walk down to the Duarte you would see that type of chair for sale everywhere. It was November, the mangoes were thudding from the trees. Despite his dim eyesight, Abuelo saw Papi coming the moment he stepped onto Sumner Welles. Abuelo sighed, he'd had it up to his cojones with this spat. Papi hiked up his pants and squatted down next to the rocking chair.

I am here to talk to you about my life with your daughter, he said, removing his hat. I don't know what you've heard but I swear on my heart that none of it is true. All I want for your daughter and our children is to take them to the United States. I want a good life for them.

Abuelo searched his pockets for the cigarette he had just put away. The neighbors were gravitating towards the front of their houses to listen to the exchange. What about this other woman? Abuelo said finally, unable to find the cigarette tucked behind his ear.

It's true I went to her house, but that was a mistake. I did nothing to shame you, viejo. I know it wasn't a smart thing to do, but I didn't know the woman would lie like she did.

Is that what you said to Virta?

Yes, but she won't listen. She cares too much about what she hears from her friends. If you don't think I can do anything for your daughter then I won't ask to borrow that money.

Abuelo spit the taste of car exhaust and street dust from his mouth. He might have spit four or five times. The sun could have set twice on his deliberations but with his eyes quitting, his farm in Azua now dust and his familia in need, what could he really do?

Listen Ramón, he said, scratching his arm hairs. I believe you. But Virta, she hears the chisme on the street and you know how that is. Come home and be good to her. Don't yell. Don't hit the children. I'll tell her that you are leaving soon. That will help smooth things between the two of you.

Papi fetched his things from the puta's house and moved back in that night. Mami acted as if he were a troublesome visitor who had to be endured. She slept with the children and stayed out of the house as often as she could, visiting her relatives in other parts of the Capital. Many times Papi took hold of her arms and pushed her against the slumping walls of the house, thinking his touch would snap her from her brooding silence, but instead she slapped or kicked him. Why the hell do you do that? he demanded. Don't you know how soon I'm leaving?

Then go, she said.

You'll regret that.

She shrugged and said nothing else.

In a house as loud as ours, one woman's silence was a serious thing. Papi slouched about for a month, taking us to kung fu movies we couldn't understand and drilling into us how much we'd miss him. He'd hover around Mami while she checked our hair for lice, wanting to be nearby the instant she cracked and begged him to stay.

One night Abuelo handed Papi a cigar box stuffed with cash. The bills were new and smelled of ginger. Here it is. Make your children proud.

You'll see. He kissed the viejo's cheek and the next day had himself a ticket for a flight leaving in three days. He held the ticket in front of Mami's eyes. Do you see this?

She nodded tiredly and took up his hands. In their room, she already had his clothes packed and mended.

She didn't kiss him when he left. Instead she sent each of the children over to him. Say good-bye to your father. Tell him that you want him back soon.

When he tried to embrace her she grabbed his upper arms, her fingers like pincers. You had best remember where this money came from, she said, the last words they exchanged face-to-face for five years.

He arrived in Miami at four in the morning in a roaring poorly booked plane. He passed easily through customs, having brought nothing but some clothes, a towel, a bar of soap, a razor, his money and a box of Chiclets in his pocket. The ticket to Miami had saved him money but he intended to continue on to Nueva York as soon as he could. Nueva York was the city of jobs, the city that had first called the Cubanos and their cigar industry, then the Bootstrap Puerto Ricans and now him.

He had trouble finding his way out of the terminal. Everyone was speaking English and the signs were no help. He smoked half a pack of cigarettes while wandering around. When he finally exited the terminal, he rested his bag on the sidewalk and threw away the rest of the cigarettes. In the darkness he could see little of Northamerica. A vast stretch of cars, distant palms and a highway that reminded him of the Máximo Gomez. The air was not as hot as home and the city was well lit but he didn't feel as if he had crossed an ocean and a world. A cabdriver in front of the terminal called to him in Spanish and threw his bag easily in the back seat of the cab. A new one, he said. The man was black, stooped and strong.

You got family here?

Not really.

How about an address?

Nope, Papi said. I'm here on my own. I got two hands and a heart as strong as a rock.

Right, the taxi driver said. He toured Papi through the city, around Calle Ocho. Although the streets were empty and accordion gates stretched in front of storefronts Papi recognized the prosperity in the buildings and in the tall operative lampposts. He indulged himself in the feeling that he was being shown his new digs to ensure that they met with his approval. Find a place to sleep here, the driver advised. And first thing tomorrow get yourself a job. Anything you can find.

I'm here to work.

Sure, said the driver. He dropped Papi off at a hotel and charged him five dollars for half an hour of service. Whatever you save on me will help you later. I hope you do well.

Papi offered the driver a tip but the driver was already pulling away, the dome atop his cab glowing, calling another fare. Shouldering his bag, Papi began to stroll, smelling the dust and the heat filtering up from the pressed rock of the streets. At first he considered saving money by sleeping outside on a bench but he was without guides and the inscrutability of the nearby signs unnerved him. What if there was a curfew? He knew that the slightest turn of fortune could dash him. How many before him had gotten this far only to get sent back for some stupid infraction? The sky was suddenly too high. He walked back the way he had come and went into the hotel, its spastic neon sign obtrusively jutting into the street. He had difficulty understanding the man at the desk, but finally the man wrote down the amount for a night's stay in block numbers. Room cuatro-cuatro, the man said. Papi had as much difficulty working the shower but finally was able to take a bath. It was the first bathroom he'd been in that hadn't curled the hair on his body. With the radio tuned in and incoherent, he trimmed his mustache. No photos exist of his mustache days but it is easily imagined. Within an hour he was asleep. He was twenty-four. He didn't dream about his familia and wouldn't for many years. He dreamed instead of gold coins, like the ones that had been salvaged from the many wrecks about our island, stacked high as sugar cane.

Even on his first disorienting morning, as an aged Latina snapped the sheets from the bed and emptied the one piece of scrap paper he'd thrown in the trash can, Papi pushed himself through the sit-ups and push-ups that kept him kicking ass until his forties.

You should try these, he told the Latina. They make work a lot easier.

If you had a job, she said, you wouldn't need exercise.

He stored the clothes he had worn the day before in his canvas shoulder bag and assembled a new outfit. He used his fingers and water to flatten out the worst of the wrinkles. During the years he'd lived with Mami, he'd washed and ironed his own clothes. These things were a man's job, he liked to say, proud of his own upkeep. Razor creases on his pants and resplendent white shirts were his trademarks. His generation had, after all, been weaned on the sarto-rial lunacy of the Jefe, who had owned just under ten thousand ties on the eve of his assassination. Dressed as he was, trim and serious, Papi looked foreign but not mojado.

That first day he chanced on a share in an apartment with three Guatemalans and his first job washing dishes at a Cuban sandwich shop. Once an old gringo diner of the hamburger-and-soda variety, the shop now filled with Óyeme's and the aroma of lechón. Sandwich pressers clamped down methodically behind the front counter. The man reading the newspaper in the back told Papi he could start right away and gave him two white ankle-length aprons. Wash these every day, he said. We stay clean around here.

Two of Papi's flatmates were brothers, Stefan and Tomás Hernández. Stefan was older than Tomás by twenty years. Both had families back home. Cataracts were slowly obscuring Stefan's eyes; the disease had cost him half a finger and his last job. He now swept floors and cleaned up vomit at the train station. This is a lot safer, he told my father. Working at a fábrica will kill you long before any tíguere will. Stefan had a passion for the track and would read the forms, despite his brother's warnings that he was ruining what was left of his eyes, by bringing his face down to the type. The tip of his nose was often capped in ink.

Eulalio was the third apartment-mate. He had the largest room to himself and owned the rusted-out Duster that brought them to work every morning. He'd been in the States close to two years and when he met Papi he spoke to him in English. When Papi didn't answer, Eulalio switched to Spanish. You're going to have to practice if you expect to get anywhere. How much English do you know?

None, Papi said after a moment.

Eulalio shook his head. Papi met Eulalio last and liked him least.

Papi slept in the living room, first on a carpet whose fraying threads kept sticking to his shaved head, and then on a mattress he salvaged from a neighbor. He worked two long shifts a day at the shop and had two four-hour breaks in between. On one of the breaks he slept at home and on the other he would handwash his aprons in the shop's sink and then nap in the storage room while the aprons dried, amidst the towers of El Pico coffee cans and sacks of bread. Sometimes he read the Western dreadfuls he was fond of—he could read one in about an hour. If it was too hot or he was bored by his book, he walked the neighborhoods, amazed at streets unblocked by sewage and the orderliness of the cars and houses. He was impressed with the transplanted Latinas, who had been transformed by good diets and beauty products unimagined back home.

They were beautiful but unfriendly women. He would touch a finger to his beret and stop, hoping to slip in a comment or two, but these women would walk right on by, grimacing.

He wasn't discouraged. He began joining Eulalio on his nightly jaunts to the bars. Papi would have gladly shared a drink with the Devil rather than go out alone. The Hernández brothers weren't much for the outings; they were hoarders, though occasionally they cut loose, blinding themselves on tequila and beers. The brothers would stumble home late, stepping on Papi, howling about some morena who had spurned them to their faces.

Eulalio and Papi went out two, three nights a week, drinking rum and stalking. Whenever he could, Papi let Eulalio do the buying. Eulalio liked to talk about the finca he had come from, a large plantation near the center of his country. I fell in love with the daughter of the owner and she fell in love with me. Me, a peon.

Can you believe that? I would fuck her on her own mother's bed, in sight of the Holy Mother and her crucified Son. I tried to make her take down that cross but she wouldn't hear of it. She loved it that way. She was the one who lent me the money to come here. Can you believe that? One of these days, when I got a little money on the side I'm going to send for her.

It was the same story, seasoned differently, every night. Papi said little, believed less. He watched the women who were always with other men. After an hour or two, Papi would pay his bill and leave. Even though the weather was cool, he didn't need a jacket and liked to push through the breeze in shortsleeved shirts. He'd walk the mile home, talking to anyone who would let him. Occasionally drunkards would stop at his Spanish and invite him to a house where men and women were drinking and dancing. He liked those parties far better than the face-offs at the bars. It was with these strangers that he practiced his fledgling English, away from Eulalio's gleeful criticisms.

At the apartment, he'd lie down on his mattress, stretching out his limbs to fill it as much as he could. He abstained from thoughts of home, from thoughts of his two bellicose sons and the wife he had nicknamed Melao. He told himself, Think only of today and tomorrow. Whenever he felt weak, he'd take from under the couch the road map he bought at a gas station and trace his fingers up the coast, enunciating the city names slowly, trying to copy the awful crunch of sounds that was English. The northern coast of our island was visible on the bottom right-hand corner of the map.

He left Miami in the winter. He'd lost his job and gained a new one but neither paid enough and the cost of the living room floor was too great. Besides, Papi had figured out from a few calculations and from talking to the gringa downstairs (who now understood him) that Eulalio wasn't paying culo for rent. Which explained why he had so many fine clothes and didn't work nearly as much as the rest. When Papi showed the figures to the Hernández brothers, written on the border of a newspaper, they were indifferent. He's the one with the car, they said, Stefan blinking at the numbers. Besides, who wants to start trouble here? We'll all be moving on anyway.

But this isn't right, Papi said. I'm living like a dog for this shit.

What can you do? Tomás said. Life smacks everybody around.

We'll see about that.

There are two stories about what happened next, one from Papi, one from Mami: either Papi left peacefully with a suitcase filled with Eulalio's best clothes or he beat the man first, and then took a bus and the suitcase to Virginia.

Papi logged most of the miles after Virginia on foot. He could have afforded another bus ticket but that would have bitten into the rent money he had so diligently saved on the advice of many a veteran immigrant. To be homeless in Nueva York was to court the worst sort of disaster. Better to walk 380 miles than to arrive completely broke. He stored his savings in a fake alligator change purse sewn into the seam of his boxer shorts. Though the purse blistered his thigh, it was in a place no thief would search.

He walked in his bad shoes, froze and learned to distinguish different cars by the sounds of their motors. The cold wasn't as much a bother as his bags were. His arms ached from carrying them, especially the meat of his biceps. Twice he hitched rides from truckers who took pity on the shivering man and just outside of Delaware a K-car stopped him on the side of I-95.

These men were federal marshals. Papi recognized them immediately as police; he knew the type. He studied their car and considered running into the woods behind him. His visa had expired five weeks earlier and if caught, he'd go home in chains. He'd heard plenty of tales about the Northamerican police from other illegals, how they liked to beat you before they turned you over to la migra and how sometimes they just took your money and tossed you out toothless on an abandoned road. For some reason, perhaps the whipping cold, perhaps stupidity, Papi stayed where he was, shuffling and sniffing. A window rolled down on the car. Papi went over and looked in on two sleepy blancos.

You need a ride?

Jes, Papi said.

The men squeezed together and Papi slipped into the front seat. Ten miles passed before he could feel his ass again. When the chill and the roar of passing cars finally left him, he realized that a fragile-looking man, handcuffed and shackled, sat in the back seat. The small man wept quietly.

How far you going? the driver asked.

New York, he said, carefully omitting the Nueva and the Yol.

We ain't going that far but you can ride with us to Trenton if you like. Where the hell you from pal?

Miami.

Miami. Miami's kind of far from here. The other man looked at the driver. Are you a musician or something?

Jes, Papi said. I play the accordion.

That excited the man in the middle. Shit, my old man played the accordion but he was a Polack like me. I didn't know you spiks played it too. What kind of polkas do you like?

Polkas?

Jesus, Will, the driver said. They don't play polkas in Cuba.

They drove on, slowing only to unfold their badges at the tolls. Papi sat still and listened to the man crying in the back. What is wrong? Papi asked. Maybe sick?

The driver snorted. Him sick? We're the ones who are about to puke.

What's your name? the Polack asked.

Ramón.

Ramón, meet Scott Carlson Porter, murderer.

Murderer?

Many many murders. Mucho murders.

He's been crying since we left Georgia, the driver explained. He hasn't stopped. Not once. The little pussy cries even when we're eating. He's driving us nuts.

We thought maybe having another person inside with us would shut him up—the man next to Papi shook his head—but I guess not.

The marshals dropped Papi off in Trenton. He was so relieved not to be in jail that he didn't mind walking the four hours it took to summon the nerve to put his thumb out again.

His first year in Nueva York he lived in Washington Heights, in a roachy flat above what's now the Tres Marías restaurant. As soon as he secured his apartment and two jobs, one cleaning offices and the other washing dishes, he started writing home. In the first letter he folded four twenty-dollar bills. The trickles of money he sent back were not premeditated like those sent by his other friends, calculated from what he needed to survive; these were arbitrary sums that often left him broke and borrowing until the next payday.

The first year he worked nineteen-, twenty-hour days, seven days a week. Out in the cold he coughed explosively, feeling as if his lungs were tearing open from the force of his exhales and in the kitchens the heat from the ovens sent pain corkscrewing into his head. He wrote home sporadically. Mami forgave him for what he had done and told him who else had left the barrio, via coffin or plane ticket. Papi's replies were scribbled on whatever he could find, usually the thin cardboard of tissue boxes or pages from the bill books at work. He was so tired from working that he misspelled almost everything and had to bite his lip to stay awake. He promised her and the children tickets soon. The pictures he received from Mami were shared with his friends at work and then forgotten in his wallet, lost between old lottery slips.

The weather was no good. He was sick often but was able to work through it and succeeded in saving up enough money to start looking for a wife to marry. It was the old routine, the oldest of the postwar maromas. Find a citizen, get married, wait, and then divorce her. The routine was well practiced and expensive and riddled with swindlers.

A friend of his at work put him in touch with a portly balding blanco named el General. They met at a bar. El General had to eat two plates of greasy onion rings before he talked business. Look here friend, el General said. You pay me fifty bills and I bring you a woman that's interested. Whatever the two of you decide is up to you. All I care is that I get paid and that the women I bring are for real. You get no refunds if you can't work something out with her.

Why the hell don't I just go out looking for myself?

Sure, you can do that. He patted vegetable oil on Papi's hand. But I'm the one who takes the risk of running into Immigration. If you don't mind that then you can go out looking anywhere you want.

Even to Papi fifty bucks wasn't exorbitant but he was reluctant to part with it. He had no problem buying rounds at the bar or picking up a new belt when the colors and the moment suited him but this was different. He didn't want to deal with any more change. Don't get me wrong: it wasn't that he was having fun. No, he'd been robbed twice already, his ribs beaten until they were bruised. He often drank too much and went home to his room, and there he'd fume, spinning, angry at the stupidity that had brought him to this freezing hell of a country, angry that a man his age had to masturbate when he had a wife, and angry at the blinkered existence his jobs and the city imposed on him. He never had time to

sleep, let alone to go to a concert or the museums that filled entire
sections of the newspapers. And the roaches. The roaches were so
bold in his flat that turning on the lights did not startle them. They
waved their three-inch antennas as if to say, Hey puto, turn that shit
off. He spent five minutes stepping on their carapaced bodies and
shaking them from his mattress before dropping into his cot and still
the roaches crawled on him at night. No, he wasn't having fun but
he also wasn't ready to start bringing his family over. Getting legal
would place his hand firmly on that first rung. He wasn't so sure he
could face us so soon. He asked his friends, most of whom were in
worse financial shape than he was, for advice.

They assumed he was reluctant because of the money. Don't be
a pendejo, hombre. Give fulano his money and that's it. Maybe you
make good, maybe you don't. That's the way it is. They built these
barrios out of bad luck and you got to get used to that.

He met el General across from the Boricua Cafeteria and handed
him the money. A day later the man gave him a name: Flor de Oro.
That isn't her real name of course, el General assured Papi. I like to
keep things historical.

They met at the cafeteria. Each of them had an empanada and a
glass of soda. Flor was businesslike, about fifty. Her gray hair coiled
in a bun on top of her head. She smoked while Papi talked, her
hands speckled like the shell of an egg.

Are you Dominican? Papi asked.

No.

You must be Cuban then.

One thousand dollars and you'll be too busy being an American
to care where I'm from.

That seems like a lot of money. Do you think once I become a
citizen I could make money marrying people?

I don't know.

Papi threw two dollars down on the counter and stood.

How much then? How much do you have?

I work so much that sitting here is like having a week's vacation.
Still I only have six hundred.

Find two hundred more and we got a deal.

Papi brought her the money the next day stuffed in a wrinkled
paper bag and in return was given a pink receipt. When do we get
started? he asked.

Next week. I have to start on the paperwork right away.

He pinned the receipt over his bed and before he went to sleep, he checked behind it to be sure no roaches lurked. His friends were excited and the boss at the cleaning job took them out for drinks and appetizers in Harlem, where their Spanish drew more looks than their frumpy clothes. Their excitement was not his; he felt as if he'd moved too precipitously. A week later, Papi went to see the friend who had recommended el General.

I still haven't gotten a call, he explained. The friend was scrubbing down a counter.

You will. The friend didn't look up. A week later Papi lay in bed, drunk, alone, knowing full well that he'd been robbed.

He lost the cleaning job shortly thereafter for punching the friend off a ladder. He lost his apartment and had to move in with a familia and found another job frying wings and rice at a Chinese take-out joint. Before he left his flat, he wrote an account of what had happened to him on the pink receipt and left it on the wall as a warning to whatever fool came next to take his place. Ten cuidado, he wrote. These people are worse than sharks.

He sent no money home for close to six months. Mami's letters would be read and folded and tucked into his well-used bags.

Papi met her on the morning before Christmas, in a laundry, while folding his pants and knotting his damp socks. She was short, had daggers of black hair pointing down in front of her ears and lent him her iron. She was originally from La Romana, but like so many Dominicans had eventually moved to the Capital.

I go back there about once a year, she told Papi. Usually around Pascua to see my parents and my sister.

I haven't been home in a long long time. I'm still trying to get the money together.

It will happen, believe me. It took me years before I could go back my first time.

Papi found out she'd been in the States for six years, a citizen. Her English was excellent. While he packed his things in his nylon bag, he considered asking her to the party. A friend had invited him to a house in Corona, Queens, where fellow Dominicans were celebrating la Noche Buena together. He knew from a past party that up in Queens the food, dancing and single women came in heaps.

Four children were trying to pry open the plate at the top of a dryer to reach the coin mechanism underneath. My fucking quarter is stuck, a kid was shouting. In the corner, a student, still in medical greens, was trying to read a magazine and not be noticed but as soon as the kids were tired of the machine, they descended on him, pulling at his magazine and pushing their hands into his pockets. He began to shove back.

Hey, Papi said. The kids threw him the finger and ran outside. Fuck all spiks! they shrieked.

Niggers, the medical student muttered. Papi pulled the drawstring shut on his bag and decided against asking her. He knew the rule: Strange is the woman who goes strange places with a complete stranger. Instead, Papi asked her if he could practice his English on her one day. I really need to practice, he said. And I'd be willing to pay you for your time.

She laughed. Don't be ridiculous. Stop by when you can. She wrote her number and address in crooked letters.

Papi squinted at the paper. You don't live around here?

No but my cousin does. I can give you her number if you want.

No, this will be fine.

He had a grand time at the party and actually avoided the rum and the six-packs he liked to down. He sat with two older women and their husbands, a plate of food on his lap (potato salad, pieces of roast chicken, a stack of tostones, half an avocado and a tiny splattering of mondongo out of politeness to the woman who'd brought it) and talked about his days in Santo Domingo. It was a lucid enjoyable night that would stick out in his memory like a spike. He swaggered home around one o'clock, bearing a plastic bag loaded with food and a loaf of telera under his arm. He gave the bread to the shivering man sleeping in the hallway of his building.

When he called Nilda a few days later he found out from a young girl who spoke in politely spaced words that she was at work. Papi left his name and called back that night. Nilda answered.

Ramón, you should have called me yesterday. It was a good day to start since neither of us had work.

I wanted to let you celebrate the holiday with your family.

Family? she clucked. I only have a daughter here. What are you doing now? Maybe you want to come over.

I wouldn't want to intrude, he said because he was a sly one, you had to admit that.

She owned the top floor of a house on a bleak quiet street in Brooklyn. The house was clean, with cheap bubbled linoleum covering the floors. Nilda's taste struck Ramón as low-class. She threw together styles and colors the way a child might throw together paint or clay. A bright orange plaster elephant reared up from the center of a low glass table. A tapestry of a herd of mustangs hung opposite vinyl cutouts of African singers. Fake plants relaxed in each room. Her daughter Milagros was excruciatingly polite and seemed to have an endless supply of dresses more fit for quinceañeras than everyday life. She wore thick plastic glasses and sat in front of the television when Papi visited, one skinny leg crossed over the other. Nilda had a well-stocked kitchen and Papi cooked for her, his stockpile of Cantonese and Cuban recipes inexhaustible. His ropa vieja was his best dish and he was glad to see he had surprised her. I should have you in my kitchen, she said.

She liked to talk about the restaurant she owned and her last husband, who had a habit of hitting her and expecting that all his friends be fed for free. Nilda wasted hours of their study time caught between the leaves of tome-sized photo albums, showing Papi each stage of Milagros's development as if the girl were an exotic bug. He did not mention his own familia. Two weeks into his English lessons, Papi kissed Nilda. They were sitting on the plastic-covered sofa, in the next room a game show was on the TV, and his lips were greasy from Nilda's pollo guisado.

I think you better leave, she said.

You mean now?

Yes, now.

He drew on his windbreaker as slowly as he could, expecting her to recant. She held open the door and shut it quickly after him. He cursed her the entire train ride back into Manhattan. The next day at work, he told his co-workers that she was insane and had a snake coiled up in her heart. I should've known, he said bitterly. A week later he was back at her house, grating coconuts and talking in English. He tried again and again she had him leave.

Each time he kissed her she threw him out. It was a cold winter and he didn't have much of a coat. Nobody bought coats then, Papi told me, because nobody was expecting to stay that long. So I kept going back and any chance I got I kissed her. She would tense up and tell me to leave, like I'd hit her. So I would kiss her again and she'd say, Oh, I really think you better leave now. She was a crazy lady. I kept it up and one day she kissed me back. Finally. By then

I knew every maldito train in the city and I had this big wool coat and two pairs of gloves. I looked like an Eskimo. Like an American.

Within a month Papi moved out of his apartment into her house in Brooklyn. They were married in March.

Although he wore a ring, Papi didn't act the part of the husband. He lived in Nilda's house, shared her bed, paid no rent, ate her food, talked to Milagros when the TV was broken and set up his weight bench in the cellar. He regained his health and liked to show Nilda how his triceps and biceps could gather in prominent knots with a twist of his arm. He bought his shirts in size medium so he could fill them out.

He worked two jobs close to her house. The first soldering at a radiator shop, plugging holes mostly, the other as a cook at a Chinese restaurant. The owners of the restaurant were Chinese-Cubans; they cooked a better arroz negro than pork fried rice and loved to spend the quiet hours between lunch and dinner slapping dominos with Papi and the other help on top of huge drums of shortening. One day, while adding up his totals, Papi told these men about his familia in Santo Domingo.

The chief cook, a man so skinny they called him Needle, soured. You can't forget your familia like that. Didn't they support you to send you here?

I'm not forgetting them, Papi said defensively. Right now is just not a good time for me to send for them. You should see my bills.

What bills?

Papi thought a moment. Electricity. That's very expensive. My house has eighty-eight light bulbs.

What kind of house are you living in?

Very big. An antique house needs a lot of bulbs, you know.

Come mierda. Nobody has that many light bulbs in their house.

You better do more playing and less talking or I'm going to have to take all your money.

These harangues must not have bothered his conscience much because that year he sent no money.

Nilda learned about Papi's other familia from a chain of friends that reached back across the Caribe. It was inevitable. She was upset and Papi had to deliver some of his most polished performances to convince her that he no longer cared about us. He'd been fortunate in that when Mami reached back across a similar chain of immigrants to locate Papi in the north, he'd told her to direct her letters to the restaurant he was working at and not to Nilda's home.

As with most of the immigrants around them, Nilda was usually at work. The couple saw each other mostly in the evenings. Nilda not only had her restaurant, where she served a spectacular and popular sancocho with wedges of cold avocado, but she also pushed her tailoring on the customers. If a man had a torn work shirt or a pant cuff soiled in machine oil, she'd tell him to bring it by, that she'd take care of it, cheap. She had a loud voice and could draw the attention of the entire eatery to a shabby article of clothing and few, under the combined gaze of their peers, could resist her. She brought the clothes home in a garbage bag and spent her time off sewing and listening to the radio, getting up only to bring Ramón a beer or change the channel for him. When she had to bring money home from the register, her skills at secreting it away were uncanny. She kept nothing but coins in her purse and switched her hiding place each trip. Usually she lined her bra with twenty-dollar bills as if each cup was a nest but Papi was amazed at her other ploys. After a crazy day of mashing platanos and serving the workers, she sealed nearly nine hundred dollars in twenties and fifties in a sandwich bag and then forced the bag into the mouth of a Malta bottle. She put a straw in there and sipped on it on her way home. She never lost a brown penny in the time she and Papi were together. If she wasn't too tired she liked to have him guess where she was hiding the money and with each wrong guess he'd remove a piece of her clothing until the cache was found.

Papi's best friend at this time, and Nilda's neighbor, was Jorge Carretas Lugones, or Jo-Jo as he was commonly known in the barrio. Jo-Jo was a five-foot-tall Puerto Rican whose light skin was stippled with moles and whose blue eyes were the color of larimar. On the street, he wore a pava, angled in the style of the past, carried a pen and all the local lotteries in his shirt pockets, and would have struck anyone as a hustler. Jo-Jo owned two hot dog carts and co-owned a grocery store that was very prosperous. It had once been a tired place with rotting wood and cracked tiles but with his two brothers he'd pulled the porquería out and rebuilt it over the four months of one winter, while driving a taxi and working as a translator and letter-writer for a local patrón. The years of doubling the price on toilet paper, soap and diapers to pay the loan sharks were over. The coffin refrigerators lining one wall were new, as were the bright green lottery machine and the revolving racks of junk food at the end of each short shelf. He was disdainful of anyone who had a regular crowd of parasites loafing about their stores, discussing the taste of yuca and their last lays. And though this neighborhood was rough (not as bad as his old barrio in San Juan where he had seen all his best friends lose fingers in machete fights), Jo-Jo didn't need to put a grate over his store. The local kids left him alone and instead terrorized a Pakistani family down the street. The family owned an Asian grocery store that looked like a holding cell, windows behind steel mesh, door reinforced with steel plates.

Jo-Jo and Papi met at the local bar regularly. Papi was the man who knew the right times to laugh and when he did, everyone around him joined in. He was always reading newspapers and sometimes books and seemed to know many things. Jo-Jo saw in Papi another brother, a man from a luckless past needing a little direction. Jo-Jo had already rehabilitated two of his siblings, who were on their way to owning their own stores.

Now that you have a place and papers, Jo-Jo told Papi, you need to use these things to your advantage. You have some time, you don't have to break your ass paying the rent, so use it. Save some money and buy yourself a little business. I'll sell you one of my hot dog carts cheap if you want. You can see they're making steady plata. Then you get your familia over here and buy yourself a nice house and start branching out. That's the American way.

Papi wanted a negocio of his own, that was his dream, but he balked at starting at the bottom, selling hot dogs. While most of the men around him were two-times broke, he had seen a few, fresh off the boat, shake the water from their backs and jump right into the lowest branches of the American establishment. That leap was what he envisioned for himself, not some slow upward crawl through the mud. What it would be and when it would come, he did not know.

I'm looking for the right investment, he told Jo-Jo. I'm not a food man.

What sort of man are you then? Jo-Jo demanded. You Dominicans got restaurants in your blood.

I know, Papi said, but I am not a food man.

Worse, Jo-Jo spouted a hard line on loyalty to familia which troubled Papi. Each scenario his friend proposed ended with Papi's familia living safely within his sight, showering him with love. Papi had difficulty separating the two threads of his friend's beliefs, that of negocios and that of familia, and in the end the two became impossibly intertwined.

With the hum of his new life Papi should have found it easy to bury the memory of us but neither his conscience, nor the letters from home that found him wherever he went, would allow it. Mami's letters, as regular as the months themselves, were corrosive slaps in the face. It was now a one-sided correspondence, with Papi reading and not mailing anything back. He opened the letters wincing in anticipation. Mami detailed how his children were suffering, how his littlest boy was so anemic people thought he was a corpse come back to life; she told him about his oldest son, playing in the barrio, tearing open his feet and exchanging blows with his so-called friends. Mami refused to talk about her condition. She called Papi a desgraciado and a puto of the highest order for abandoning them, a traitor worm, an eater of pubic lice, a cockless, ball-less cabrón. He showed Jo-Jo the letters, often at drunken bitter moments, and Jo-Jo would shake his head, waving for two more beers. You, my compadre, have done too many things wrong. If you keep this up, your life will spring apart.

What in the world can I do? What does this woman want from me? I've been sending her money. Does she want me to starve up here?

You and I know what you have to do. That's all I can say, otherwise I'd be wasting my breath.

Papi was lost. He would take long perilous night walks home from his jobs, sometimes arriving with his knuckles scuffed and his clothes disheveled. His and Nilda's child was born in the spring, a son, also named Ramón, cause for fiesta but there was no celebration among his friends. Too many of them knew. Nilda could sense that something was wrong, that a part of him was detained elsewhere but each time she brought it up Papi told her it was nothing, always nothing.

With a regularity that proved instructional, Jo-Jo had Papi drive him to Kennedy to meet one or the other of the relatives Jo-Jo had sponsored to come to the States to make it big. Despite his prosperity, Jo-Jo could not drive and did not own a car. Papi would borrow Nilda's Chevy station wagon and would fight the traffic for an hour to reach the airport. Depending on the season, Jo-Jo would bring either a number of coats or a cooler of beverages taken from his shelves—a rare treat since Jo-Jo's cardinal rule was that one should never prey on one's own stock. At the terminal, Papi would stand back, his hands pressed in his pockets, his beret plugged on tight, while Jo-Jo surged forward to greet his familia. Papi's English was good now, his clothes better. Jo-Jo would enter a berserk frenzy when his relatives stumbled through the arrival gate, dazed and grinning, bearing cardboard boxes and canvas bags. There would be crying and abrazos. Jo-Jo would introduce Ramón as a brother and Ramón would be dragged into the circle of crying people. It was a simple matter for Ramón to rearrange the faces of the arrivals and see his wife and his children there.

He began again to send money to his familia on the Island. Nilda noticed that he began to borrow from her for his tobacco and to play the lotteries. Why do you need my money? she complained. Isn't that the reason you're working? We have a baby to look after. There are bills to pay.

One of my children died, he said. I have to pay for the wake and the funeral. So leave me alone.

Why didn't you tell me?

He put his hands over his face but when he removed them she was still staring skeptically.

Which one? she demanded. His hand swung clumsily. She fell down and neither of them said a word.

Papi landed a union job with Reynolds Aluminum in West New York that paid triple what he was making at the radiator shop. It was nearly a two-hour commute, followed by a day of tendon-ripping labor, but he was willing—the money and the benefits were exceptional. It was the first time he had moved outside the umbra of his fellow immigrants. The racism was pronounced. The two fights he had were reported to the bosses and they put him on probation. He worked through that period, got a raise and the highest performance rating in his department and the shiniest schedule in the entire fábrica. The whites were always dumping their bad shifts on him and on his friend Chuito. Guess what, they'd say, clapping them on the back. I need a little time with my kids this week. I know you wouldn't mind taking this or that day for me.

No, my friend, Papi would say. I wouldn't mind. Once Chuito complained to the bosses and was written up for detracting *from the familial spirit of the department*. Both men knew better than to speak up again.

On a normal day Papi was too exhausted to visit with Jo-Jo. He'd enjoy his dinner and then settle down to watch Tom and Jerry, who delighted him with their violence. Nilda, watch this, he'd scream and she'd dutifully appear, needles in mouth, baby in her arms. Papi would laugh so loud that Milagros upstairs would join in without even seeing what had occurred. Oh, that's wonderful, he'd say. Would you look at that! They're *killing* each other!

One day, he skipped his dinner and a night in front of the TV to drive south with Chuito into New Jersey to a small town outside of Perth Amboy. Chuito's Gremlin pulled into a neighborhood under construction. Huge craters had been gouged in the earth and towering ziggurats of tan bricks stood ready to be organized into buildings. New pipes were being laid by the mile and the air was tart with the smell of chemicals. It was a cool night. The men wandered around the pits and the sleeping trucks.

I have a friend who is doing the hiring for this place, Chuito said.

Construction?

No. When this neighborhood goes up they'll need superintendents to watch over things. Keep the hot water running, stop a leaking faucet, put new tile in the bathroom. For that you get a salary and free rent. That's the kind of job worth having. The towns nearby are quiet, lots of good gringos. Listen Ramón, I can get you a job here if you like. It would be a good place to move. Out of the city, safety. I'll put your name at the top of the list and when this place is done you'll have a nice easy job.

This sounds better than a dream.

Forget dreams. This is real, compadre.

The two men inspected the site for about an hour and then headed back toward Brooklyn. Papi was silent. A plan was forming. Here was the place to move his familia if it came from the Island. Quiet and close to his job. Most important, the neighborhood would not know him or the wife he had in the States. When he reached home that night he said nothing to Nilda about where he had been. He didn't care that she was suspicious and that she yelled at him about his muddy shoes.

Papi continued to send money home and in Jo-Jo's lockbox he was saving a tidy sum for plane tickets. And then one morning, when the sun had taken hold of the entire house and the sky seemed too thin and blue to hold a cloud, Nilda said, I want to go to the Island this year.

Are you serious?

I want to see my viejos.

What about the baby?

He's never gone, has he?

No.

Then he should see his patria. I think it's important.

I agree, he said. He tapped a pen on the wrinkled place mat. This sounds like you're serious.

I think I am.

Maybe I'll go with you.

If you say so. She had reason to doubt him; he was real good at planning but real bad at doing. And she didn't stop doubting him either, until he was on the plane next to her, rifling anxiously through the catalogs, the vomit bag and the safety instructions.

He was in Santo Domingo for five days. He stayed at Nilda's familia's house on the western edge of the city.

It was painted bright orange with an outhouse slumped nearby and a pig pushing around in a pen. Homero and Josefa, tíos of Nilda, drove home with them from the airport in a cab and gave them the "bedroom." The couple slept in the other room, the "living room."

Are you going to see them? Nilda asked that first night. They were both listening to their stomachs struggling to digest the heaping meal of yuca and hígado they had eaten. Outside, the roosters were pestering each other.

Maybe, he said. If I get the time.

I know that's the only reason you're here.

What's wrong with a man seeing his familia? If you had to see your first husband for some reason, I'd let you, wouldn't I?

Does she know about me?

Of course she knows about you. Not like it matters now. She's out of the picture completely.

She didn't answer him. He listened to his heart beating, and began to sense its slick contours.

On the plane, he'd been confident. He'd talked to the vieja near the aisle, telling her how excited he was. It is always good to return home, she said tremulously. I come back anytime I can, which isn't so much anymore. Things aren't good.

Seeing the country he'd been born in, seeing his people in charge of everything, he was unprepared for it. The air whooshed out of his lungs. For nearly four years he'd not spoken his Spanish loudly in front of the Northamericans and now he was hearing it bellowed and flung from every mouth.

His pores opened, dousing him as he hadn't been doused in years. An awful heat was on the city and the red dust dried out his throat and clogged his nose. The poverty—the unwashed children pointing sullenly at his new shoes, the familias slouching in hovels—was familiar and stifling.

He felt like a tourist, riding a guagua to Boca Chica and having his and Nilda's photograph taken in front of the Alcázar de Colón. He was obliged to eat two or three times a day at various friends of Nilda's familia; he was, after all, the new successful husband from the North. He watched Josefa pluck a chicken, the wet plumage caking her hands and plastering the floor, and remembered the many times he'd done the same, up in Santiago, his first home, where he no longer belonged.

He tried to see his familia but each time he set his mind to it, his resolve scattered like leaves before a hurricane wind. Instead he saw his old friends on the force and drank six bottles of Brugal in three days. Finally, on the fourth day of his visit, he borrowed the nicest clothes he could find and folded two hundred dollars into his pocket. He took a guagua down Sumner Welles, as Calle XXI had been renamed, and cruised into the heart of his old barrio. Colmados on every block and billboards plastering every exposed wall or board. The children chased each other with hunks of cinder block from nearby buildings—a few threw rocks at the guagua, the loud pings jerking the passengers upright. The progress of the guagua was frustratingly slow, each stop seemed spaced four feet from the last. Finally, he disembarked, walking two blocks to the corner of XXI and Tunti. The air must have seemed thin then, and the sun like a fire in his hair, sending trickles of sweat down his face. He must have seen people he knew. Jayson sitting glumly at his colmado, a soldier turned grocer. Chicho, gnawing at a chicken bone, at his feet a row of newly shined shoes. Maybe Papi stopped there and couldn't go on, maybe he went as far as the house, which hadn't been painted since his departure. Maybe he even stopped at our house and stood there, waiting for his children out front to recognize him.

In the end, he never visited us. If Mami heard from her friends that he was in the city, with his other wife, she never told us about it. His absence was a seamless thing to me. And if a strange man approached me during my play and stared down at me and my brother, perhaps asking our names, I don't remember it now.

Papi returned home and had trouble resuming his routine. He took a couple of sick days, the first three ever, and spent the time in front of the television and at the bar. Twice he turned down negocios from Jo-Jo. The first ended in utter failure, cost Jo-Jo "the gold in his teeth," but the other, the FOB clothing store on Smith Street, with the bargain basement buys, the enormous bins of factory seconds and a huge layaway shelf, pulled in the money in bags. Papi had recommended the location to Jo-Jo, having heard about the vacancy from Chuito, who was still living in Perth Amboy. London Terrace Apartments had not yet opened.

After work Papi and Chuito caroused in the bars on Smith and Elm Streets and every few nights Papi stayed over in Perth Amboy. Nilda had continued to put on weight after the birth of the third Ramón and while Papi favored heavy women, he didn't favor obesity and wasn't inclined to go home. Who needs a woman like you? he told her. The couple began to fight on a regular schedule. Locks were changed, doors were broken, slaps were exchanged but weekends and an occasional weekday night were still spent together.

In the dead of summer, when the potato-scented fumes from the diesel forklifts were choking the warehouses, Papi was helping another man shove a crate into position when he felt a twinge about midway up his spine. Hey asshole, keep pushing, the other man grunted. Pulling his work shirt out of his Dickies, Papi twisted to the right, then to the left and that was it, something snapped. He fell to his knees. The pain was so intense, shooting through him like fireballs from Roman candles, that he vomited on the concrete floor of the warehouse. His co-workers moved him to the lunchroom. For two hours he tried repeatedly to walk and failed. Chuito came down from his division, concerned for his friend but also worried that this unscheduled break would piss off his boss. How are you? he asked.

Not so good. You have to get me out of here.

You know I can't leave.

Then call me a cab. Just get me home. Like anyone wounded, he thought home could save him.

Chuito called him the taxi; none of the other employees took time to help him walk out.

Nilda put him in bed and had a cousin manage the restaurant. Jesú, he moaned to her. I should've slowed down a little. Just a little bit longer and I would've been home with you. Do you know that? A couple of hours more.

She went down to the botánica for a poultice and then down to the bodega for aspirin. Let's see how well the old magic works, she said, smearing the poultice onto his back.

For two days he couldn't move, not even his head. He ate very little, strictly soups she concocted. More than once he fell asleep and woke up to find Nilda out, shopping for medicinal teas, and Milagros over him, a grave owl in her large glasses. Mi hija, he said. I feel like I'm dying.

You won't die, she said.

And what if I do?

Then Mama will be alone.

He closed his eyes and prayed that she would be gone and when he opened them, she was and Nilda was coming in through the door with another remedy, steaming on a battered tray.

He was able to sit up and call in sick by himself on the fourth day. He told the morning-shift manager that he couldn't move too well. I think I stay in bed, he said. The manager told him to come in so he could receive a medical furlough. Papi had Milagros find the name of a lawyer in the phone book. He was thinking lawsuit. He had dreams, fantastic dreams of gold rings and a spacious house with caged tropical birds in its rooms, a house awash with sea winds. The woman lawyer he contacted only worked divorces but she gave him the name of her brother.

Nilda wasn't optimistic about his plan. Do you think the gringo will part with his money like that? The reason they're so pale is because they're terrified of not having any plata. Have you even spoken to the man you were helping? He's probably going to be a witness for the company so that he won't lose his job the same way you're going to lose yours. That maricón will probably get a raise for it, too.

I'm not an illegal, he said. I'm protected.

I think it's better if you let it drop.

He called Chuito to sound him out. Chuito wasn't optimistic either. The boss knows what you're trying to yank. He no like it, compadre. He say you better get back to work or you're quitted.

His courage failing, Papi started pricing a consultation with an independent doctor. Very likely, his father's foot was hopping about in his mind. His father, José Edilio, the loudmouthed ball-breaking vagrant who had never married Papi's mother but nevertheless had given her nine children, had attempted a similar stunt when he worked in a hotel kitchen in Río Piedras. Jose had accidentally dropped a tin of stewed tomatoes on his foot. Two small bones broke but instead of seeing a doctor, Jose kept working, limping around the kitchen. Every day at work, he'd smile at his fellow workers and say, I guess it's time to take care of that foot. Then he'd smash another can on it, figuring the worse it was, the more money he'd get when he finally showed the bosses. It saddened and shamed Papi to hear of this while he was growing up. The old man was rumored to have wandered the barrio he lived in, trying to find someone who would take a bat to the foot. For the old man that foot was an investment, an heirloom he cherished and burnished, until half of it had to be amputated because the infection was so bad.

After another week and with no calls from the lawyers, Papi saw the company doctor. His spine felt as if there were broken glass inside of it but he was given only three weeks of medical leave. Ignoring the instructions on the medication, he swallowed ten pills a day for the pain. He got better. When he returned to the job he could work and that was enough. The bosses were unanimous, however, in voting down Papi's next raise. They demoted him to the rotating shift he'd been on during the first days of the job.

Instead of taking his licks, he blamed it on Nilda. Puta, was what he took to calling her. They fought with renewed vigor; the orange elephant was knocked over and lost a tusk. She kicked him out twice but after probationary weeks at Jo-Jo's allowed him to return. He saw less of his son, avoiding all of the daily routines that fed and maintained the infant. The third Ramón was a handsome child who roamed the house restlessly, tilted forward and at full speed, as if he were a top that had been sent spinning. Papi was good at playing with the baby, pulling him by his foot across the floor and tickling his sides, but as soon as the third Ramón started to fuss, playtime was over. Nilda, come and tend to this, he'd say.

The third Ramón resembled Papi's other sons and on occasion he'd say, Yunior, don't do that. If Nilda heard these slips she would explode. Maldito, she'd cry, picking up the child and retreating with Milagros into the bedroom. Papi didn't screw up too often but

he was never certain how many times he'd called the third Ramón
with the second son Ramón in mind.

With his back killing him and his life with Nilda headed down
the toilet, Papi began more and more to regard his departure as
inevitable. His first familia was the logical destination. He began to
see them as his saviors, as a regenerative force that could redeem his
fortunes. He said as much to Jo-Jo. Now you're finally talking
sense, panín, Jo-Jo said. Chuito's imminent departure from the
warehouse also emboldened Ramon to act. London Terrace
Apartments, delayed because of a rumor that it had been built on a
chemical dump site, had finally opened.

Jo-Jo was only able to promise Papi half the money he needed.
Jo-Jo was still throwing away money on his failed negocio and
needed a little time to recover. Papi took this as a betrayal and said
so to their friends. He talks a big game but when you're at the final
inning, you get nada. Although these accusations filtered back to
Jo-Jo and wounded him, he still loaned Papi the money without
comment. That's how Jo-Jo was. Papi worked for the rest of it,
more months than he expected. Chuito reserved him an apartment
and together they began filling the place with furniture. He started
taking a shirt or two with him to work, which he then sent to the
apartment. Sometimes he'd cram socks in his pockets or put on two
pairs of underwear. He was smuggling himself out of Nilda's life.

What's happening to your clothes? she asked one night.

It's that damn cleaners, he said. That bobo keeps losing my
things. I'm going to have to have a word with him as soon as I get
a day off.

Do you want me to go?

I can handle this. He's a very nasty guy.

The next morning she caught him cramming two guayaberas in
his lunch pail. I'm sending these to be cleaned, he explained.

Let me do them.

You're too busy. It's easier this way.

He wasn't very smooth about it.

They spoke only when necessary.

Years later Nilda and I would speak, after he had left us for good,
after her children had moved out of the house. Milagros had children of her own and their pictures crowded on tables and walls.
Nilda's son loaded baggage at JFK. I picked up the picture of him

with his girlfriend. We were brothers all right, though his face
respected symmetry.

We sat in the kitchen, in that same house, and listened to the
occasional pop of a rubber ball being batted down the wide channel
between the building fronts. My mother had given me her address
(Give my regards to the puta, she'd said) and I'd taken three trains
to reach her, walked blocks with her address written on my palm.

I'm Ramón's son, I'd said.

Hijo, I know who you are.

She fixed café con leche and offered me a Goya cracker. No
thanks, I said, no longer as willing to ask her questions or even to
be sitting there. Anger has a way of returning. I looked down at my
feet and saw that the linoleum was worn and filthy. Her hair was
white and cut close to her small head. We sat and drank and finally
talked, two strangers reliving an event—a whirlwind, a comet, a
war—we'd both seen but from different faraway angles.

He left in the morning, she explained quietly. I knew something
was wrong because he was lying in bed, not doing anything but
stroking my hair, which was very long back then. I was a
Pentecostal. Usually he didn't lay around in bed. As soon as he was
awake he was showered and dressed and gone. He had that sort of
energy. But when he got up he just stood over little Ramón. Are
you OK? I asked him and he said he was just fine. I wasn't going
to fight with him about it so I went right back to sleep. The dream
I had is one I still think about. I was young and it was my birthday
and I was eating a plate of quail's eggs and all of them were for me.
A silly dream really. When I woke up I saw that the rest of his
things were gone.

She cracked her knuckles slowly. I thought that I would never
stop hurting. I knew then what it must have been like for your
mother. You should tell her that.

We talked until it got dark and then I got up. Outside the local
kids were gathered in squads, stalking in and out of the lucid clouds
produced by the street-lamps. She suggested I go to her restaurant
but when I got there and stared through my reflection in the glass
at the people inside, all of them versions of people I already knew,
I decided to go home.

December. He had left in December. The company had given
him a two-week vacation, which Nilda knew nothing about. He
drank a cup of black café in the kitchen and left it washed and dry-

ing in the caddy. I doubt if he was crying or even anxious. He lit a cigarette, tossed the match on the kitchen table and headed out into the angular winds that were blowing long and cold from the south. He ignored the convoys of empty-cabs that prowled the streets and walked down Atlantic. There were less furniture and antique shops then. He smoked cigarette after cigarette and killed his pack within the hour. He bought a carton at a stand, knowing how expensive they would be abroad.

The first subway station on Bond would have taken him to the airport and I like to think that he grabbed that first train, instead of what was more likely true, that he had gone out to Chuito's first, before flying south to get us.

MISTRESS (2002)

Lara Vapnyar

In "Mistress," Lara Vapnyar tells the story of the adaptation to Brooklyn of a three-generation family of recent immigrants from Russia. Vapnyar herself was born in Moscow in 1971; she moved with her husband to Brooklyn in 1994. After she entered the graduate program at the City University of New York, she began writing (in English) wry short stories as well as novels. She lives with her children in Staten Island and has taught writing at NYU and Columbia University.

THE DERMATOLOGIST HAD a mistress. For the past few weeks, it had been the main topic of conversation in his white waiting room, decorated with bright dermatology posters and a lonely, lopsided palm in the corner. This afternoon, there were about eight patients, most of them Russians, seated on red patent-leather chairs, because the office was located on Kings Highway, in a Russian area of Brooklyn. The doctor even had a few Russian newspapers, along with dated issues of *Time* and *Sports Illustrated,* in a plastic magazine rack. But nobody was interested in them.

"He took her to Aroba in November. The mistress," Misha's grandmother was confiding in Russian to a gray-haired woman in a blazer, sneakers, and a long skirt. "Aru-ba," Misha corrected her mentally. He tried to read a book, but the grandmother's excited whisper filled with fat, rich words like "Aroba" or "mistress" kept him from concentrating. Sometimes she attempted to talk to a woman in a gray beret, seated next to Misha. To do that she leaned over him, putting her heavy elbow on his knee for balance. He had to press his opened book to his chest and wait until she was through, trying to hold his face away from her mixed aroma of sweat, valerian root drops and dill. "First he went on vacation with his wife, but the mistress made a scene, and he had to take her too. They are all like that, you know." The gray-haired woman nodded. At some point, other Russian patients moved closer and joined in the chat. "You mean Dr. Levy has a mistress?" "Yes," the gray-haired woman said eagerly. "He even took her to Aroba." And Misha's grandmother looked at her with reproach, because she wanted to be the one to tell about Aruba.

Every second Thursday after school, Misha had to take his grandmother to the dermatologist. He served as an interpreter, because the grandmother didn't speak English. Misha didn't mind these visits—there wasn't much to translate. Dr. Levy, a small, skinny man with dark circles under his eyes, just glanced at the sores on his grandmother's ankles, scribbled something in the chart, and asked: "How's it going?" Grandmother said "Better" in Russian, and Misha translated it into English. Misha didn't mind the eye doctor or the dentist either. He was saved from attending visits to a gynecologist by his mother and grandfather. "A nine-year-old boy has no business in a gynecologist's office," the grand-father said firmly, surprising everybody, because since they had come to America, it was a rarity to hear him argue, to hear him speak at all. Misha was happy—for some reason he was afraid of pregnant women with their inflated bellies, fat ankles, and wobbly, domineering way of walking. His mother had to take several hours off work to take the grandmother there. She complained about it and looked at Misha and the grandfather with reproach.

Nobody saved Misha from monthly visits to the internal doctor. The doctor let Misha and his grandmother into his sparkling office with cream-colored walls covered with diplomas and walked con-fidently to his large mahogany desk. He sat there tall and lean, with a thick mane of bluish-white hair, a red face, and very clean white hands, listening patiently to the grandmother's complaints. Unlike other doctors, he never interrupted her. Misha would have pre-ferred that he did. "My problem is . . .," she would begin with a sigh of anticipation. She prided herself on being able to describe her symptoms with vividness and precision. "You should've been a writer, Mother," Misha's father once said when she described her perspiration as a "heavy shower pouring from under my skin." Misha's mother looked lost. She didn't know if she should smile at the joke or scold her husband for being ironic about her mother. She chose to smile. "No, a doctor," Misha's grandmother cor-rected, oblivious to his irony. "I would've become a doctor if I hadn't devoted my life to my husband."

While she talked to the internist, Misha usually stared down, following the checkerboard of the beige-and-brown linoleum floor
with his eyes, the pattern interrupted in places by furniture legs and
his grandmother's feet in wide black sneakers. Her words were loud
and clear, emphasized by occasional groans and changes of tone. "I
can't have a bowel movement for days, but I have to go to the
bathroom every few hours. It usually happens like this. I feel the
urge and go to the bathroom immediately. I push very hard, but
nothing happens. I come out, but I feel as if a heavy rock is in there
inside me, weighing down my bowels. I go in and try again." The
grandmother pressed one of her feet hard into the floor when she
described the "heavy rock." Misha looked at her thick, dark stock-
ings. She had brought a supply of them from Russia, along with an
assortment of wide-striped garters. Misha felt the edge of his patent-
leather chair become moist and slippery under his clutched fingers.
He also felt that his whole face was blushing all over, especially his
ears. He wondered if the doctor noticed how red they were. But
he didn't look at Misha; he looked directly at the grandmother with
a patient, polite smile.

"Come on," Misha thought, "stop her. There must be other
patients waiting." But the doctor didn't move. Maybe he used
these minutes to sleep with his eyes open. "When at last it happens,
I feel exhausted, as if I had won a battle. My head aches, and I have
a heartbeat so severe that I have to take forty drops of valerian root,
lie down, and stay like that for at least an hour." When the grandmother was through, she turned to Misha. The doctor turned to
him too, keeping the same polite and patient expression on his face.
Misha thought about darting out the door, past the receptionist,
past the waiting room, onto the street. He thought about rushing
out the window, a large clean window with a plastic model of a
split human head on a windowsill. He could see himself falling into
the grass, then rising to his feet and running away from the office.
But he didn't jump. He just sat there, thinking how to avoid men-
tioning "heavy rock" or the grandmother's sitting in the bathroom.
"Um . . . she . . . my grandmother . . . her problem is . . . she has
a . .. she often gets a headache and her heart beats very fast." The
doctor smiled at Misha approvingly and wrote a prescription with
his beautiful, very clean hands. "Tylenol!" his grandmother later
complained loudly to the other patients in the waiting room.
"Look at these American doctors! I tell him that I am constipated

and he gives me Tylenol! Can you believe that?" The Russian patients sympathized eagerly. Misha hid his burning ears behind *The Great Pictorial Guide to the Prehistoric World*. He wished they would switch to the safer subject of the dermatologist's mistress.

Once they saw her. She flung the door open and walked straight into Dr. Levy's office, not smiling, staring ahead. She was a stout woman in her late thirties, with short reddish-brown hair, in tight white jeans and a shiny leather jacket. She was clomping her high-heeled boots and jingling her gold bracelets as she walked, swinging her car keys in her hand. Everybody in the room stopped talking and followed her with their eyes, even Misha. She had a beautiful mouth, painted bright red. "Shameless!" somebody hissed in Russian. Maybe it was Misha's grandmother.

* * *

AT HOME, Misha did his homework in their long white kitchen, because in his mother's opinion this was the only place that had proper light for him to work and wasn't too drafty. For about a year, the four of them—he, his mother, his grandfather, and his grandmother—had been living in this one-bedroom apartment with unevenly painted walls, faded brown carpet, and secondhand furniture. Everything in the apartment seemed to belong to some-body else. Misha and his mother slept in the bedroom, Misha on a folding bed. The grandmother and grandfather slept on the sofa bed in the living room. Or rather it was the grandmother who slept, snoring softly. The grandfather seemed to be awake all night. Whenever Misha woke up, he heard the old man tossing and groaning or pacing heavily on the creaky kitchen floor.

In Russia, they'd had separate apartments. They even lived in different cities. His grandparents lived in the south of Russia, in a small town overgrown with apple and peach trees. Misha and his parents lived in Moscow. Then his father left to live with another woman. In Moscow, Misha had his own room, a very small one, not bigger than six square meters, where the wallpaper was pat-terned with tiny sailboats. Misha had his own bed and his own desk with a lamp shaped like a crocodile. His books were shelved neatly above the desk, and his toys were kept in two plywood boxes beside his bed. When his parents argued, they used to say, "Misha, go to your room!" But during the last months before his father left, they didn't have time to send him to his room. They argued almost constantly: they started suddenly, without any warning, in the middle of a matter-of-fact conversation, during dinner, or while playing chess, or while watching TV, and stopped after Misha had gone to bed, or maybe they didn't stop at all. Misha went to his room himself. He sat on a little woven rug between his bed and his desk, playing with his building blocks and listening to the muffled sounds of his parents yelling. He played very quietly.

Misha liked doing his homework, although he would never have admitted that. He laid out his glossy American textbooks so that they took up nearly the entire surface of the table. He loved coloring maps, drawing diagrams, solving math problems: he even loved spelling exercises—he was pleased with the sight of his handwriting, the sight of the firm, clear, rounded letters. Most of all, he loved that during homework time nobody bothered him. "Shh! Michael's studying," everybody said. Even his grandmother, who usually cooked dinner while Misha was studying, was silent, or almost silent—she quietly hummed a theme from a Mexican soap opera that she watched every day on the Spanish channel. Her Spanish was not much better than her English, but she said that in Mexican shows you didn't need words to understand what was going on. The other thing she loved to watch on TV was the weather reports, where you didn't need words either: a picture of the sun meant a good day, raindrops meant drizzle, rows of raindrops meant heavy rain. Misha's mother was against subscribing to a Russian TV channel, because she thought it would prevent them from adjusting to American life. For the same reason, she insisted that everybody call Misha "Michael." Misha's mother was well adjusted. She watched the news on TV, rented American movies, and read American newspapers. She worked in Manhattan and wore the same clothes to work that Misha had seen in the magazines in the waiting room, but her skirts were longer and the heels of her shoes weren't as high.

The problem with the homework was that it took Misha only about forty minutes. He tried to prolong it as much as he could. He did all the extra math problems from the section called "You Might Try It." He brought his own book and read it, pretending that it was an English assignment. He stopped from time to time as if he had a problem and had to think it over, but in truth he just sat there, watching his grandmother cook.

She took all these funny packages, string bags, plastic bags, paper bags, bowls, and wrapped plates out of the refrigerator and put them on the counter, never forgetting to sniff at each of them first. Then she opened the oven with a loud screech, gasping and saying, "Sorry, Michael," took out saucepans and skillets, put them on the stove, filled some of them with water and greased others with chicken fat (she always kept some chicken fat handy, not trusting oil). While the saucepans and skillets gurgled and hissed on the stove, the grandmother washed and chopped the contents of packages and bowls, using two wooden boards—one for meat, the other for everything else. Misha always marveled at how fast her short and swollen fingers moved. In a matter of seconds, handfuls of colorful cubes disappeared in the saucepans and skillets under chipped enameled lids. "I was wise," the grandmother often said to her waiting-room friends. "I brought all the lids here. In America, it's impossible to find a lid that fits." The women agreed, something was definitely wrong with American lids.

To make ground meat, the grandmother used a hand-operated metal meat-grinder, also transported from Russia. She had to summon the grandfather into the kitchen, because the grinder was too heavy. She couldn't turn the handle herself; she couldn't even lift it. The grandfather put his newspaper down and came in obediently, shuffling his slippered feet as he walked, with the same tired, resigned expression that he had worn when he followed the grandmother home from the Russian food store, carrying bulging bags printed with a stretched red THANK YOU. He took off his dark checkered shirt and put it on the chair. (The grandmother insisted that he do that. "You don't want pieces of raw meat all over your shirt!") He put an enameled bowl of meat cubes in front of him and secured the grinder on the windowsill. He stood leaning over it, dressed in a white undershirt and dark woolen trousers. He had brought to America five good suits that he used to wear to work in Russia. Now he wore the trousers at home and the jackets hung in a closet with mothballs in their pockets. The grandfather took hold of the rusty meat-grinder handle and turned it slowly, with effort at first, then faster and faster. His flabby pale shoulders were shaking and tiny beads of sweat came out on his puffy cheeks, his long rounded nose, and his shiny head. The grandmother sometimes tore herself away from her cooking to offer comments: "What have you got, crooked fingers?" or "Here, you dropped a piece again" or "I hope I will have this meat ground by next year." She had never talked to him like that in Russia. In Russia, when he came home from work, she rushed to serve him dinner and put two spoonfuls of sour cream into his shchi herself. The grandfather slurped the soup loudly and talked a lot during dinner. Now he didn't even answer the grandmother back. He just stood there, clutching the meat-grinder handle with yellowed knuckles, turning it even faster, which made his face redden and the blue twisted veins on his neck bulge. His stare was focused on something far away, out the window. Misha thought that maybe he wanted to jump, like Misha had wanted to in the doctor's office. But their apartment was on the sixth floor.

While the food was cooking, the grandmother went to get her special ingredient, dill. She kept darkened, slightly wilted bunches spread out on an old newspaper on the windowsill. She took one and crushed it into a little bowl with her fingers, to add it to every dish she cooked. At dinner, everything had the taste of dill: soup, potatoes, meat stew, salad. In fact, dinner hardly tasted like anything else but dill—the grandmother didn't trust spices; she put very little salt in their food and no pepper at all. Misha watched how she moved from one saucepan to another, dressed in a square-shaped dark cotton dress, drying her moist red face and her closely cropped gray hair with a piece of cloth, sweeping potato peels off the counter, groaning when one fell to the floor and she had to pick it up. He couldn't understand why she put so much work into the preparation of this food, which was consumed in twenty minutes, in silence, and didn't even taste good.

Misha couldn't pretend to be busy with his homework forever. Eventually, the grandmother knew that he was done. She watched a weather report on TV and if nothing indicated a natural disaster sent Misha to a playground with his grandfather. "Go, go," she would yell at the grandfather, who sat on the sofa in his unbuttoned checkered shirt, buried in a Russian newspaper. "Go, walk with the boy, make yourself useful for a change!" And the grandfather would stand up, groaning, go to the bathroom mirror to check if he should shave, and usually decide against it. Then he would button his shirt, tuck it into his trousers, and say gloomily: "Let's go, Michael." Misha knew that after they left, the grandmother would take over the Russian newspaper. She would put her glasses on (she had two pairs, both made from cheap plastic, one light blue, the other pink), and slump on the sofa, making the springs creak. She would sit there with her feet planted far apart and read the classifieds section, the singles ads. She would circle some with a red marker she had borrowed from Misha, to show them later to Misha's mother, who would laugh at first, then get irritated, then get upset and yell at the grandmother.

All the way to the playground, while they passed red brick apartment buildings and rows of private houses with little boys in yarmulkes and little girls in long flowery dresses playing on the sidewalks, Misha's grandfather walked a few steps ahead, with his hands folded against his back, staring down at his feet, never saying a word.

Back in Russia, it was different, maybe because Misha was younger then. When he spent summers at his grandparents' place, the grandfather took him to a park willingly, without being asked. He talked a lot while they strolled along the paths of a dark, dense forest: about trees, animals, about how fascinating even the most ordinary things that surround us could be. Little Misha didn't try to grasp the meaning of his words. They just reached him along with other noises: the rustle of a tree, a bird's squawk, a nasty scrape of gravel as he ran his sandal-clad toes through it. It was the sound of the grandfather's voice that was important to him. They walked slowly, Misha's little hand lying securely in the grandfather's big sweaty one. From time to time, Misha had to release his hand and wipe it against his pants, but then he hurried to take the grandfather's hand again.

Now, once they reached the playground and stepped on its black spongy floor, the grandfather said, "Okay, go play, Michael." Then he strolled around the place, searching for Russian newspapers left behind on the benches. He usually found two or three. He walked to a big flat tree stump, in the farthest corner from the domino tables where a heated crowd of old Russian men gathered, and where old Russian women sat on benches discussing their own ailments and other people's mistresses. There, for the full hour that they spent in the playground, the grandfather sat unmoving, except to turn the newspaper pages. Misha didn't know how he was supposed to play. Three-year-olds on their tricycles rode all over the soft black surface of the playground. The slide was occupied by shrieking six-year-olds, and the swings were filled with little babies rocked by their mothers, or with fat teenage girls who had to squeeze their bottoms tightly to fit between the chains. Misha usually walked to the tallest slide, stepping over dabs of chewing gum and pools of melted ice cream. He climbed up to the very top and crawled into a plastic hut. There he sat huddled on a low plastic bench. Sometimes he brought a book with him. He liked thick, serious books about ancient civilizations, archaeological expeditions, and animals who'd become extinct millions of years ago. But most of the time, it was too noisy to read. Then Misha simply stared down at the playground that seemed to move and stir like a big restless animal, and at his immobile grandfather.

The notice about the English class was printed in bold black letters on pink neon paper. The color was so bright that it arrested everyone's gaze no matter where it was lying. Since the beginning of March, it could be seen lying anywhere in the apartment: on the kitchen table, in the bedroom on a crumpled pillow, on the toilet floor between a broom and a Macy's catalog, stuffed under the sofa (the grandmother pulled it out from there, blew the pellets of dust off it, smoothed it with her hands, and scolded the grandfather angrily). Everybody studied it, read it, or at least looked at it. They were discussing whether the grandfather should go. He fit the description perfectly. Any legal immigrant who had lived in the country less than two years and possessed basic knowledge of English was invited to attend a three-month-long class on American conversation. "Rich in Idioms" was printed in letters bigger than the rest. "Free of Charge," in even bigger letters. "It's an excellent program, Father!" Misha's mother raved at dinner, removing the bones from the catfish stew on her plate. "Taught by American teachers, real teachers, native speakers! Not by Russian old ladies, who confuse all the tenses and claim that it's classic British grammar." At first, the grandfather tried to ignore her. But Misha's mother was persistent. "You're rotting alive, Father! Think how wonderful it would be if you had something to do, something to look forward to." Misha's grandmother clattered dishes, moved chairs with a screech, and often interrupted this conversation with questions like "Where are the matches? I just put them right here" or "Do you think this fish is overcooked?" She was offended that nobody suggested that she go to the class, even though she knew that the words "basic knowledge of English" hardly applied to her. The best she could do was spell her first name. The last name required Misha's help. But Misha's mother couldn't be distracted by the grandmother's questions or the clattering of dishes. "You'll begin to speak in no time, Father. You know grammar, you have vocabulary, you just need a push." The grandfather only bent his neck lower and sipped his tea, muttering that it was all nonsense and that in their area of Brooklyn you hardly ever needed English. "What about yours and mother's appointments?! Michael and I are tired of taking you there all the time. Right, Michael?" As she said this, Misha's mother moved their large porcelain teapot, preventing her from seeing Misha's face across the table. Misha nodded. It was decided that the grandfather would go.

On the first day of class, the grandfather took one of his jackets from a hanger and put it on, on top of his usual checkered shirt. He asked Misha if he had a spare notebook. Misha gave him a notebook with a marble cover, a sharp pencil, and a ballpoint pen. The grandfather put it all in a plastic THANK YOU bag. In the hall, he took the box with his Russian leather shoes from the top shelf of the closet and asked Misha if they needed shining. Misha did not know, and the grandfather shoved the box back and put his sneakers on. He shuffled out to the elevator, holding the THANK YOU bag under his arm.

From then on, two nights a week—the class was held on Mondays and Wednesdays—they had dinner without the grandfather. His absence didn't make much difference, except maybe that Misha's mother and the grandmother bickered a little more. It usually started with a clipping from a Russian newspaper, a big colorful ad—come TO OUR PARTY AND MEET YOUR DESTINY. PRICE: FIFTY DOLLARS (FOOD AND DRINK INCLUDED)—and ended with Misha's mother yelling: "Why do you want to marry me off? So you can drive the next one away?" and the grandmother reaching for a bottle of valerian root drops. "I never said a bad word to your husband," the grandmother said plaintively. "You said plenty of your words to me. Didn't spare money in long-distance calls!" "I only wanted to open your eyes!" Then Misha's mother rushed out of the kitchen, and the grandmother yelled after her, carefully counting the drops into her teacup: "How can you be so ungrateful! I came to America to help you. I left everything and came here for your sake!"

Misha's mother had come to America for Misha's sake. She said it to him once, after she got back from a parent-teacher conference. She returned home and said, "Come with me to the bedroom,

Michael." He went, feeling his hands grow sweaty and his ears turn red, although he knew that he hadn't done anything bad at school. His mother sat on the edge of the bed and removed her high-heeled shoes, then pulled off her pantyhose. "The teacher says you don't talk, Michael. You don't talk at all. Not in class, not during the recess." She was rubbing her pale feet with small, crooked toes. "Your English is fine, you have excellent marks on your tests. You have excellent marks in every subject. Yet you're not going to make it to the top of the class!" She left her feet alone and began to cry, her black eye makeup running around her eyes. She said to him, sniffling, that he—his future—was the only reason she came to America. Then she went into the bathroom to wash her face, leaving her rolled-up pantyhose on the floor—two soft, dark circles joined together. From the bathroom, she yelled to him: "Why don't you talk, Michael?"

It wasn't true that he didn't talk at all. When asked a question, he gave an accurate answer, but he tried to make it as brief as possible. He never volunteered to talk. He registered everything that was said in class; he made comments and counterarguments in his head; he even made jokes. But something prevented these already-formed words from coming out of his mouth. He felt the same way when his father called on Saturdays. Misha spent a whole week preparing for his call; he had thousands of things to tell him. In his head, he related everything that had happened to him at school; he described his classmates, his teachers. He wanted to talk about things he had read in books, about lost cities, volcanoes, and weird animals. In his head, Misha even laughed, imagining how he would tell his father all the funny stories he read about dinosaurs, and how his father would laugh with him. But when his father called, Misha went numb. He answered questions but never volunteered to speak and never asked anything himself. He sat with the phone on his bed, facing the wall and picking at old layers of paint with his fingernail. He could hear his father's impatient, disappointed breathing on the other end of the line. Misha thought that his reluctance to talk might explain why his father had not called in several weeks.

Now the grandfather had to do his homework too. Misha came home from school and found him sitting at the kitchen table in Misha's usual place with his notebooks and dictionaries spread across the table. The grandfather would even cut himself little colorful cards out of construction paper and copy down difficult words from the dictionary: an English word on one side, the Russian meaning on the other. He studied seriously and couldn't be bothered during that time. The grandmother had to go to the Russian food store alone, and she brought back smaller, lighter bags because she couldn't carry heavy things. Nobody used the meat-grinder now. It was stored in a cupboard along with other useless things brought from Russia: baking sheets, funny-shaped molds, a small, dented samovar, a gadget for removing sour cherrystones. The grandmother wasn't happy about this. She muttered that she had the whole household on her shoulders and threw looks of reproach at her husband. Misha's mother said: "Please leave him alone—Father has to learn something. It's only for three months anyway." Misha wondered if the grandfather enjoyed his home-work as much as he did. He also wondered if the grandfather cheated like he did, pretending that his homework took much more time than it really did.

About three weeks after the class started, the grandfather made up his mind and took the box with his leather shoes down from the shelf. He went to a shoe store and bought a small bottle of dark brown shoe polish. To do that, he had to look up the English term for "shoe polish" in the dictionary. Before each class, he polished his shoes zealously with a piece of cloth. "I don't want the teacher to think that Russians are pigs," he mumbled in response to the grandmother's stare. He squatted with his head down, and his face and neck became very red, as red as they were when he said that he wasn't making enough progress and had to come for extra lessons on Saturdays. The grandmother was putting things away in a cup-board when he said that. She shut the white cupboard door with a satisfied boom. "All that studying and you are not making prog-ress!" One evening the grandfather got up from the sofa, put on his jacket, put some money in the pocket, walked to Kings Highway, and came back with a new shirt, a light-blue one with dark-blue stripes. "It was on sale," he explained to the grandmother.

"'It was on sale!' was all he said to me," Misha's grandmother announced in the dermatologist's waiting room. "If I didn't know him, I would have thought *he* had a mistress." Her listeners, two Russian women, one wearing a thick knitted beret of a lustrous purple color and the other a plain black one, nodded to her

sympathetically. "But I do know him." The grandmother grinned
and raised one brow to emphasize her words. She looked meaning-
fully at the women, leaned closer to them, and whispered something. "That—for several years now," she added. The woman in a
purple beret said: "But this is good, this is better." The grandmother considered her words and said: "Yes, yes, this is better, of
course."

Misha imagined his grandfather with a mistress, with the dermatologist's mistress, because she was the only mistress he'd seen. He
imagined his grandfather strolling with her along the Sheepshead
Bay embankment with other couples, one of her hands sticking out
of the shiny leather sleeve holding his grandfather's hand, her other
hand swinging car keys. Then he imagined her kissing the grandfather on the cheek and leaving a mark with her bright red lipstick.
The grandfather would wrinkle his nose and rush to wipe it off, the
way Misha always did when his mother kissed him after work. The
image of his serious grandfather rubbing his cheek vigorously made
Misha smile.

Sheepshead Bay was the place where the grandfather took Misha
for his evening walks now. For a few weeks after the class began,
they continued to go to the playground, but the Russian newspapers were abandoned. The grandfather took his colorful word cards
with him instead. He spread them on the stump, securing each with
a small stone to prevent the wind from scattering them. Sometimes
he read the words slowly, in whispers, or with his lips moving or
with his eyes. But more often he just looked around with an
incredulous expression as if he were seeing all this for the first time.
Then one day the grandfather said that he was going to take
Michael to Sheepshead Bay to look at the ships and breathe the
fresh ocean air. The grandmother protested at first, saying that it
was a long walk, and it was windy there, and the boy might catch
cold. But the grandfather was firm, almost as firm as he used to be
back in Russia. He said that the boy needed exercise and that was
that.

On Sheepshead Bay, they didn't stop to look at the ships. They
crossed the creaky wooden bridge and proceeded along the
embankment, passing fishermen, tall trees, and chipped green
benches occupied by lonely-looking women. At the end of the
path, they turned back and repeated their route three or four times.
The grandfather walked ahead, maybe a little faster than usual,

limping slightly in his stiff leather shoes. He stared ahead, sometimes turning to look in the direction of the trees and benches. A
few times, Misha had the impression that the grandfather nodded
to somebody on one bench. Once he slipped on a fish head on the
pavement and almost fell while looking in that direction. Misha
made frequent stops to look at the fishermen's shiny tackles, the fish
heads and tails they used for bait, and the insides of their white
plastic buckets, which were usually empty. When the wind was so
strong that it chilled Misha's ears and tried to tear his little Yankees
cap off his head, there were sharp, dark waves in the water, and
Misha could see fish jumping with big splashes. He watched as
somebody pulled out his fishing rod, following it with his eyes,
holding his breath and licking his lips. He hoped to see a fish being
caught at least once. When the grandfather's class was over, Misha
was sure that they wouldn't come here anymore. He would have
to go back to the plastic hut on the playground, which would get
hot in summer and smell of burnt rubber.

The grandmother had all her appointments written down on a big
wall calendar. It hung next to the refrigerator, a bright spot on a
pale kitchen wall. It was called "Famous Russian Monasteries,"
printed in Germany and sold on Brighton Beach. Below the beautiful, glossy picture of the Zagorsk Monastery, with golden cupolas
floating in the brilliantly blue sky, was the schedule for June. The
fifteenth, the date when the grandfather's class would end, was
circled with Misha's red marker. "See, you didn't want to go, but
when it's over you will miss it, Father," Misha's mother said when
she passed the calendar on her way to dump her plate in the sink.
The grandfather only shrugged. He didn't look moved in any way
by her words. It was the grandmother who looked moved, even
animated, every time June 15 was mentioned. The great things
were to be done then. The grandmother spoke about the ten
pounds of cucumbers she wanted the grandfather to bring for her
from Brighton Beach. "They are twenty-nine cents per pound
there! I will make pickles." She also spoke about the plums and
apricots she needed for jam, about sour cherries to make sour
cherry dumplings, about little hard pears for marinating, about
apples for apple pies. She threw longing looks in the direction of
the locked-up meat-grinder, telling about a wonderful recipe she
heard in the dentist's office. "I'll make zrazy. Anna Stepanovna says

that they come out much better with scallions instead of onions. I'll need a lot of ground beef for them." Then she found a Russian travel agency, which offered discounted tours to elderly people. "We'll go to Boston, to Washington, to Philadelphia. Women in waiting rooms talk about their trips nonstop, and I just sit there too shy to open my mouth. And you will have to go with me," she said to the grandfather. "I won't go alone, as if I weren't married. They put unmarried women on bad seats in the back, next to the toilet." Misha thought that maybe for his grandmother it wasn't such a bad idea to sit next to the toilet, but he didn't say anything. The grandfather didn't say anything either. He only buried himself deeper in his textbook.

On June 2, a weather report on TV showed a neat gray cloud and dense oblique rows of raindrops. "Heavy showers," the grandmother announced, turning the TV off and walking into the kitchen where Misha and the grandfather were doing their homework, or rather sitting with their textbooks open. "You're staying home tonight." The sky in the window was mostly gray with a few patches of blue. Misha looked further down. People weren't carrying umbrellas, and the gray asphalt of the road was dry and dusty. He looked at his grandfather. The grandfather examined the sky carefully, then lifted the window up a few inches to stick out his arm. The howling gushes of cold wind dashed in, but the arm, although covered with goose bumps, stayed dry. "We'll come back before the rain starts," he said. The grandmother shrugged.

The first raindrops started falling as soon as they left the building. They made dark marks on the pavement but missed Misha and his grandfather. Then a raindrop fell right on the tip of Misha's nose. He wiped it off. Close to Sheepshead Bay, the grandfather stopped and stuck out his open palm. Some drops landed on it. "It's not rain, is it, Michael?" the grandfather asked, turning to Misha and wiping his damp face with his damp palm. Misha shrugged. They both looked in the direction of the bay. It was very close, they could see the ships, and the dirty-gray high waves, and the tops of the trees bending low under the pressure of wind. Newspaper pages, probably left on the benches, were flying up. "It's not a heavy rain. Let's make one round. Okay?" Misha nodded, holding tight to his cap. They crossed the street, the only ones to walk in the direction of the park. Most people hurried out. Big round raindrops were now falling fast, hitting the pavement one after another with a smacking sound and turning small wet spots into intricate ornaments, then into puddles. The grandfather stopped hesitantly and looked in the direction of the benches. There was nobody there. "I think we'd better head home, Michael," the grandfather said. "It's starting to rain."

The heavy downpour reached them while they were waiting for the streetlight to turn to green. With all the wind's howling and the sounds of rain, they didn't immediately hear somebody calling for them. Or rather, Misha heard, but he didn't grasp at once that it was his grandfather's name being called. "Grigory Semyonovich! Grigory Semyonovich!" Nobody had used his surname since they left Russia. A small old woman in a brown raincoat, holding a plastic bag above her head, was running to them, stumbling in black water-resistant boots too wide for her. Misha pulled the grandfather on the sleeve, making him stop and turn. "Grigory Semyonovich! Come to my place, come quickly, the boy will catch cold," she said breathlessly, trying to position her plastic bag above Misha's head.

* * *

Her place was on the top floor of a three-story brownstone across the street from the park. They walked up a dark staircase that smelled of something unpleasant. "Cats?" thought Misha, who had never smelled a cat. The woman led the way. She was still out of breath and spoke in short, abrupt sentences. "Poor boy. Grigory Semyonovich. How could you. In weather like this. I was there on a bench. But I left. As soon as the rain started. I saw you from across the street. I'm worried about the boy." The grandfather was also out of breath, and silent.

Inside, Misha had only a moment to notice that the apartment was very small and dimly lit before a big rough towel, smelling of unfamiliar soap, covered his face and shoulders and back. He felt the woman's swift little hands rubbing his body. He became ticklish and wanted to sneeze.

"My name is Elena Pavlovna. We go to school together, your grandfather and I," the woman said after Misha and the grandfather had refused dry sweatpants but accepted dry socks and their shoes had been stuffed with newspapers and put to dry in the bathroom. They were drinking hot chocolate at the one-legged round table in the tiny kitchen. Misha's grandfather and Elena Pavlovna had made the hot chocolate together. The grandfather poured boiling water from the kettle, holding it by the wooden handle with both hands. Elena Pavlovna put the mix into three yellow mugs and moved them closer to the kettle. They said "Thank you," "Please," and "Would you" to each other and smiled frequently. They spoke like characters in the Chekhov adaptations that Misha's mother loved to watch in Russia, yet Misha could feel that with his grandfather and Elena Pavlovna it wasn't an act. "What's your name?" Elena Pavlovna asked. "Michael," said Misha. "Michael?! You don't look like a Michael. Misha would suit you better. Can I call you Misha?" Misha nodded, blowing with pleasure on his too-hot drink (at home the grandmother would usually add a bit of cold milk) and biting into a cookie with delicious raspberry jam inside. "Store-bought," Elena Pavlovna said. "I don't bake. Why bother when there are so many delicious things sold in bakeries? Right? But that's not the real reason. I am simply a very bad cook." Misha could see that she wasn't ashamed to admit this.

Her apartment was smaller than theirs. One room and a kitchen. It was furnished just like theirs: a hard brown sofa from a cheap Russian furniture store, a scratched coffee table and a chest of drawers retrieved from the trash, heavy lamps bought at a garage sale. Delicate Russian tea set and books in a dark cabinet with glass doors. Misha read the titles of the same books they had brought from Russia—Chekhov, Pushkin, historical novels with dark, gloomy covers, Maupassant and Flaubert translated into Russian, thick dictionaries, Russian-English and English-Russian. Some titles were obscured by two big photographs. One showed two serious, curly-headed girls, both older than Misha. "My grand-daughters," Elena Pavlovna said with a sigh. "They live in California with my son." On the other picture, in black and white, was a smiling young man in a uniform. "Her son," Misha thought, but Elena Pavlovna said that it was her husband.

Elena Pavlovna had a braid, a thin gray braid coiled on the back of her head. Misha had never seen an old woman with a braid before. The hair coming out of the braid framed her face with a crown of fluffy grayish-white curls. Her skin was dry and thin, with neat little wrinkles that looked as though they were drawn on her face with a pencil. Her eyes were small and dark. They misted over as she read them her sister's letter from Leningrad. "Everything is the same: the Neva, the embankment, the Winter Palace; only you, Lenochka, are gone." The grandfather patted her hand when she said that. She wore a blue woolen dress with a high collar covering her neck and a large amber brooch. "Want to look at my brooch, Misha?" she asked, unpinning it. "My mother said that there was a fly inside." Misha held the large, unpolished piece of amber in his hands. It was cool and smooth on top, rough on the edges. There was a strange black mass inside with thin sprouts looking a little like an insect's legs. "I am not sure myself, maybe it's just a crack," Elena Pavlovna said. "Do you know, Misha, what amber is?" "Yes," he answered eagerly, turning the piece of amber in his hands. "It's hardened tree tar; flies could get stuck in it while it was still soft and gluey. Yes, I think it is a fly, only a deformed one." Misha raised his eyes off the brooch and blushed, seeing that both Elena Pavlovna and his grandfather looked pleased with what he said.

Outside, everything was wet and brightened by the rain. The trees released showers of raindrops on their heads when they passed under them. They walked very fast, close to each other, their wet shoes squishing on the black, wet asphalt. They had left Elena Pavlovna's apartment as soon as the rain ended. Their shoes were still damp, but they took the sodden newspapers out and put the shoes on. Elena Pavlovna didn't protest, didn't say that they must wait, that Misha might catch cold from wearing damp shoes. On the staircase, she took his hand in her dry, small one and said: "Come again, Misha." But Misha doubted that he would ever see her again. He also knew that she wasn't to be mentioned at home. They would probably have to say that they waited until the rain was over in the hallway of some building or inside a deli. Elena Pavlovna, a woman with a gray braid and an amber brooch, would be his and the grandfather's secret. For some reason, Misha felt an urge to take his grandfather's hand, but then he thought that nine-year-old boys don't walk holding their grandfathers' hands. Instead, he began talking about the formation of amber, about volcanoes, about chameleons, about dinosaurs that swallowed big rocks to help them grind their food, about crocodiles that did this too. He talked nonstop, breathlessly, sputtering, chuckling in excitement, interrupting one story to tell the next. He looked at his grandfather, whose eyes were focused on Misha, who nodded in amazement and muttered from time to time: "Imagine!" or "Imagine what living things have to come up with to survive!" And Misha wanted to tell him more, to hear the "Imagine!" again and again. Close to their building, the grandfather suddenly stopped, interrupting a story about comodo dragons. "Misha," he said, sounding a little out of breath. "You know what, my class won't be over on June fifteenth. I mean it will, but I'll find another class, then another. Misha, there are a lot of free English programs in Brooklyn. You have no idea how many!" A big raindrop fell on the grandfather's head from the tree. It ran down his forehead, lingered on his large nose, and hung on the tip. The grandfather shivered and shook his head like a horse. Misha laughed.

SIRENS OF GOWANUS (2013)

Simon Rich

Simon Rich (b. 1984) was raised in New York City, where he continues to live. While a student at Harvard, he began publishing humor pieces in The New Yorker; *he has written novels, screenplays, collections of humor, and a book of short stories.*

BRENT WAS WALKING HOME from band practice when he heard a girl singing. He recognized the song immediately; it was that new Arcade Fire song, his favorite track off their new album. He put down his amp and listened as she belted out the chorus. It was a busy night on Smith Street but her crisp, clear voice pierced easily through the clatter.

He heaved his amp over his shoulder and headed toward the singer. She had moved on to another tune by now—a b-side by Big Star. The streetlamps grew sparser as he neared the Gowanus Canal, but he was able to spot her in the moonlight. She was under the Carroll Street bridge, sitting on a round, smooth rock. Her silky eyelashes fluttered as she sang. And whenever she hit a high note, she playfully splashed the water with her feet. She was naked from the waist up, two large breasts protruding from her slender, birdlike frame.

Brent was trying to figure out what to say to her when she called out his name.

"I'm sorry," he said. "Do I know you?"

She bashfully turned away, her pale cheeks crimsoning in the moonlight.

"Not exactly," she said. "But I've been to a couple of your shows. You're in the Fuzz, right?"

Brent's eyes widened with amazement. His band had only formed a few months ago. No one had ever recognized him before.

Even when he headlined at Club Trash, he'd had to show his ID at the door.

"I can't believe you've heard of me," he admitted.

The girl let loose a high-pitched musical laugh.

"I haven't just *heard* of you!" she cried. "I *worship* you!"

She took a deep breath and broke into one of his songs— the final track on the Fuzz's self-released EP.

Brent moved closer to the water. He knew the Gowanus Canal was filthy. He'd read once online that its water was so putrid it had somehow tested positive for gonorrhea. But it looked so lovely in the moonlight, a solid strip of blue, weaving elegantly through the city.

Brent talked to her for hours that night—about music and art and "the scene." When the sun started to rise, he gave her his cell phone number and wobbled off toward the F train. He'd barely walked a block when she texted him: "I hope U come back 2morrow!" Brent shook his head, laughing with giddiness. He could hardly believe his luck.

"Dude, that girl's trouble."

Brent scoffed.

"What are you talking about?"

His roommate Rob turned toward him, muting the TV to emphasize his words' importance.

"She's a fucking siren," he said. "She lures people out to that rock and, like, eats their flesh."

Brent rolled his eyes.

"I'm serious," Rob said. "Remember Stanley? The bassist in Dustin's band? She ate his face off."

"You can't judge someone by their past relationships. Like, okay, she killed Stanley. But how do you know what was going on between them? You weren't there. Maybe if you heard Thelxiepeia's take on what happened, you'd side with her."

Rob sighed.

"It's your life," he said. "I just don't want to see you get hurt."

Brent decided to invite her to Bar Tabac. It was a great first-date restaurant: not too expensive but classy enough to show a girl you were trying. It was also convenient—halfway between his apartment and her rock.

"I'd love to see you!" she cooed over the phone. "But I'm not super into French food."

Brent suggested a few alternatives—Thai, Italian, Mexican— but she balked at all of them.

"Where do *you* want to eat?" he asked.

Her breathing grew strangely thick.

"At my place," she said.

Brent couldn't believe it; he'd only known the girl for two days and she was already inviting him over! He called his drummer to cancel band practice. He needed to go buy a swimsuit.

"How's this one?" Brent asked Rob, holding up a purple Speedo.

"If you swim to that rock," he said, "she's going to kill you."

Brent ignored him and turned to his other roommate, Jeff.

"What do *you* think?"

"I think you're going to die," Jeff said.

Brent threw up his hands in frustration.

"Why do you guys always have to be so negative?"

"Just tell me this," Jeff said. "That rock she was sitting on. Did you see any bones on it?"

Brent sighed. There had been a few bones.

"Okay," Rob said. "I take it from your silence that you saw bones. Did she say anything about where they came from?"

"I didn't ask," Brent admitted.

"Why not?" Jeff asked.

"I just met her!" Brent said. "I don't know what kind of food issues she has! I didn't want to make her uncomfortable. I'm trying not to blow this."

He walked in silence to the checkout line. How could he explain his situation to those cynical morons? How could he explain the way this beautiful girl made him feel? They'd only met once and he already caught himself daydreaming about their future. He could easily picture them moving in together someday. His apartment was tiny, and so was her rock, but maybe they could find a bigger place? Brent visualized their wedding. They'd have it outside, on the shores of the Gowanus. He was pretty sure Thelxiepeia was a gentile, based on her hair color and the number of times she'd mentioned Zeus. But he didn't care about that kind of stuff.

"Do you need a bag?" the cashier asked him as he paid for his purple Speedo.

"That's okay," Brent said. "I'm going to put it on right now."

Brent hurried toward the water, his roommates both struggling to keep up.

"There's still time to cancel," Jeff said.

"Yeah," Rob said. "Just text her saying you're sick. The three of us can go get wings."

Brent spun around swiftly, his cheeks flushed with rage.

"Look," he said. "I'm not an idiot, okay? I know the odds are against us. I know she's a siren. I know she's eaten people. I know she's five thousand years older than me. But I *really* like her."

His eyes grew moist.

"I think," he said, "I might even be in *love* with her."

Her voice sounded in the distance. She was singing a Magnetic Fields tune—something off *69 Love Songs*. She was almost up to the chorus when two more voices suddenly joined her. Brent's roommates looked out onto the Gowanus. Apparently, Thelxiepeia had invited some friends over.

"Holy shit," Rob whispered as the three topless girls sang on. "Those girls are hot."

Jeff said nothing; he just stared at the water in silence, his lips slightly parted.

The girls finished singing and waved hello, playfully splashing the water with their feet.

"Are you Rob Swieskowski?" the one on the left asked. "I love your YouTube comedy videos."

Rob blushed.

"I can't believe you've seen those."

"And you're Jeff Selsam!" the other siren interrupted. "Actuary of the Month at Chapman and Chapman Life Insurance."

Jeff's eyes widened.

"How did you know?"

The sirens nodded at each other and then broke into a Beatles song, their voices braided perfectly in harmony. They smiled at the men, beckoning them closer.

And closer.